You're About to Become a
Privileged
Woman.

INTRODUCING
PAGES & PRIVILEGES™.
It's our way of thanking you for buying
our books at your favorite retail store.

GET ALL THIS FREE
WITH JUST ONE PROOF OF PURCHASE:

◆ Hotel Discounts up to 60% at home and abroad

◆ Travel Service - Guaranteed lowest published
airfares plus 5% cash back on tickets

◆ $25 Travel Voucher

◆ Sensuous Petite Parfumerie collection ($50 value)

◆ Insider Tips Letter with sneak previews of
upcoming books

◆ Mystery Gift (if you enroll before 6/15/95)

You'll get a FREE personal card, too.
It's your passport to all these benefits– and to
even more great gifts & benefits to come!
There's no club to join. No purchase commitment. No obligation.

As a Privileged Woman, you'll be entitled to all these Free Benefits. And Free Gifts, too.

To thank you for buying our books, we've designed an exclusive FREE program called *PAGES & PRIVILEGES*™. You can enroll with just one Proof of Purchase, and get the kind of luxuries that, until now, you could only read about.

Big HOTEL DISCOUNTS

A privileged woman stays in the finest hotels. And so can you—at up to 60% off! Imagine standing in a hotel check-in line and watching as the guest in front of you pays $150 for the same room that's only costing you $60. Your *Pages & Privileges* discounts are good at Sheraton, Marriott, Best Western, Hyatt and thousands of other fine hotels all over the U.S., Canada and Europe.

Free DISCOUNT TRAVEL SERVICE

A privileged woman is always jetting to romantic places.
When you fly, just make one phone call for the lowest published airfare at time of booking—or double the difference back! PLUS—

you'll get a $25 voucher to use the first time you book a flight AND 5% cash back on every ticket you buy thereafter through the travel service!

Mikelle was stunned

She shook her head disbelievingly. "That's it. Now I know I'm not imagining things."

Greg stared at her, a wary look in his eyes. "What aren't you imagining?"

"Your unusual interest in my son, that's what," she answered. "Ever since I first saw you in the grocery store, you've been eyeballing my baby. It makes a mother paranoid, you know? I've even wondered if you booked a room at my inn just to be near Jamie."

Greg laughed. "You're right. You are being paranoid."

Mikelle frowned. "If you aren't out to kidnap Jamie, why all the soft gazes and worried questions about my son? I want an explanation, Greg, and I want it now."

Dear Reader,

This month, a new "Rising Star" comes out to shine, as American Romance continues to search the heavens for the best new talent...the best new stories.

Let me introduce you to Emily Dalton.

Although Emily has written several historical and Regency romances, she is pleased to have penned her first contemporary romance for Harlequin American Romance. Emily lives in Bountiful, Utah, a charming hillside community where it's still safe to walk at night. She is a wife and mother of two boys who are dangerously close to driving age. Her two biggest weaknesses are an addiction to dark chocolate truffles and to crafts boutiques.

Turn the page and catch a "Rising Star!"

Sincerely,

Debra Matteucci
Senior Editor & Editorial Coordinator
Harlequin Books
300 East 42nd Street, 6th Floor
New York, NY 10017

Emily Dalton

MAKE ROOM FOR DADDY

Harlequin Books

TORONTO • NEW YORK • LONDON
AMSTERDAM • PARIS • SYDNEY • HAMBURG
STOCKHOLM • ATHENS • TOKYO • MILAN
MADRID • WARSAW • BUDAPEST • AUCKLAND

To B from D—
Thanks for putting the zipper in my wedding dress and thanks for being a great friend all these years.

ISBN 0-373-16586-2

MAKE ROOM FOR DADDY

Prologue

"Gave you a start, didn't I, Greg?"

Greg rubbed his unshaven jaw and leaned against the doorframe. "You do look a hell of a lot like Connie."

Hayley flashed a grin. Her teeth gleamed white against tanned skin and pale coral lipstick. "Well, she is my big sister." She tossed back a mane of straight blond hair, just like Connie used to do. "Aren't you going to invite me in?"

"I don't suppose you're selling Girl Scout cookies?" he murmured ruefully as he moved aside. Hayley glided past and into his apartment. He caught a whiff of her perfume. Obsession, the scent Connie used to wear.

"Does this look like a uniform?" she quipped.

No, Hayley was hardly wearing a uniform. She was dressed to kill in a short flirty skirt, tailored jacket and high heels. She looked like a million bucks, which was probably just about what her daddy gave her for an annual allowance. She sat down on the couch and crossed her long, coltish legs, which were the trademark of the Van der Linden women from Newport. The legs and the money.

"I'm not selling anything, Greg," she said.

Could have fooled me, he thought. He remained standing and looked Hayley straight in the eye. He was not about to let a pair of Van der Linden legs distract him...again. He had a bad feeling about this unexpected visit. Just minutes ago he was happily watching the baseball play-offs and drinking beer. He was even dressed for the part in a comfortable T-shirt, sweatpants and cotton tube socks. It was rare that he took time just to bum around the house. "Why are you here, Hayley?"

Hayley shook her head reprovingly. "Where are your manners, Greg? Aren't you going to offer me a drink or something?"

Greg folded his arms across his chest. He could feel a muscle ticking at the corner of his right eye. "Is this a social call? If I remember right, the last time we talked you had some highly colorful pet names for me."

Hayley waved a manicured hand and laughed dismissively. "I was angry. I was reacting out of misplaced loyalty to Connie."

Greg raised a brow. "Misplaced?"

Hayley's smile fell away. She ran a bright coral fingernail along the glass-topped table next to the sofa, following the movement with her eyes. "I've grown up a lot in the last year and a half. I've also learned a lot, especially about Connie."

She stole a glance at him from under thick, dark lashes. It wasn't a seductive look. In fact, the expression in Hayley's eyes surprised the hell out of him. She seemed to be struggling with painful emotions. She looked vulnerable...and he hated that.

"Look, Hayley," he said, dragging a hand through his hair, still damp and unruly from his shower. "You're making me nervous. Why don't you just get to the point?" He paused. "Connie's okay, isn't she?"

He rued the day he'd ever met Constance Van der Linden, but he didn't wish her anything worse than gritty sand in her bikini. He was never one for holding grudges, but he wasn't a fool, either. He didn't want to come within ten feet of his ex-girlfriend. Just being in the same room with her look-alike sister was unnerving enough.

Hayley's lips quirked up on one side. "Connie's fine. She's got a new boyfriend. One of the Newport crowd. Someone she overlooked till now, I suppose."

Greg sighed. "Then why are you here? I'm sure Connie's had several boyfriends since we broke up. And your sister's love life is no concern of mine." He realized she wasn't listening. She was taking a slow visual cruise down his six-foot, four-inch frame.

"I don't get it," she said at last. "Even in your grubbies you're a doll, Greg. You have a great body." Her gaze lifted to his face, ignoring his discouraging scowl. "You have gorgeous blond hair and eyes to die for." She squinted. "Are they green or gray?"

When he didn't answer, she flicked a quick glance around the room. Black-and-white art deco design dominated the living room. He arranged his furniture as he arranged his life—sleekly and simply. "You've got money, too," she said, sighing, "and you own your own architectural firm in downtown Manhattan."

"Your point, Hayley?" prompted Greg, impatient with Hayley's game . . . whatever it was. He thought longingly of his den, where comfort, not style, was the order of the day. He thought of his cushy reclining chair and a bottle of beer waiting for him in front of a fifty-two-inch TV.

She stood up and walked to the French doors that led to his twenty-fifth-floor balcony, and Greg reluctantly followed her outside. She leaned on the railing and stared out into the bright sunshine of a simmering September afternoon. "You've even got a view of Central Park. No wonder Connie didn't want to let you go!" She turned and looked at him.

Greg shrugged. "The breakup had been coming for a long time. All we did was fight. We weren't meant to be together, that's all."

Hayley smiled slyly. "I'll bet you say that about all the girls."

Again, Greg thought it best not to reply. She was alluding to his reputation as a love-'em-and-leave-'em ladies' man, an unfortunate tag he'd learned to live with. Although he'd earned his reputation by avoiding commitment, he never intentionally led women to think there was a chance for something permanent. If he was a cad, he was an honest one.

"She wanted to marry you."

Greg frowned. "I never—"

"She was determined to marry you. That's why she—" Hayley broke off and returned her gaze to the panoramic view of Central Park.

"Why she . . . what?" The bad feeling that had trailed Hayley into the room along with her heady perfume was growing stronger. Greg's stomach twisted with apprehension.

"She got pregnant, Greg."

Greg felt as though he'd been sucker punched in the gut. He could barely breathe. "What the hell are you talking about, Hayley? Connie was on the Pill. It was understood—"

"She thought it might make a difference. She thought you might—"

"Be forced to marry her out of a sense of responsibility," Greg finished grimly. "Then why didn't she tell me?"

"Because you made it pretty clear that things were over between you two. Connie wasn't used to rejection. She was so angry with you, she decided to keep the pregnancy a secret."

Greg rubbed his jaw distractedly, trying to take it all in. Him, a father. It was something he'd never aspired to. In fact, he'd guarded against it in every relationship he'd ever had.

His parents went through a bitter divorce when he was six and his father was given custody of Greg, their only child. Greg never saw his mother again, and over the years his dad was barely there, too busy building his career to pay much attention to a child. Greg had learned early that children were an encumbrance to the smooth flow of things. Why would he want such a complication in his own life?

"So, did she . . . ?"

"Yes, she had the baby," said Hayley. "Nine months ago. But she didn't keep it. She gave it up for adoption."

The word *adoption* left Greg with a hollow feeling in his chest. It had such a ring of finality to it. He told himself he ought to be completely happy with the news, because Connie wouldn't have made a very stable or loving mother. Wherever his child was, he or she was better off far away from Connie and her jet-set crowd. So, why did he still feel uneasy?

"Don't you want to know whether it's a boy or a girl?"

Greg looked up, surprised. "Yeah. I guess so."

"It's a boy."

A son. "Why did you decide to tell me about the baby?"

Hayley shrugged. "You had a right. Connie was wrong to keep the fact of your paternity from you, and especially to give the baby up for adoption without your knowledge or consent."

"How was she able to do that? If I was named as the child's father on the birth certificate, surely the lawyers were obligated to contact me before—"

"Connie told the lawyers she didn't know who the father was," interrupted Hayley. "The birth certificate reads 'father unknown.'"

Greg felt his jaw tighten. "Is that possible?"

"No," Hayley answered firmly. "Connie didn't lie about that part of it, Greg. She had no reason to hide the truth from me. The baby is yours, all right."

Greg did not reply. He couldn't. He was still visualizing those words on the birth certificate. *Father unknown.*

"Anyway," continued Hayley, "all this has been gnawing at me for months. I had to tell you to relieve my conscience." She looked searchingly at him. "And I thought you might want to...you know...do something about it."

Greg raised his brows. "Like what? It's enough to know he's been placed in a good home." He paused, then asked, "Connie did make sure he was put with good people, didn't she?"

Hayley shrugged again. "I don't know any of the details. If you want details, Greg, you'll have to ask Connie."

Greg felt himself cringing. "Not likely," he said flatly.

Abruptly Hayley turned and walked back into the living room. "Well, I'm going now. I've done my duty. You know as much as I do. Now maybe I'll get a decent night's sleep."

Greg followed her to the door. "You've been losing sleep over this, Hayley?"

With her hand on the doorknob, she turned and grinned sheepishly. "Yeah. Can you believe it?"

Greg smiled back. "Then maybe you aren't as much like Connie as it appears."

"God, I hope not," she retorted, then opened the door and left. He watched those long legs swing as she walked to the elevator. Damn, just like her big sister. Connie had been about as deep as a puddle of spilled milk, but she'd kept his hormones in a spin for over a year. He hated remembering their time together. He'd been dazzled by her beauty, her pedigree and her money, but after a year he'd realized he was becoming as shallow as she was. It scared the hell out of him.

At the elevator, Hayley turned and waved breezily as if she hadn't just given him the biggest shock of his life. When the elevator closed, he went inside and stood for a minute in a daze. If not for the faint lingering scent of Obsession, Greg might believe that the past few minutes hadn't really happened.

He closed the French doors to the balcony on his way to the den. Sighing, he eased into the cushiony lounge chair and picked up his beer. But the baseball players on the wide-screen TV had lost their appeal. He couldn't concentrate.

Damn. He was a father. But it really made no difference, he told himself. Life would go on just as before. If Connie had done things right, his son was in a good home with committed parents who had plenty of time and love just for him. Greg's fingers clenched tightly around the narrow neck of the beer bottle.

If Connie had done things right... But had she?

Chapter One

Greg nursed his third cup of coffee, alternately checking his watch and looking impatiently toward the door of the small bistro just off Fifth Avenue. One hand drummed a staccato beat against the white linen cloth that covered the circular table, and the other raked through his thick blond hair. He had agreed to meet Mr. Smith at three o'clock, and it was already three-thirty. But then, Mr. Smith was always late.

Nothing irritated Greg more than doing business with someone habitually tardy. He tossed back the last dregs of his coffee, wishing he'd ignored the early-afternoon hour and ordered Scotch instead. Whiskey might have given a good chin punch to the butterflies doing a jig in his stomach.

Butterflies and business didn't mix. But Greg knew that his business with Mr. Smith, who was reputed to be one of the best private investigators in New York City, really wasn't business at all. His dealings with Mr. Smith were painfully personal, and important enough to keep him rooted to his chair even though he never waited for anyone more than fifteen minutes—not even a potential client. But today Mr. Smith had promised to have the information he'd hired him to dig up. Today Greg would find out who was raising his son.

Ever since Hayley's surprise visit nearly a month ago, he'd tried to put her shocking revelation out of his mind. His son was already calling some other guy "Daddy," and that was fine with Greg. He had no intention of disrupting the domestic tranquillity of the child's adoptive home. But he had to make sure it was a good home.

Hiring a P.I. to find the child, then to conduct a thorough investigation into the adoptive parents' background and current circumstances, was all Greg intended to do. Then he'd be satisfied. Then he could go on with his life without worrying about the kid's future.

The waiter had refilled Greg's cup. Now, as he lifted the cup to his lips, his hand shook and he spilled the dark, scalding liquid on his silk tie. Cursing, he dabbed at the maroon paisley swirls that complemented his gray suit and crisp white shirt. He couldn't remember ever feeling this out of control, this rattled. Life had been as smooth as chiffon pie till—

"Mr. Chandler?"

Greg's head jerked up and he found Mr. Smith, in his usual wrinkled khaki pants, worn corduroy jacket and scuffed loafers, standing by the table. He was a rumpled Columbo—without the trench coat and squint.

"Sit down, Mr. Smith," he ordered, "and tell me what you found out." Mr. Smith sat down. Greg leaned back in his chair and crossed his long legs, ankle meeting knee in a negligent pose that belied his inner turmoil. Just then the waiter walked up and handed Mr. Smith a menu.

Much to Greg's irritation, the detective studied the menu at great length, as if the information he was about to impart was less important than the soup of the day. Finally he sent the waiter away without ordering, patted his paunchy stomach and said with a sigh, "I'd kill for something greasy, but the wife's got me on a diet of rice cakes, fresh fruit and vegetables. Have you ever eaten rice cakes, Mr. Chandler? The damn things taste like Styrofoam."

"Can we get to the point, Mr. Smith?" Greg leaned forward, steepled his fingers, and glared across the table. He was past politeness.

"Whatever you say, Mr. Chandler." Mr. Smith slumped in his chair and hooked his thumbs in his belt loops. "His name is James Bennet. Goes by Jamie."

Some new feeling, a feeling Greg didn't understand and didn't have the patience to analyze, was choking him. "They named him James?" He swallowed hard, pushing past the painful emotion. "Who are these Bennets? Where do they live? Are there other children?"

Mr. Smith raised a hand to stem the flow of questions. "Slow down, Mr. Chandler. I've got it all right here for you in this envelope." He reached inside a beat-up briefcase and pulled out a manila envelope. Then he stood, apparently ready to leave.

Greg curbed his impatience to rip open the envelope and devour its contents, and instead reached for his checkbook. Mr. Smith again raised a restraining hand. "I'll send you a bill."

"What if I want to know more? How can I be sure this envelope contains all the information I need?"

"I'm not worried." Mr. Smith smiled smugly. "Satisfaction guaranteed, remember?"

"Right." Greg's eyes drifted back to the envelope. Inside were facts about people he didn't know, but who were raising his son. More than likely they'd be angry and concerned if they knew he'd paid a detective to dig up every detail of their private lives. What would he do if he found out something negative about the couple who'd adopted his son? What *could* he do?

Suddenly remembering Mr. Smith, Greg raised his head. But the private investigator had already gone. Greg shrugged, dismissing the man from his mind.

He ripped open the envelope, pulled out three neatly typed sheets of paper and two photographs. One was of a woman in her late twenties, he guessed, dressed in a casual madras skirt and thongs, her dark hair pulled back in a ponytail. She was sitting on a beach, building a sand castle with the questionable help of a sturdy-looking toddler wielding a plastic shovel. They were both laughing. The other picture was a close-up of the toddler. Towheaded, chubby-cheeked and smiling, he looked like a Gerber baby.

The painful constriction in Greg's throat returned. He forced himself to be objective as he continued to examine the picture. An attractive child, he supposed, but being an only child himself and a thirty-five-year-old bachelor, what did he know?

Then it struck him. Where was *Mr.* Bennet? Where was the *daddy?* He reached for the paper and started to read. Skimming past less important details, he read that Mr. Bennet was dead—thirteen months dead—

killed in a boating accident off Nantucket Island before the adoption was even finalized. A widow was raising his son!

He told himself that single mothers were not that uncommon, but a gnawing uncertainty rumbled in his stomach. Was Mrs. Bennet capable of raising a child alone? And the child would be alone, too, without other siblings in the family. He remembered his own loneliness as a child.

He glanced again at the baby in the photo and at the smiling brunette. Could she be everything the child needed? If he could give her points for looks, she'd have it made. But good-looking women were sometimes just attractive packaging. Connie had certainly taught him that.

Then his gaze returned to the baby, his baby, his *son*. There was that damned lump in his throat again! He started again at the beginning of the document, reading every detail of the Bennets' lives with an urgent interest, anxious for reassurance that Jamie was being raised in a wonderful environment.

Ten minutes later, with a grim set to his jaw and a determined glint in his gray-green eyes, he threw a twenty-dollar bill on the table and headed for the nearest pay phone to make reservations for the first flight to Nantucket Island in the morning. Mikelle Bennet ran a bed-and-breakfast called the Little Gray Lady on the island.

Other details about her personal preferences led him to believe she was a liberal. She was an artist and a vegetarian. Her politics were probably as green as her main dishes. All that was acceptable, of course, even though he was a conservative and a dedicated carnivore—cholesterol be damned.

There was nothing really objectionable about the woman except her single state, but there was also nothing solid that could reassure him of her ability to raise a child alone. Would she have time for Jamie? Or would she be too busy whipping up bran muffins for her bed-and-breakfast clientele?

Weaving his tall frame through swarms of New Yorkers, Greg Chandler knew one thing for sure. He had to see his son and his son's adoptive parent and make up his own mind about Mikelle's suitability as a mother. He wouldn't make an effort to meet them, he'd only observe them as a stranger would—in the park, or at the beach, or wherever she went with Jamie.

A pesky little voice told him that the pictures ought to be proof enough that Mikelle Bennet was a loving mother, and that maybe—just maybe—he was making this trip out of an overwhelming curiosity to see his son. But Greg didn't allow himself time to question his impulsive decision to fly to Nantucket. He'd get a good look at Mikelle and Jamie together, *then* he'd examine his feelings. Hell, already this fatherhood thing was complicating his life!

NO SHOPPING MALLS, no high rises, neon signs, billboards, or even stoplights. Driving along Nantucket Town's cobblestoned main street, Greg was struck by the island's nostalgic charm. Sporadic sprinkles of rain spotted the road like a giant case of measles, and sea-salted breezes wafted through the open window of the car. He had rented a Jeep Cherokee wagon at the small airport and was now headed for the Little Gray Lady, which he knew he could find easily by the address provided in Mr. Smith's report.

With the interest of an architect, he looked appreciatively at all the stately old homes and quaint little shops. The sidewalks were brick, and wavy from the passage of time and the tread of decades of footsteps. Gilt-leaved elm trees lined the meandering street.

He turned left on Quaker Road, then right on Vestal Street, and there it was. The Little Gray Lady. The gray, two-story inn reflected the Georgian style of late-eighteenth-century England. A raised porch graced the front of the white-shuttered, many-windowed house, and two slender columns held up the slight overhang that protected the porch.

A rooftop structure, popularly called a widow's walk, could be seen in all its quaint charm atop the shingles. Greg thought he saw a telescope up there, too, and remembered from Mr. Smith's report that Jim Bennet had had an interest in astronomy.

He realized he'd gawked long enough and drove on around the block, then turned again on Vestal Street and parked on the opposite side of the road from the bed-and-breakfast and about three houses down. He'd brought *The New York Times* to read while he waited and a sandwich from the airport snack bar to use as a prop if someone suspected him of staking out the neighborhood for the purpose of theft. If questioned, he'd say he'd pulled over to eat lunch.

Greg unfolded the newspaper and laid it on the steering wheel. He unwrapped a tuna on rye and put it on the dashboard. Then he simply waited and watched. He had no real interest in the paper or the sandwich. It was eleven o'clock in the morning, a perfect time for the owner of a bed-and-breakfast to run errands or take her child on an outing. All the guests would have eaten and been on their way by now—

He sat up straight. Someone was coming out of a side door and walking toward the garage. Even from a distance, he recognized Mikelle Bennet from her picture. She was wearing jeans and a red, oversize top. Her dark hair skimmed her shoulders. Propped on her right hip was a toddler. *Jamie.*

Greg's heart skipped a beat. He strained to see, but within seconds they had disappeared into the garage. He folded the paper, stashed the sandwich, started the car engine and shifted into gear. A blue Volvo station wagon backed down the gravel driveway and onto the street. He saw the back of Jamie's head in the front seat. The child was sitting quite tall and Greg realized that Jamie must be strapped into a special infant car seat. That pleased him. She obviously understood the danger of transporting a baby loose in the car. He followed them at a discreet distance, pulling in behind when they stopped at a small grocery store.

Greg waited till they'd gone inside, then got out of the car. He locked the doors, although he'd noticed that Mikelle hadn't locked hers. He frowned, wondering if she was too trusting. Inside the store he looked around and spotted Mikelle and Jamie in the produce department. *Figures,* he thought. *She's probably planning some sort of broccoli casserole for dinner.*

He got himself a shopping cart and wheeled it toward the artichokes. That was one vegetable he liked, each leaf dipped in a bowl of melted butter. Besides, Mikelle and Jamie were just three feet away—yeah, he'd been right—at the broccoli.

While pretending to be engrossed in picking out a perfect artichoke, Greg surreptitiously got his first close-up look at his son. He was a big baby, dressed in a blue corduroy jumpsuit and miniature basketball shoes. The kid looked older than ten months, but what the hell did he know? Jamie was nearing his first birthday and this was the first time Greg had ever laid eyes on him.

The kid squirmed a lot, too. Greg was glad Mikelle had strapped him snugly in the shopping cart's baby seat. He was alternately beating Mikelle's car keys against the metal bars of the shopping cart in rhythm to some incoherent baby chatter, then lifting them to his mouth and sucking on the leather key ring. Greg wondered if that was such a good idea. Leather was porous, wasn't it? Ripe for germs. How sanitary could that key ring be?

Suddenly Jamie caught Greg looking at him and smiled. The big eyes crinkled, the pink cheeks puffed out like little balloons and the drooling mouth spread wide to display a couple of tiny white teeth. Greg thought his heart would literally melt. He went all oozy inside. He found himself smiling back and fighting the urge to pick up Jamie then and there. Such strong emotions scared him to death.

"Excuse me, young man," said a querulous voice, "but I'd sure like to get to those artichokes. You aren't picking out a bride, you know. No need to be so choosy."

Startled, Greg looked around and found himself confronted by a short elderly woman in a straw hat and a bright pink sweat suit. He and his cart were completely blocking access to the artichoke bin. "Sorry," he mumbled, then hurriedly stuffed three artichokes into a paper bag and tossed it into the cart, moving on to the plum tomatoes.

His cart had a bum wheel, something he hadn't noticed at first. It made a *kerblunk, kerblunk* sound as he pushed it, and was also difficult to steer.

Greg was embarrassed. He felt the heat creeping up his neck. He wasn't being very effective at being inconspicuous...or being objective, either. He thought Jamie was one adorable kid. The little guy was smiling at the lady in pink now. He wondered if Jamie was always so good-natured.

Then he glanced up at Mikelle and discovered her watching him with curiosity. As soon as their gazes met, however, they both looked abruptly away. He concentrated on the plum tomatoes, rolling them in his fingers like a gourmet cook searching for prize marinara fixings. But averting his eyes didn't keep him from listening.

"Hi, Annabelle," said Mikelle to the pink lady. She had a nice voice. Low pitched, melodic. Good for reading Dr. Seuss and singing lullabies.

"Mikelle!" exclaimed Annabelle. "I didn't see you standing there, honey. Can't see much farther than my nose these days. Doing your shopping, eh? How's things at the Gray Lady?"

"Business is a little off right now," said Mikelle.

Visions of financial ruin danced through Greg's head. Damn, how was she going to be able to help Jamie with college tuition? And what if he wanted to go to medical school, or got a hankering to practice law, or—

"It's always been a mystery to me why there aren't more mainlanders on the island in the fall. It's the most beautiful time of the year. Right now I've only got a retired couple from Kansas.''

"Well, business will pick up. Just use the extra time to play with Jamie." There was a pause and Greg heard Jamie laugh. It was a delightful sound, all gurgly and happy. He slid a covert look their way and saw Annabelle tickling his son under his plump chin. Unfortunately, Mikelle saw him looking and looked back. This time her eyes held a hint of suspicion.

He put several tomatoes in a bag and moved to the cucumbers, still close enough to hear everything the women were saying. "Jamie's grown so much," said Annabelle. "He's been a godsend to you, hasn't he, Mikelle?"

"Without Jamie this last year would have been horrible," said Mikelle, so softly Greg had to strain to hear her. It struck him then that he'd never thought about Mikelle's loss at Jim Bennet's death, but only how it effected Jamie. His sympathy was belatedly stirred.

"Will you be at bingo Friday night?"

"Not this week, Annabelle," said Mikelle. "Jamie and I are going to the Johnsons' for a barbecue. They've got a little boy just two months older than Jamie. The two of them have a ball together." Her voice got softer and higher pitched. "Don't you, Jamie? Don't you just love to play with Tyler?"

Greg braved a look. Mikelle was bending, her face at Jamie's level, her hands propped on her knees. Mother and son were smiling like idiots at each other and Jamie was kicking his legs like crazy. He reached out and gently tapped her cheek with his palm. Greg knew that fat little baby hand had to be covered with drool, judging by the way Jamie had been gumming the key ring. But Mikelle didn't seem to mind at all. Come to think of it, he wouldn't mind, either. He felt his heart ache with a new kind of yearning. He moved on to the cantaloupes, trying to get a handle on his emotions.

"Say 'bye-bye to Annabelle," said Mikelle. Greg tried not to look again, but he couldn't help it. Mikelle was waving to Annabelle and Jamie was paying rapt attention. "Don't be shy, Jamie. You do this at home all the time. Say 'bye-bye," Mikelle coaxed again.

Mikelle's face was animated. Greg wondered if his mother had ever looked that way at him, had been so encouraging with his first words, his first steps, his first anything. He held his breath. He felt as if he were at a Little League game and his kid was up for bat. Jamie finally lifted his hand and waved at Annabelle, a little voice calling out, "'Ba-bye."

Mikelle, Annabelle and Greg were all delighted. Only he couldn't beam and share a smile with someone, the way Mikelle and Annabelle were doing. He had nothing to grin at but a cantaloupe, and anyone watching him would think he was either crazy or a pervert.

Mikelle said goodbye to Annabelle and moved out of the produce section. Greg waited a few seconds, then followed. He noticed with chagrin that his cart looked as though it had collided with a vegetable truck; it was already half-full.

For the next few aisles, Greg continued to stay close to Mikelle and Greg, but not too close. Mikelle was kept busy taking grocery items out of Jamie's grabby little hands, things he'd snatched from shelves and out of the cart. He'd either try to eat the item, gum it, shake it, or rip it apart.

Mikelle finally gave him a plastic bottle of juice. He held it in one hand while he sucked down the juice, and continued to grab things with his free hand. *Resourceful*, thought Greg with pride.

Mikelle was quick—Greg had to grant her that—but she wasn't quick enough to stop Jamie from pulling a small jar of pickles off the shelf. Greg cringed as the crash resounded through the store and sent pickle juice spraying in all directions. Greg's trousers were lightly splattered, even though he was standing ten feet away.

Jamie popped the bottle out of his mouth, looked down at the mess, and said, "Uh-oh."

"Cleanup on aisle four," called Mikelle in a beleaguered voice.

Greg had to hold back his laughter. But maybe Mikelle didn't find the situation as amusing as he did. He glanced at her and was relieved to see her ruffling Jamie's hair, a wry smile on her lips. She was patient with Jamie and apparently resigned to the fact that active children sometimes wreak havoc.

A teenage boy with a freckled face showed up with a mop and a smile. "Hi, Mrs. Bennet," he said cheerfully. "When I heard glass breaking I thought you might be in the store."

Mikelle flicked Greg an embarrassed look. He turned and pretended to be reading the nutrition label on a box of stuffing. Later, when she caught him ogling Jamie again, her look was more irritated and suspicious than embarrassed. He added to the ever growing mound of groceries by picking up three boxes of Lucky Charms and moved on. He knew she probably thought he was stalking them for the purpose of kidnapping, or trying to pick her up.

Finally, Mikelle was done shopping, although she hadn't bought nearly as much as Greg had. He thought it might be pushing things if he got in the same checkout line, but then found out he had no choice. There was only one cash register servicing the entire store. He reminded himself that he was in Nantucket, not New York. People around here weren't in as big a hurry as where he came from.

He lined up his cart, which had become extremely difficult to navigate with the loopy wheel and so much food in it, behind Mikelle's. Mikelle went around to the counter to write her check and was immediately engaged in conversation by a chatty cashier.

"I got off easy today, Colleen. He just broke a jar of pickles," Mikelle replied. "It was a small jar of Nallys' baby dills." Mikelle kept one eye on the cashier and one eye on Jamie, who sat facing Greg.

Greg was very pleased with this arrangement. He picked up a copy of the *National Intruder* with a picture on the front of Madonna holding hands with Elvis. He couldn't care less that Elvis had been hiding all this time in Madonna's basement. He simply planned to use the scandal sheet for a screen.

Holding it in front of his face, he peeked over and around the pages to look at his son. Jamie found this game of hide-and-seek vastly entertaining and burst out with one of his throaty baby laughs.

"Excuse me?"

Greg slowly lowered the paper. Mikelle was standing right in front of him, so close he could smell her light cologne. The scent reminded him of roses on a rainy day—fresh, floral. And what was that other smell? Ah, yes. Pickle juice.

"Yes?" he said, trying to look innocent. Mikelle smiled. He was mesmerized for an instant by the way her lips—devoid of lipstick but still looking pink and dewy—stretched over straight, white teeth. But then he realized that the smile didn't reach her eyes. The expression in her gray eyes was wary, edgy. He thought this must be how protective mothers looked just before they lost control and dented the head of a suspected kidnapper with a king-size can of wax beans.

"You must be new around here," she said pleasantly enough.

"Er...yes."

"Where did you buy?"

"I didn't buy. I'm just visiting."

She flicked a look over him; at his dress slacks and pullover polo shirt. "You're staying at the Executive Inn, right?"

He grinned sheepishly. "Right. There's a hot tub in every room, you know."

She looked pointedly at the cart full of food. "I hope you got a suite with a kitchen. That's enough food to feed a small principality."

"I'm here with friends," he lied. He smiled engagingly and lied some more for good measure. "We're gourmet cooks, actually, stocking up for a weekend of culinary competition." He wondered if heating up take-out Chinese qualified him for the status of gourmet cook.

"You're having a cooking contest?" She looked surprised and gave him a sort of incredulous once-over. "What's your specialty? And don't tell me one of the ingredients of your favorite dish is Lucky Charms."

He forced a laugh, casting a nervous glance at the three boxes of "magically delicious" cereal he'd thrown into the cart. "The Lucky Charms are for energy. Slaving over a hot stove saps a person's sugar reserves."

"I see," she said dubiously, a smile twitching at the corners of her mouth. He could tell he was about as convincing as a three-dollar bill. Even he had a hard time imagining gourmet cooks chowing down on a kids' cereal. "I thought at first you must be doing the shopping for your wife, who was home herding a houseful of children."

The alarming vision he'd conjured up prompted him to blurt out the truth. "I'm not married."

She raised her brows. "You could have fooled me. I noticed how much you've been looking at my little boy. I was sure you had children of your own."

Greg slid the *National Intruder* back in its slot and shoved his hands into his pockets. "No, I don't. But your little Jamie makes me wish I did."

He immediately realized his blunder.

"How did you know his name is Jamie?" she demanded, her smile gone now.

Think fast, Chandler. "I heard you talking to that pink lady."

"Pink lady?"

"You know, the one in produce."

Her expression relaxed a little. "Oh. Annabelle." But by the shrewd look in her eyes, he could tell she was still sizing him up, trying to figure out just what kind of man he was. He could clear that up for her in a heartbeat. He was a very confused man...a bungling bozo trying to think on his feet at least as fast as she did.

He braced himself for another question, but was saved from further interrogation by the cashier calling out, "You're all bagged up and ready to go, Mikelle."

Mikelle and Greg both turned and saw that she was indeed ready to go. And so was Jamie. He was tired of sitting in that cart and was bouncing his bottom up and down on the seat, squealing, "Go! Go! Go!" Ah, another word he seemed to have mastered.

"Yes, you'd better go, Mikelle," said Greg. "Jamie's a tad on the impatient side." *Just like his old man.*

When she looked surprised, Greg hooked a thumb at the cashier. "I heard your name from her. You know... Colleen. You see, it's not so difficult to discover people's names around here. You just have to do a little eavesdropping." He smiled, striving to dredge up some charm from the overflowing buckets of it he was supposed to have as one of New York's premier lady-killers.

He must have made a little impact, because she smiled genuinely this time and extended her hand. "I may be crazy to divulge this willingly, but I have a feeling you'd find out anyway if you really wanted to. The whole name is Mikelle Bennet. And you are...?"

Greg took her hand and shook it. "Greg Chandler. Pleased to officially meet you." He noticed that her hand was slender and finely boned and fit quite nicely in his. Too nice to let go.

"What's holding up this line?" demanded the same querulous voice that had shooed him away from the artichokes. Greg let go of Mikelle's hand and turned to see Annabelle, her wrinkled sunburned face glowering at him from under her straw hat. "Oh, it's you again. Lordy, you're one to dally, aren't you?"

"Sorry," he murmured, then turned back to Mikelle with a rueful shake of his head. She smiled with amused sympathy, then moved around the counter and began pushing her cart toward the door. "Good luck with your culinary competition, Mr. Chandler," she called as she walked away. "If you and your gourmet friends are ever back on the island again, you ought to try my bed-and-breakfast, the Little Gray Lady. The food's great and you don't have to cook it. Comfortable beds, too. 'Bye-bye, now."

"Bye," he called after them, waving. To his surprise, Jamie waved back and said, "'Ba-bye."

Nothing could have touched Greg more or helped him make up his mind faster. Mikelle was definitely going to see him again, but without his fictitious friends. And he was toying with the idea of actually staying at the Little Gray Lady.

While the cashier rang up his groceries, Greg tried to understand what was happening to him. The answer came quickly enough—he was falling in love with his son. But what he was hoping to accomplish by personally acquainting himself with Mikelle and Jamie was not too clear in his slightly overtaxed brain. However, in the past few weeks it seemed as though his heart and not his brain was making all the decisions. Trouble was, hearts frequently made risky choices, choices that ended up hurting people.

"That'll be one-hundred-seventy-two dollars and twenty-three cents," said the cashier.

Now that hurt. "Are you sure?"

"These fingers never make a mistake," Colleen assured him, rolling his receipt into a paper tube thick enough to beat off a New York mugger. He'd never spent so much money on groceries in his life. Luckily he'd brought plenty of cash.

Once the groceries were loaded into the Cherokee and he was sitting behind the wheel, it struck him that he had no place to store the stuff. He had not rented a suite at the Executive Inn. His room had a hot tub, but no kitchen facilities. There was only a minibar that was already crammed with little booze bottles and tiny five-dollar packages of peanuts and candy. He realized then how obsessed he'd become, how oblivious to everything except this new experience called fatherhood.

But at the moment his most pressing problem was the possible reenactment of the melting of the ice age in the back seat of his rented Jeep. He'd spent considerable time in the freezer section of the store and he vaguely remembered at least two half gallons of Rocky Road ice cream. What the hell was he going to do with all this food?

Driving down the street, he suddenly saw the answer to his dilemma. He flipped on his blinker and prepared to turn.

Chapter Two

"I hope you prepared lots of food for tea, Rose. That guest from New York arrives this afternoon and a few dainty finger sandwiches will probably only whet his appetite."

Sunlight filtered through the windows of the large kitchen decorated in soft country blues. "No one ever leaves my table hungry, Mikelle," said Rose, punching a fist into a crockery bowl of inflated dough. The yeast hissed and the dough deflated like a punctured inner tube. "But I'll make extra of everything just to be sure. How do you know this man's a big eater?"

Mikelle hiked a sleeping Jamie farther up on her shoulder. He was big for a baby nearly eleven months old, as tall as some two-year-olds. Mikelle often thought his biological father must be some sort of Goliath type. "All you have to do is look at him to figure that out. I met him two weeks ago at the grocery store. His cart was piled so high he could barely push it."

She grinned ruefully at the memory. "He said he was shopping for some cooking contest with friends, but I'll believe that story when pigs fly. I suspect he's full of blarney, as you Irish say."

Rose raised an interested brow. "A big man with a charmin' way about 'im, is he?"

"I never said he was charming," Mikelle corrected quickly. "But he is tall. At least six-four."

Rose pursed her lips consideringly. "How old?"

"Oh, early thirties, I guess."

"A good age," mused Rose, and Mikelle didn't have to ask what Rose thought it was good for. "Handsome?"

"Most women would think so."

Now both of Rose's eyebrows shot up, but she said nothing as she greased her hands with virgin olive oil, removed the tan ball of bread dough from the bowl and dropped it onto the floured countertop. Mikelle waited. She knew the other shoe would drop any second.

"And did he have a gold band on the third finger of his left hand?"

Mikelle laughed. "You're so predictable, Rose. As a matter of fact, he did mention he wasn't married." Jamie was sliding down Mikelle's T-shirt again like butter on a hot cob of corn. She placed one foot on a kitchen chair and eased Jamie's bottom down to rest on her knee, relieving her aching arms from some of the strain of supporting his full weight. Now his cheek rested against her chest, a soft baby snore lisping from his slightly parted lips.

"But don't get any ideas," she told Rose firmly. "He didn't look like my type at all. Besides—"

Rose was pounding, slapping and kneading the dough as if it were the devil himself, but she stopped to give Mikelle a keen look. "Besides what?"

Mikelle shrugged, though she felt far less nonchalant than she pretended. "I don't know. Sometimes I wish I'd never mentioned the Gray Lady to him. There's something about him that makes me nervous. At the store he sort of hung around in our general vicinity the whole time. It was almost like he was following us."

"He was interested, Mikelle," said Rose with exasperation. "He probably wanted to meet you, but was too shy to say anything."

"Believe me," Mikelle said wryly, "this guy doesn't strike me as the shy type. Besides, I got the feeling he was more interested in Jamie. Every time I caught him glancing my way, he was looking at Jamie, not me. After a while I started having visions of Jamie's face on milk cartons." Mikelle didn't really believe Greg was a kidnapper, but she did think his obvious interest in Jamie was unusual.

Rose raised her floured hands. "So what if he looked at Jamie? Everyone looks at Jamie. He's a beautiful baby. Maybe this Mr. Chandler just likes kids. Whoever you hook up with, Mikelle, has got to like kids."

"Rose, I thought you already had my matrimonial future planned," chided Mikelle. "You've been hoping for me and Frank to get together for months."

Rose resumed her kneading. "Humph! I'm about to give up on Frank. If he can't light a fire in you, maybe he needs some competition to get him more— shall we say—motivated?"

Mikelle didn't want Frank more "motivated." She liked her relationship just the way it was. While she had gone out with several men, Frank was the only one she'd continued to see beyond the first date or two. And that was because he was more of a friend.

He didn't rush her. He seemed to understand that five years of marriage couldn't be forgotten overnight.

"When is this charming New Yorker going to be here?" Rose's question recalled Mikelle to the matters at hand. She was grateful to Rose for her stalwart practicality.

Rose was sixty-one, a first-generation American from County Cork, Ireland, a widow of six years, and a mother of four grown children. She had a lot of wisdom stored in her canny brain and she had shared that wisdom with Mikelle over the past year, becoming not only her cook, housekeeper and sometime baby-sitter, but also a valued friend. She'd stood by her, cried with her, and prodded her through the black depression after Jim's death at sea.

Rose had been Mikelle's support, and Jamie had been her saving grace. Raising the baby both she and Jim had wanted so desperately had given Mikelle a new lease on life.

"He flew in on the one-thirty flight," Mikelle replied briskly, checking her watch. "He ought to show up any time now. I'll go lay Jamie down and change for tea."

"Wear a skirt, Mikelle," advised Rose. "Maybe he's a leg man."

Mikelle chuckled and repositioned Jamie so that his head was cradled in the crook of her arm. "Rose, you're incorrigible. Just call me when he gets here, okay? I'll need a shower before I change clothes."

"Put on some rouge," called Rose as Mikelle slowly climbed the back stairs. "You're a little pale today."

Mikelle just shook her head.

GREG OPENED THE GATE of the wrought-iron fence that enclosed the tiny front yard of the Little Gray Lady. Striding up the cobbled walkway, he hoped he looked more casual and relaxed than he felt. The last two weeks, although filled with work, had seemed to drag on endlessly. And now that he was finally back in Nantucket, he was adrift in a sea of nerves.

Stepping onto the porch, Greg paused momentarily to admire the door knocker. It was a brass replica of a sixteenth-century galleon, its sails full-blown and flapping in the ocean air. Then he gathered his resolve and gave the knocker three sharp raps against the door. Would Mikelle answer? Would she be holding Jamie in her arms?

The door opened and a short, rounded woman in an apron stared over her bifocals at him. "Mr. Chandler?" she asked, wiping her hands on a dishcloth.

"Yes." The woman stepped back and Greg stepped forward onto the hardwood floor of a spacious entry hall. A wonderful aroma permeated the air. Bread baking, or maybe cinnamon rolls. A hodgepodge of antique furniture lined the walls, Queen Anne mostly, all in rich cherrywood.

"Mrs. Bennet will be down in a minute," the woman said with a slight Irish accent. Her voice and manner were respectful and polite, but her sharp blue eyes scrutinized him. "My name is Rose. If you ever need anything— Ah, here is Mrs. Bennet."

Greg followed Rose's gaze to the stairs and watched as Mikelle slowly descended. She was putting on earrings—dangling, turquoise-colored things that looked like Indian beadwork. She wore a denim jumper that buttoned down the front and flowed from a fitted waist to a full skirt. Like the last time he saw her, her chestnut hair bobbed in a glossy pageboy. She wore just a touch of makeup.

Greg was used to New York businesswoman with their high heels, narrow-skirted power suits and high-tech hair. Mikelle gave off a most unsettling impression of softness all over.

Greg's eyes slipped down to Mikelle's long, tanned legs. From the pearl-polished toenails peeping out of the open-toed sandals she wore, he could tell she wasn't wearing nylons. But her legs looked as smooth as a Porsche dealer's softest chamois. He could just imagine his hand circling the trim ankle, easing up the firm, rounded calf, dipping into the satin hollow behind her knee....

What was he thinking? Hell, his blood was percolating like a river of lava! He was here to see Jamie and to observe Mikelle Bennet's mothering skills, not to check out her legs. He forced himself to focus.

"So glad you took me up on my offer," said Mikelle, walking toward him with an outstretched hand.

Greg was sure he looked totally blank. "Er...your offer?" Her hand fit just as neatly in his as it had that first time they shook hands.

"At the grocery store two weeks ago. I mentioned the Gray Lady and suggested you stay here on your next visit. Isn't that why you're here, forgoing the pleasures of the 'hot tub in every room' Executive Inn?"

"Yes, I guess I never thought about the advantages of staying at a bed-and-breakfast...till I met you," he answered. Listening to himself, he nearly winced. He sounded like a third-rate lothario delivering a come-on line, but it was better she thought he was coming on to her than to suspect his true motives.

"But you didn't bring along your clutch of gourmet cooks," she said.

"No, they were too busy rustling up knock-'em-dead recipes for our next bake-off." Suddenly Greg realized that he was still clasping her hand. There was a trace of anxiousness in her eyes...eyes as gray as the Little Gray Lady herself. He let go.

She smiled nervously. "So all that food you bought turned into something delicious?"

Greg smiled back, glad to be able to say something completely truthful. "The people who ate that food really appreciated it."

"I'm glad," she replied, more composed now that he'd released her hand. "You said on the phone that you were here on business?"

"Yes. I'm an architect." Greg began his rehearsed speech. "I have a client who's looking to build on the island. He's very particular. He wants a secluded spot and he wants the house designed to fit in perfectly with its surroundings. I'll be looking at lots of real estate. I don't usually find sites for clients, but this client is special. It may take me a while, so that's why I'd like my stay here to be open-ended. I'll be coming and going at odd hours—no set business itinerary."

"Sounds like a perfect way to do business to me," said Mikelle. "You'll really know the island by the time you leave."

And hopefully I'll really know you, he thought. For a second he allowed himself to admire how smooth her skin looked, then reminded himself that the things he needed to know about Mikelle had nothing to do with her appearance. He was here to be reassured that he could leave Jamie in this woman's care for the entire duration of his son's formative years. Then he was going to go on with his own life— the slightly hedonistic life he'd enjoyed so thoroughly before Hayley had dropped that bombshell several weeks ago.

"Tea will be served in the parlor in half an hour, so I'll show you to your room and let you get settled in," she said, turning and moving to the stairs. He picked up his suitcase and followed closely behind, finding the feminine sway of her hips as she ascended the stairs a little too interesting.

Mikelle was glad to be given a short reprieve as she turned her back on Greg Chandler, though his close proximity behind her was still pretty unnerving. When they'd shook hands just now, she'd felt her insides lurch, as if she'd taken a speed bump too fast. She'd had the same reaction at the grocery store, but had shrugged it off as a hormone fluctuation. No one had made her pulse skitter like that since Jim.

"This is your room," she said, opening the first door on the right at the top of the stairs and breaking into her usual speech. "A sea captain by the name of Obed Barney built this house in 1807. He filled the house with treasures he'd acquired during his numerous voyages. I tried to give this room the same kind of feel it might have had when Captain Barney slept here."

Greg smiled politely and stepped past her. He stood in the center of the room, his long, well-shaped hands resting on his hips. There among the antiques and the big brass bed, with restored photos of early Nantucket citizens scattered on the patterned wallpaper,

Mikelle could easily imagine him in the tight-fitting breeches and tall boots of Captain Barney's time.

Even in brown corduroy slacks that hugged his slim thighs and hips, and a light brown suede-and-leather jacket, he was a presence to be reckoned with. Broad shoulders and a sleek well-proportioned body saved him from the gawkiness that sometimes came with extra height. He was very attractive. *Too* attractive.

He turned and raised a tawny brow. "Will I be sleeping alone?" Mikelle drew a shaky breath. "Or does Captain Barney still pay visits to his old haunt, so to speak?"

"As far as I know, the house isn't haunted," she replied, angry with herself for reacting so strongly to his perfectly innocent words. Or had they been so innocent? Judging by the gleam in his eye, she was beginning to suspect Greg Chandler of being a hardened flirt.

Suddenly Mikelle was more than a little anxious to return to the kitchen and the comfortable safety of Rose's company. "Tea is at three every day," she said, reverting to her most businesslike manner. "However, when you eat breakfast is entirely up to you."

"Even if I get a craving for bacon at one o'clock in the morning?"

How could she remain businesslike when he smiled like that? "There's an all-night Domino's downtown. I've heard they make a mean Canadian-bacon pizza that should take care of any cravings you might have in the middle of the night."

She couldn't believe it! She was playing right into his hands!

He laughed. "You've just heard it's good, eh? But—that's right—you're a vegetarian, aren't you?"

Mikelle's smiled faltered. "How did you know?"

"You told me," he answered smoothly.

Her eyes locked with his. "When did I tell you?"

"At the store. We were talking about cooking...." He cocked his head to the side. "Don't you remember?"

"Actually, I don't."

He laughed, slow and easy. "Well, if you didn't tell me, how could I know?"

He was right, she told herself quickly. She was being ridiculous and paranoid. What did she think he'd done—hired a private detective to dig up information about her? She'd obviously mentioned she was a vegetarian.

"I guess I say a lot of things I don't remember," she offered ruefully.

He shrugged. "We all do."

"Back to breakfast... Just ring down in the morning and let us know when you want it served. There's a brochure on the desk that explains everything, use of the phone, et cetera." She smiled politely and started to leave.

Greg didn't like the feel of his size-twelve foot in his mouth. He was beginning to think a Harvard education had been sadly wasted on an idiot like himself. He was going to have to be a lot more careful. He knew many things about Mikelle from Smith's report, but he had to act as if he knew nothing.

Despite his attraction to Mikelle, Greg had never forgotten his purpose for coming to Nantucket. He'd been wondering all along where Jamie was. Sleeping, maybe? In the kitchen, throwing mashed tofu and organically grown spinach against the walls?

He followed her into the hall. She stood hesitantly at the top of the stairs. He guessed he made her nervous. Well, that made two of them. "Do you have other guests?"

"There are only two other guests staying here now, honeymooners from Montana. Very nice . . . but a little preoccupied."

"Is that their room?" He pointed to the closed door next to his.

"Yes, I only have three rooms I rent out. The one next to theirs is unoccupied, and mine and Jamie's room is the far one across the hall. It's the most private." She got a keen look in her eyes and added, "You remember Jamie, don't you? The little terror throwing pickle jars on the floor of the grocery store?"

Greg played nonchalant. "Sure, I remember him. You two bunk together, huh?"

"Until he's older. I'm a widow, so there's no problem with waking a husband during the night if I have to get up with Jamie." A stricken look flashed in her gray eyes for half a second, like lightning against a leaden sky. With such a young child, most people would assume that Jim Bennet's passing was fairly recent and would offer condolences or ask questions. Greg remained silent, and he sensed that Mikelle was grateful for his restraint. Besides, he didn't want to see that stricken look again.

"Remember, tea's at three. See you there," she said in a rush, then turned and began descending the stairs.

"Will Jamie be there?"

Where was his brain? He could have kicked himself for blurting that out, especially when Mikelle's brow wrinkled with puzzlement.

"Of course he doesn't drink tea," she answered lightly, though he knew she was wondering about his interest in her son again. "But when Jamie's awake he's attached to me like a wart to a witch's nose. He'll be there." She paused, studying him curiously. "You seem to like children, Greg. Come from a large family?"

"Nope, I'm an only child," he replied. Her responding look was barely disguised confusion. He thought it best to retreat.

Inside his room with the door shut, he thought he heard Mikelle walk down the hall to the room she shared with Jamie. He'd probably worried her into cutting short the poor kid's nap and taking him downstairs with her.

Greg sat down on the bed and cupped his chin in his hands. *Damn! Damn! Damn!*

He was going to have to be much more subtle, exercise more restraint where Jamie was concerned, or she'd never trust him within ten feet of the kid. She was skittish, which suggested a bit of paranoia. But she was protective, and he couldn't fault her for that.

The quick and powerful attraction he felt for Jamie's adoptive mom was entirely unexpected and might prove to be a nuisance. On the other hand, he could use it to his advantage. An attraction for the mom was a good excuse to be with the kid who was attached to her "like a wart to a witch's nose." Would it be dishonest to flirt with her, woo her a little? Or was the prospect of wooing her too appealing and therefore too dangerous?

MIKELLE WAS LATE for tea. And so were the honeymooners. Greg occupied himself by looking at the artwork on the walls of the parlor, where a lavish feast was laid out on a low table in the center of a cozy grouping of antique sofas and chairs.

The paintings were all watercolors of Nantucket. There were creamy beach scenes, vivid cranberry bogs, bright pastel beds of flowers in front of weathered cottages. The images evoked the nostalgic charm of the island and the essence of a lazy, sun-washed summer day. He squinted at the minuscule signature of the artist and confirmed his suspicion that the paintings were Mikelle's. Instantly his respect for her increased. She had talent. Lots of it. Perhaps she could pass on some of that expertise to Jamie.

Greg turned as the door opened and Mikelle appeared. Bent nearly double, she was holding on to Jamie's hands, guiding him ahead of her as he took one tottering step after another.

Greg tried to lessen the broad smile that spread uncontrollably over his face. Damn, Jamie had grown so much in just the last two weeks! "He's learning how to walk?"

Mikelle looked up, startled, a strand of hair falling over one eye. "Oh, I didn't know you were in here."

She didn't look or sound very happy to see him. He glanced at his watch. "Well, it is ten after three."

"Is it? Jamie and I got busy, I guess." She continued to guide Jamie till they reached a sofa. She transferred his hands to the plush sofa arm, which he immediately grabbed hold of. Mikelle watched to make sure he was balanced, then turned to look at Greg. "He's been walking around the furniture for the past couple of weeks. I think he's ready to strike out on his own, but he had a bad fall a few days ago and I think he's a little nervous."

Greg felt his anxiety rise like a geyser. "A bad fall?"

"He fell forward and bumped his head on a table. He got a pretty nasty-looking knot, but the doctor said it was just a bad bruise. I think his confidence was shaken a little."

Greg was struggling with a multitude of disturbing emotions. Was Mikelle really careful enough? Jamie was an active kid. She should be on her guard constantly. Knocks to the head were nothing to sneeze at.

He also hated to think that Jamie's confidence had been affected. If it were up to him, he'd work with him continually till that confidence was restored. But, he reminded himself, it *wasn't* up to him.

It would be nice if Jamie's face lit up with recognition when he saw him, but Greg knew realistically that a child of his age wouldn't have a long memory. Still, he wished Jamie would just look up and acknowledge his presence, instead of being so thoroughly engrossed in the process of making his way around the couch toward the tea table. Damn, he was cute. He wished he could pick him up....

But Greg had promised himself to show less interest in Jamie, thereby reassuring Mikelle that he wasn't a kidnapper or something equally awful. It would be easier, however, to show interest in something else if there was something more interesting in the room than his son and his son's adopted mother.

Mikelle wasn't trying to make conversation, either. She seemed uncomfortable, and she kept her eyes glued to Jamie. Greg was beginning to think this whole idea of coming to Nantucket was a big mis-

take, when the parlor door slowly eased open to re-
veal the honeymooners.

How did he know they were the honeymooners?
Well, while they appeared to be slowly inching their
way into the room, they were simultaneously enjoying the sort of passionate clench one usually saw only
on the covers of romance novels. They were kissing
and groping like two teenagers behind the school
bleachers during a football game.

Even for honeymooners, Greg thought their conduct was a little excessive, though admittedly hu-
morous. Didn't they know they were being observed
by two—no, three—pairs of curious eyes? Even Jamie was standing still, his gaze fixed on the torrid
couple.

Mikelle was hoping the Austins would show a little
restraint after she'd told them last night that there
would be another guest in the inn. Apparently she'd
been too optimistic. "Ahem!" she said loudly.

Lyn and Cary Austin jumped guiltily apart, and
Mikelle trained her eyes on the fireplace behind the
sofa. She didn't want to watch as the honeymooners
hastily straightened their clothes, and she definitely
didn't want to look at Greg.

"Oh, M-Mikelle," stuttered Lyn, pushing a strand
of coffee-colored hair behind her ear. "We didn't expect you to be in here already."

Mikelle saw Greg glance at his watch again, a rueful expression on his face. Unlike herself, she supposed he was one of those punctual types who hated
anybody or anything to be late.

"Sorry," muttered Cary, tucking the tail of his
Western-cut shirt into his jeans. Cary was tall and
lean, with hair a shade darker than his wife's and a

neatly trimmed mustache. He nodded toward Greg by way of notice and sheepishly explained, "We're on our honeymoon."

"I was warned that there were honeymooners in the inn," Greg returned amiably, extending his hand. The men shook hands and Mikelle released the breath she'd been holding. She snatched a glance at Greg and was relieved to see the amused twinkle in his sea green eyes. *Sea green* eyes? Now where had that come from? Next thing she knew, she'd be drowning in his limpid pools!

"Where are you from?" Greg asked them.

"Montana," said Cary. He smiled broadly. "Big sky country. Rancher. Cary Austin and my wife, Lyn. You?"

"Architect. Manhattan. Greg Chandler."

And possible kidnapper, added Mikelle silently, though she still didn't really believe it. But why did he seem so interested in Jamie? And why did he make her feel so uncomfortable if there wasn't something...dangerous about him? That was it. For some reason, he seemed to represent a danger to her and Jamie, but she couldn't imagine why.

"Lyn's got the traveling bug," continued Cary. "Said she wanted to see a bit of the country before I got her barefoot, pregnant and in the kitchen." He turned and winked at his blushing bride.

Mikelle had no doubt that the pregnant part was not far from being realized...the lucky girl. She'd give anything to have the experience of being pregnant.

"Lyn read about Nantucket in the travel section of the *Butte Gazette* and had to come. I'm glad she did. Great place."

Mikelle raised a brow. How would Cary know what Nantucket was like? They'd hardly left the inn since they'd got there four days ago! They'd be gone in a couple of days, she told herself. Surely she could tolerate their moonstruck behavior that long. All that kissing and cuddling just reminded her of what she'd been missing since Jim died. But until Greg Chandler showed up, she hadn't felt so deprived.

"I'll ring for the tea," said Mikelle, picking up Jamie as he was about to grab a handful of clotted cream. "Why don't you all sit down?"

"No need. Tea is here." Rose bustled into the room with a tray laden with three different teapots. She set the tray on the table that was already groaning under platters of food. She'd taken Mikelle seriously when she'd told her to make more food for Greg.

"Oh, it all looks so good," exclaimed Lyn, sitting on the couch beside her husband. "I'm so hungry I could eat a cow!"

"Must be the sea air," said Greg, darting Mikelle a sly look that clearly said, *or all the exercise.* He sat down in a wing chair opposite the Austins. He wore a cream-colored cable-knit sweater, the sleeves of which he'd pushed up to just below his elbows. His forearms were lightly furred with blond hair and were strong and sinewy. "Aren't you going to join us?"

Greg looked pointedly at Mikelle as she continued to stand and hold a squirming Jamie. "Sure," she said, recalling her wayward thoughts. Greg Chandler was hard on her concentration. She sat down in the chair next to his. "I'll pour the tea. What does everyone want? Orange pekoe, chamomile, or Earl Grey?"

While the Austins debated on their choice for tea, Mikelle struggled with Jamie. He wanted whatever he could get his hands on. Although he'd already been fed in the kitchen, she was going to give him some bits from the table as soon as she was done playing hostess and pouring the tea. Probably because she'd cut short his nap today, he was not being very patient. She'd been besieged by an uncontrollable surge of protectiveness earlier, and had taken him out of his bed a half hour sooner than usual.

"Jamie, honey, settle down," she soothed. He made a squawk of protest and reached for the muffin plate.

"I'll hold him," offered Greg.

Mikelle cast him a troubled look. Jamie had started crying in earnest now. "I wouldn't dream of bothering you with Jamie," she said.

"It wouldn't be a bother," he said, casually enough.

Mikelle looked over at Rose, who was headed back to the kitchen. "Rose, could you take Jamie for just a minute?"

Rose glanced over her shoulder. "Sorry, Mikelle," she said breezily. "I've got bread in the oven ready to come out." She paused at the door and inclined her head toward Greg. "Mr. Chandler offered to hold him. Why don't you let him?"

Well, for starters, she thought, *because I don't trust him.*

"I'll hold Jamie," said Lyn. "I love babies."

The situation was becoming awkward. She couldn't very well hand Jamie over to Lyn after declining Greg's offer.

"Maybe he's just hungry," said Greg, reaching for a chocolate-covered cookie.

"He just ate," said Mikelle, a little defensively.

"Oh, so you don't want him to have the cookie?"

Mikelle thought she detected a suggestion of hurt in Greg's voice. She glanced quickly at him, and the guarded look in his eyes confirmed this suspicion. She decided she was being ridiculous again. "Of course he can have it," she said. Then, in an attempt to overcome the completely irrational sense of danger she felt about Greg Chandler, she stood up and put Jamie in his lap. "And if you're such a glutton for punishment, Greg," she said lightly, "you can hold him."

By now Jamie was having an out-and-out temper tantrum. If holding a screaming, squirming baby didn't cure this only-child New Yorker of his fascination with her son, nothing would, thought Mikelle.

The minute Jamie realized he was sitting in someone else's lap besides Mom's, being gently restrained by hands twice the size of hers, he stopped crying. As he twisted around to see just who it was that was holding him, he and Greg Chandler faced off.

Mikelle wasn't sure which one of them looked more uncertain, Greg or Jamie. But one thing she was sure of, her plan to prove to herself that Greg was perfectly harmless hadn't worked. The sense of danger was still there... and stronger than ever.

Chapter Three

Coming face-to-face with your posterity was more unsettling than Greg ever imagined—even when your posterity's face was mottled and streaked with tears. Fear, pride, curiosity and a strange possessiveness mixed and exploded in Greg's chest.

Up close, Greg could see that Jamie's eyes were already turning into the same gray-green color as his own. And, holding him for the first time, Greg realized how big he really was. Thinking of Connie, of her sleek, model-thin figure, he almost felt sympathy for the discomfort she must have experienced packing around this future basketball dunker for nine months.

God, what was he doing here? Was he really here to check out Jamie's adopted parent, or because he was driven by an instinctive need to bond with his son? His *son,* for Christ's sake!

Greg realized that everyone was watching and Jamie's face was starting to crumple again. The poor kid probably didn't know what to think of an adult who simply stared at him like a stooge. He had to act quickly or Jamie would be snatched out of his arms in a heartbeat.

"Hey, Jamie, how'd you like a cookie?"

Jamie took only a cursory glance at the cookie before he grabbed it and stuck it in his mouth. Quickly taking advantage of this promising beginning, Greg settled Jamie in the crook of his elbow. He plucked a snowy white handkerchief out of his trouser pocket and wiped Jamie's face and nose with it, a process that Jamie protested against by squirming energetically. But Greg was sure that while he'd lose points with Jamie for wiping his nose, he'd gain points with Mikelle.

Jamie settled down again, content with his cookie and seemingly fascinated by the person holding him. Greg wanted to believe that they'd developed an instant rapport, but he knew Jamie was probably just a little awed and would be yelling for his mom any second.

He turned to Mikelle. "You'd better pour the tea while he's quiet. I don't expect this to last, do you?"

Mikelle seemed to stir from her own reverie. "Probably not. Although I've never seen him settle down so fast. And with a stranger, at that." She turned away and began pouring the tea.

A stranger, thought Greg. Yeah, that's exactly what he was. And that's exactly what he would remain. So, why did he want to hold on to Jamie just a little tighter?

"He's quite a kid, isn't he?" said Cary. "Professional-basketball material."

"A heartbreaker when he's grown-up," added Lyn, munching on a scone.

A heartbreaker now, thought Greg.

"Despite the occasional temper tantrum, he's a sweetheart, just like his father," said Mikelle in a soft tone.

Greg was startled at first, then realized she was talking about Jim Bennet, not Jamie's biological father.

Mikelle excused herself and went into the kitchen to refill the sugar bowl. Jamie watched her go with an anxious look in his eyes, but Greg quickly handed him another cookie.

Lyn leaned toward Greg and said, "It's a shame her husband died before the kid was born."

Cary shook his head. "It's a damned shame he had to die at all. Mikelle's good people."

At first Greg was surprised by their comments. Obviously they didn't know that Jamie was adopted. But then, why should Mikelle advertise the fact? Besides, when it came right down to it, biology didn't mean diddly squat if you weren't there for someone.

Having finished the second cookie in record time, Jamie turned to Greg, wiggled his fingers and grunted. Greg, ready to do anything to keep Jamie happy and in his lap, reached for another cookie.

"How many is that, Greg?" said Mikelle as she reentered the room.

"Well . . . er . . . three, I guess."

"Two is enough," said Mikelle firmly, setting down the full sugar bowl. "Too much chocolate makes him hyper." She sat down and smiled at Jamie. "And, as you can tell, Jamie's already got enough energy to keep me hopping all day." Jamie smiled back, gooey chocolate crumbs falling out of the corners of his mouth.

Hoping to hold Jamie for as long as possible, Greg tried to think of another diversion. He knew Jamie liked keys, but he'd left his set upstairs on the dresser. Then he remembered the tiny mirror he was storing in his wallet until he could return it to his secretary. He'd found the mirror on the floor of his car yesterday after he'd given Ms. Barnes a ride home from work. She must have dropped it.

Greg pulled out his wallet and opened it. Immediately interested, Jamie reached for the expensive leather billfold.

"You don't have any coins in there, do you?" asked Mikelle warily.

"Of course not," scoffed Greg. "I know babies shouldn't play with coins. But is a little, blunt-edged mirror okay? Don't babies like to look at themselves?"

"Well, yes. But he's going to want to explore every compartment in your wallet, and he's drooling, Greg. That's not *Italian* leather, is it?"

"Geez, you're right," said Greg, laughing as Jamie plucked out two hundred-dollar bills and dropped them on the floor.

"Here, let me take him," said Mikelle. "He's making a mess. You don't want chocolate drool on your driver's license, do you?"

"Really, I don't mind," Greg insisted, trying to sound casual. But he knew he was blowing it again. He'd promised himself that he wouldn't act too interested in Jamie, then he'd offered to hold him the minute Mikelle needed her hands free. Now he was ignoring Mikelle's outstretched arms. She was probably wondering if she was going to have to pin him to the floor in a body lock to get her kid back.

The arousing image of him and Mikelle wrestling on a floor mat made Greg's mind wander for an instant, just long enough for Jamie to pull something out of a pocket of his wallet. It was something that any responsible, red-blooded bachelor would keep handy for protection, but hardly an item that Greg wanted to flaunt.

It was a package of condoms.

To make matters worse, they were the glow-in-the-dark kind, given to him by a fun-loving brunette he'd dated last spring.

"Whoa, Jamie boy," said Cary, laughing. "You won't be needing those for a few years."

Greg felt his face heat up as he gently tried to pry the package out of Jamie's hands, but Jamie held tight. He didn't hear a peep of noise coming from Mikelle, but Lyn was giggling. There was another package of generic condoms in his wallet, but naturally Jamie had been drawn to this neon green, party variety. He hadn't used them since he and the brunette quit dating. Hell, he hadn't needed any kind of protection—fluorescent or otherwise—for a while now. He'd been too caught up in this fatherhood thing to give a minute's thought to his social life.

"Were you a Boy Scout, Greg?" asked Cary, who seemed to be having a hell of a good time at Greg's expense.

"Why do you ask?" said Greg with a grim smile. He still didn't dare look at Mikelle and was trying to divert Jamie's attention away from the condoms by waving the mirror in front of his face.

"You've taken the motto Be Prepared to new heights."

Lyn gave a whoop of laughter. "You mean new *colors.* I think it's great. Who says being responsible has to be boring?"

Greg always thought of himself as a with-it kind of guy, but he was embarrassed. And if they only knew how irresponsible he'd been when Jamie was conceived, maybe they wouldn't be applauding him. But since the moment he'd set eyes on the kid, he hadn't been able to think of Jamie as a mistake. Greg had never wanted to be a father, but then he'd never known how it felt to hold your own child.

"Well, I said he'd had enough cookies, but I guess we can make an exception in this case. Like mother like son—chocolate can take Jamie's attention away from almost anything." Greg was relieved to hear Mikelle speak in a matter-of-fact voice. He looked at her, but she avoided his gaze and focused on Jamie. "Here's another cookie, Jamie. Now give the nice man his...er...pretty party balloons."

Greg held back a grin. So, the little vegetarian had a sense of humor....

Jamie dropped the condoms and grabbed the cookie. Then Mikelle picked him up and transferred him to her own lap. Her gaze met Greg's as she bent to kiss Jamie on the head. She might be amused by the incident, but by the assessing look she was giving him, he could tell she was coming to some unfortunate conclusions about his life-style. Damn those neon-colored condoms.

While Greg put his wallet back together, Lyn and Cary changed the subject. He forced himself to join in the small talk, then forced himself to eat. He was surprised to find everything delicious. In fifteen minutes, he'd polished off three muffins, two scones, and three cups of tea.

"I'm glad you like the food, Greg," said Mikelle. "I was afraid you weren't eating because you assumed, since I'm into health food, that nothing would taste good."

Greg shrugged and smiled wryly. "You assumed right. It's been my experience that if food's good for you it usually tastes like hell. But you've proved me wrong." He paused, then added, "I guess it's not fair to make assumptions when you don't know all the facts."

He wondered if she caught his double meaning. He was honestly concerned that she'd assume, because of the neon condoms, that he was a partier, a shallow skirt chaser. He wasn't. He didn't bed down with every woman he dated. And for some reason it was important to him that Mikelle understand that.

Their eyes met and locked briefly, then slid self-consciously to gaze at safer objects. Greg thought he'd never before seen such clear, yet fathomless eyes. Like a crystal ball, secrets lay within their depths. And depending on the powers you possessed, you could see nothing...or everything. What powers did he need to read Mikelle Bennet like a crystal ball?

"Don't mean to eat and run," she said, standing suddenly and hiking Jamie onto her hip. "But I have a date."

"A date?" echoed Lyn. "Great! Is he cute?"

"Oh, I don't know," said Mikelle, turning to Jamie. "Is Uncle Frank cute, Jamie?" Jamie looked sleepy and had no comment, so Mikelle turned back to Lyn. "Actually Jamie and I both have a date. We're going to the arts-and-crafts fair this afternoon with Frank Coffin, the man who owns that great little art gallery on Main Street called Impressions.''

''To be honest,'' admitted Cary, ''we haven't seen much of the town yet.''

''You should go down to the fair,'' she advised them. ''It's a beautiful day and you can easily walk there.'' She turned to Greg, her expression carefully neutral. ''You should go, too. It's the fair's last day. Surely you don't need to start work right away?''

Greg was still wrestling with the urge to wring ''Uncle Frank's'' neck. Who was this guy and how did he get to the status of uncle to Jamie? ''Maybe I will,'' said Greg, promising himself a good look at this pseudo-relative.

''But first you'd better change,'' Lyn said, her eyes brimming with laughter. ''None of Nantucket's single women will believe you're a bachelor unless you put on something different.''

Greg couldn't care less whether or not he looked like a bachelor, but Lyn had apparently decided he was a swinger and on the prowl for women wherever he went. If that was Lyn's way of thinking after seeing the condoms, had Mikelle come to the same conclusion?

He sighed and glanced down at his sweater and slacks. As he suspected, he was smeared with chocolate and dusted with sticky crumbs. His messy appearance lifted his mood. ''I guess I do look like I've been mauled by a kid with gooey fingers,'' he said. He looked like a dad. For the first time in his life, Greg found that idea rather appealing...a lot more appealing than prowling for females.

He stood up, anxious to change his clothes so he could casually bump into Mikelle at the fair and check out this Frank fellow. He followed his hostess and his droopy-eyed son to the door of the parlor, then turned to catch Cary and Lyn kissing. "Are you two coming?" he asked.

They broke apart reluctantly. "Don't think so," said Cary, his voice already husky with desire.

Greg grinned. "Didn't think you would." He dug into his pants pocket and threw Cary the glow-in-the-dark condoms. "Playing hide-and-seek with these little party favors makes the game more interesting. Have fun, kids."

As he ascended the stairs to his room, he could hear Lyn giggling. Mikelle glanced over her shoulder at him from the stair landing and tried to hide a smile. Greg felt his heart thump hard and realized that he could really enjoy playing hide-and-seek with Jamie's pretty mom....

MAIN STREET SQUARE was a three-block-long, cobblestone rectangle. Today it was a hub of activity. People ambled up and down the shop-lined sidewalks that were shaded by wineglass elm trees and lit at night by reproduction electric gaslights.

Even more people milled about in the square itself, which had been transformed into a patchwork of colorful tents, canopies, booths and food stands. Greg was wondering how the hell he was going to find Mikelle, Jamie and "Uncle Frank" in such a crowd.

He set out with determination, walking blindly past the beautiful artwork and handmade New England crafts, intent only on locating the two people who had grown overnight into the most consuming interest in his life.

Finally he caught sight of Mikelle's dark hair shining in the late-afternoon sun. She was standing in front of a large seascape with a man of medium height, slender, with light brown, curly hair. Their heads were close together as if they were conferring...or whispering sweet nothings.

Jamie was in the stroller, dangling his bottle over the side and watching the juice drip in a steady stream onto the cobbled pavement. He had on a little baseball cap to shield the fair and fuzzy top of his head from the sun. Greg was surprised Jamie hadn't gone to sleep by now; he'd looked ready to crash after eating those cookies. He hesitated for only a second, then advanced. If Frank was a significant person in Mikelle and Jamie's life, he'd better get to know him, too.

Mikelle looked up, smiled tentatively, and had barely said a polite "Hello" when Greg's arm was grabbed from behind. He looked down and saw feminine fingers curled around his bicep, the long, square-tipped nails painted chili-pepper red.

"Greg! I can't believe it— Is it really you?"

He recognized the voice and silently cursed his phenomenal bad luck. Now was not the time for a name from his little black book to suddenly materialize in the flesh.

When he turned and saw what Brenda was wearing, "in the flesh" seemed an appropriate description. She had on a top that exposed her midriff and a pair of short shorts that barely covered her...assets, so to speak. Like the girl from Ipanema, she was "tall and tan and lean and lovely." From the top of her bright blond head to the chili-pepper red toenails showing at the end of a pair of thong sandals, Brenda was a real knockout…in a flashy, sultry, feather-boa kind of way.

But contrary to the usual perception of sex goddesses, Brenda had a keen mind—especially for business—and was refreshingly honest. She didn't mince words. For about three weeks in June, Greg had found her varied attractions irresistible. Perhaps under other circumstances he might have been happy to see her.…

He forced a smile. "Brenda. What are you doing in Nantucket?"

"I might ask you the same thing. This isn't your neck of the woods." Her answering smile seemed genuine. Was it possible that despite his declining her several invitations after their last date, she'd forgiven him?

"I'm here on business," he answered. He was very aware that Mikelle was watching their exchange. "This isn't your neck of the woods, either."

She rolled one bare shoulder in that sexy way of hers and slipped her hand through his arm, hanging on to his elbow in a proprietary fashion. "I'm working, too. I've got a tent over there."

She pointed and Greg had no trouble picking out Brenda's setup. Racy lingerie waved in the Nantucket breeze, looking out of place and downright kinky between a scrimshaw booth and a cotton-candy machine. "I'm moonlighting. I do loungewear shows on the weekends, and try to hit most of the county fairs in New York State. When I was getting ready to visit my aunt in Boston, I heard about this little doo-dah and decided to mix business with pleasure. So— *voilà*—here I am."

"How's your…er…merchandise selling?"

"Great. These islanders are a lot more hip than they look."

"Sounds like you've set yourself a grueling schedule. You know what they say about all work and no play."

Suddenly there was a flirtatious gleam in her eye. "Well, when you stopped calling, I got kind of bored. I had to do something with my time."

Greg laughed. "I can't believe you're ever bored, Brenda. I've seen men trip over each other to pull out your chair. You must have lots of guys calling you."

"I do. But you were so fun, Greg, you kind of spoiled me. How lucky that I bumped into you today." She gave his arm a squeeze and lowered her voice an octave. "Are you free?"

To avoid answering, Greg turned to Mikelle with an apologetic smile. "Didn't mean to turn my back on you, Mikelle, but I—"

"But you were waylaid by a friend," she finished a little too quickly, too brightly. "Why don't you introduce your friend and I'll introduce mine?"

Greg had been hoping to keep his encounter with Brenda friendly but brief. However, Mikelle seemed to have other ideas. Introductions were made all around, and Mikelle suggested that they all have a glass of ice tea and get better acquainted.

Greg turned to Brenda. "But you can't leave your stuff, can you?" He waved vaguely in the direction of her lingerie tent.

Brenda shrugged. "Sure I can, for a little while at least. I have someone helping me."

Greg couldn't think of a polite way to get out of the situation, so he went along with the ice-tea plan, although he felt as if he were shoveling dirt on his own grave. Unless he was reading her wrong, Brenda was interested in taking up where they left off three months ago. But he wasn't. Brenda would flirt and he would have to respond without offending her, but hopefully without adding to the lothario image Mikelle might already have formed of him. For some reason, what Mikelle thought of him was fast becoming as important to Greg as what *he* thought of *her.*

There was an outdoor café down the block, and they sat around a small table topped with a beach umbrella. Mikelle picked up Jamie and held him in her lap. After Frank ordered tea, Mikelle turned to Brenda. "So, you and Greg know each other in New York."

Brenda's smile and voice were warm and rich with meaning. "Oh, yes, Greg and I know each other very well."

Greg fiddled with his napkin and said nothing. Brenda couldn't seem to help it—she oozed sensuality the way trees oozed sap. He could sense Mikelle looking at him, and he could feel the muscles in his neck tense.

"I heard you tell Greg that you're branching out from your regular job," said Frank, politely making conversation. He looked like the type of man to smooth over awkward pauses in conversation—the "nice" type. "What do you do during the week?"

"I'm a window dresser for Macy's," said Brenda. "I specialize in lingerie and swimwear. That's how I met Greg, actually. He saw me in the window late one night working on a display for the store opening in the morning, and he tapped on the glass. We were having a Valentine's Day lingerie sale and I was putting zebra-striped underwear on a mannequin. I had three more bras and pairs of matching panties hanging on my arms." She slid a coy look at Greg. "I don't know if the racy underwear attracted him or what, but he asked me for my phone number."

"And just like that you gave it to him?" asked Mikelle with an incredulous chuckle. "A man you'd never met, a strange man standing on the other side of the glass—late at night—watching you dress a mannequin in zebra underwear? In New York that's pretty risky, isn't it?"

Brenda shrugged. "What would you do if asked out by a hunk like Greg? I mean...really...just look at him."

And she did. In fact they were all looking at him, making Greg feel like a new strain of virus under a microscope.

"Well, obviously it worked out all right," said Frank cheerfully, doing his nice-guy duty by smoothing over yet another awkward pause.

"Yeah," agreed Brenda with a wistful smile. "We had a lot of fun for a while, didn't we, Greg? But we both knew it wouldn't last."

Greg raked a hand through his hair and laughed uneasily. "Brenda, really—"

Brenda leaned forward and put a hand on Greg's knee. Her breast rested against his arm and he remembered something else about Brenda, she loved to touch. "Greg, you know I don't blame you. I knew from the beginning that you weren't the type for long-term relationships." While Greg inwardly cringed, Brenda turned to Mikelle and continued matter-of-factly. "Greg has quite a reputation in New York. Everyone knows he isn't interested in marriage, but the women still can't stay away from him. He loves women and women love him, it's that simple."

Greg remembered now that Brenda's refreshing honesty sometimes ran amok. "Go easy, Brenda," he advised her dryly. "You make me sound like Don Juan."

"Oh, I didn't mean to paint you so wicked, Greg. Really. But you have to admit you could be the patron saint of confirmed bachelors." She laughed and added playfully, "Or am I the only woman you told that you saw no reason to ruin a perfectly good relationship by getting married?"

Frank smirked and Greg couldn't blame him. The situation was straight out of a second-rate sitcom. He'd find humor in the situation, too, if he didn't care so much about the opinions Mikelle was undoubtedly forming. Hell, just having Jamie present, even though he didn't understand a thing being said, made Greg feel uncomfortable.

He decided to take Frank's cue, though, and make light of things. "Didn't Shelley write 'When a man marries, dies, or turns Hindu, his best friends hear no more of him'?" Greg asked jokingly. Frank laughed, and Brenda smiled and swatted Greg in the stomach with the back of her hand.

"The solution to that is to marry your best friend," Mikelle interjected.

Greg looked at Mikelle and admired the serenity of her smile. To her, marriage was no joke. She'd had a good relationship with Jim Bennet, and for some reason that made him incredibly envious. Apparently some people were able to make marriage work.

"Didn't Shakespeare have a thing or two to say about the wedded state?" said Frank.

"He had something to say about everything else,"
Greg replied. "By the way, Brenda, have you seen the
new off-Broadway production of *Richard III?*"
Brenda, a theater enthusiast, responded eagerly, and
Greg was grateful he'd managed to change the sub-
ject.

A half hour later, Greg walked Brenda back to her
tent. It wasn't easy, but he made his excuses and tactfully declined meeting her later for dinner. She pouted
a little, then gave him a good-natured kiss on the
cheek. "You know, Greg, just because we eat together...or whatever...doesn't mean you have to
marry me," she said teasingly.

"I could do a lot worse," he answered with a grin.
He waved goodbye, then walked back to where Mikelle, Jamie and Frank still sat under the umbrella.
The shadows were getting long and Jamie was apparently getting sleepier. As he came within earshot of
Mikelle and Frank's conversation, Greg heard them
discussing how to keep the kid awake till bedtime. If
he had been a casual observer, he'd have been entirely convinced they were a happy little family of
three.

"I'll walk him around the fair for a while. That'll
wake him up," said Frank.

"You don't mind?"

"Why should I mind?"

"Then I'll meet you back at the booth in a few
minutes...okay?"

"That'll be perfect."

And it was settled just like that. Frank didn't have
to finagle time with Jamie the way Greg did. Mikelle
treated him like a trusted family member. The whole
scenario reeked of orange blossoms.

Frank turned to Greg. "It was nice meeting you, Greg. I guess I'll see you around. Good luck with your search for the perfect piece of property."

Greg mustered up a convincing smile. "Nice meeting you, too."

Frank took Jamie and hiked him up and onto his shoulders. Jamie's expression immediately changed. His grogginess vanished and was replaced by surprise, then delight. Jealousy swept through Greg like wildfire. "See ya, Mikkie. Wave 'bye to your mom, Jamie." But Jamie was too excited to notice anyone, much less take the trouble to wave.

Greg watched Frank and Jamie walk away. It irked him to see Jamie's smiling little face bobbing above this strange man's equally happy mug, although he couldn't understand why. He'd expected Jamie to have a father when he first set out to learn about his adopted parents. So, if Frank was destined to eventually fill that role, what was Greg's problem with it?

Mikelle wasn't sure how she felt about sitting alone with Greg. She had no idea what to say to him. Although he'd said he'd be back after walking Brenda to her tent, Mikelle had half expected him to disappear for the rest of the evening and perhaps all night. If he was the playboy Brenda painted him, why would he choose to sit with her, instead of taking advantage of Brenda's obvious eagerness to spend time with him? But maybe they'd made plans for later. Mikelle smiled at her own stupidity. Of course they'd made plans.

Brenda was right. Greg was definitely a hunk. Part of Mikelle could easily understand why women flocked to Greg, even though they knew there was no chance he'd ever be theirs. He'd probably broken his share of hearts, but at least he was honest and up-front with them from the beginning. Mikelle hated dishonesty above just about any character flaw a person might have. She was hard on herself, too, whenever she caught herself fudging the truth a little.

"Brenda seems very nice," she offered.

Greg's eyes flicked her way. "Yeah, she's a good kid."

Dusk was closing in and Greg seemed preoccupied. It was time to go and meet Frank and Jamie at the booth, but something kept Mikelle glued to her seat. It wasn't exactly relaxing sitting so close to over six feet of attractive male, but she felt compelled to stretch out their time together.

She admitted to herself that it was a delusive compulsion, because he wasn't even looking at her, thinking of her. His gray-green eyes restlessly scanned the thinning crowd of people still milling around the booths and tents. Was he looking for Brenda?

"Isn't it about Jamie's bedtime? Has Frank ever carried a kid that big on his shoulders? It'd be awful if he, you know, dropped Jamie or something."

Mikelle was stunned. She shook her head disbelievingly. "That's it. Now I know I'm not imagining things."

Greg turned and stared at her, a wary look in his eyes. "What aren't you imagining?"

"Your unusual interest in my son, that's what," she answered, warming to the subject. "What is it with you, Greg? Ever since I first saw you in the grocery store, you've been eyeballing my baby. It makes a mother paranoid, you know? I've even wondered if you booked into the Gray Lady just to be near Jamie."

Greg laughed. "You're right. You are being paranoid."

Mikelle frowned. "I don't like feeling this way, but if you aren't out to kidnap Jamie, why all the interest in him? You're a bachelor with no driving urge to marry, right?"

"Well, yeah, but—"

"So why the soft gazes and worried questions about my son? Marriage and babies usually go together. I want an explanation, Greg. And I want it now."

Chapter Four

For a brief, crazed moment, Greg actually considered telling Mikelle the truth. Then she'd understand. Then she'd...really have a reason to distrust him. He couldn't risk being barred from seeing his son. He wasn't ready to pack up his toothbrush, along with all his paternal impulses, and hightail it back to the Big Apple. He had to stay a little longer. So he had to lie.

"Well? I'm waiting."

He stirred the melting ice cubes at the bottom of his empty glass of tea. "You'll think I'm crazy."

She smiled. "Maybe I already do."

He grinned ruefully. "Contrary to what you might think, I don't snatch kids."

"You'd have never got your mitts on mine, but for the parenting world at large I'm very relieved."

"As you know, I'm an only child—"

"Which might account for some of your odd quirks."

"—and I don't know anything about kids from hands-on experience. All I know is what I've read and what I've seen on TV."

"Well, for starters, kids don't talk in sound bites. And their problems take a lot longer to solve in real life than they do in those sitcoms with their neat thirty-minute episodes—twenty minutes if you don't count commercials. It took me fifteen minutes this morning just to get Jamie's shoes on."

Greg blinked. "Fifteen minutes?"

"Well, after I'd played This Little Piggy Went to Market three times on each foot, changed his diaper twice and retied his laces—"

Greg laughed. "I get the picture." He liked the picture, too. "You're a great mom."

He could swear he saw Mikelle blush. Or was it just the glow of a proud mother? "Well, I have a string of pearls, but I'm no Barbara Bush. I try my best."

"It must be hard...."

"Hard?"

"Doing it alone. Raising Jamie without your husband to help."

Mikelle shrugged, looked away. A breeze stirred her bangs. "I don't think much about that. But I do think about what Jim's missing. Every new thing Jamie does makes me wish Jim were here to see it. And sometimes I think about Jamie growing up without a father."

This was Greg's chance to find out what he could about her relationship with Frank. Was he wrong to question her when the turn of conversation had left her so vulnerable? He told himself that for Jamie's sake he had the right to find out whatever he could by whatever means were available.

He cleared his throat nervously. "You could change that. You're still young, and if you don't mind me saying so, you're very attractive. Have you thought about getting married again?''

She turned to face him, her expression amused. "What? Marry and—to paraphrase Shelley—estrange some poor schnook from his friends?''

He chuckled. "I only said that to please Brenda. She thinks she has me all figured out, labeled and neatly filed under the category of confirmed bachelor.''

She lifted her chin and threw him a challenging look. "Well, aren't you?''

"We were talking about you, Mikelle. We were talking about the possibility of marriage for you, not me. What about this Frank fellow?''

She waggled a finger in front of his face. He had the wild urge to grab her finger and stick it in his mouth, but he tried to concentrate on what she was saying. "No, Greg. I distinctly remember that we were talking about you. You've managed to get as far away from the original subject as possible, but I still want to know why you're so interested in my son.''

Greg sighed. "I still say you'll think I'm crazy.''

"We've already established that.''

"I know. It's like this—'' Greg felt his hands grow clammy and he wiped them on his thighs. Telling half-truths was just like lying, and he hated all the lying. But did he have a choice? "I'm thinking of becoming a . . . father.''

Her eyes grew wide. "You mean you're thinking of getting married?''

"No, I'm definitely not getting married. And I'm not doing any of that surrogate-mother stuff, either.'' He paused, then tiptoed around the truth again. "What do you think of adoption, Mikelle?''

She laughed. "Funny you should ask. You'll be so surprised when I tell you—" Her face lit up like a delighted child about to impart a secret. She leaned close and whispered, "Jamie's adopted."

Greg was torn. She was so genuine, so damned open, it seemed criminal to keep leading her on. It was dishonest to pretend ignorance, and he wasn't sure he could keep pretending.

"Mikelle, I should tell you—"

"Mikkie?"

It took Greg about five seconds to be thankful for the interruption. They both turned to see Frank holding a fast-asleep Jamie. Jamie looked like an angel, and Frank looked . . . annoyed.

"I've been waiting at the booth. As you can see, Jamie gave up and went to sleep."

Mikelle stood up. "I'm sorry, Frank. Greg and I got to talking."

Frank glanced at Greg, then back to Mikelle, his brows furrowed. "Must have been a pretty absorbing conversation. Neither of you noticed when I walked up just now."

Greg stood, too. "The conversation wasn't all that absorbing," he said easily. "Mikelle was just being polite while I rambled on." He threw her a chagrined smile and a significant look, hoping he conveyed that he didn't want the substance of their conversation repeated. There was an answering gleam of understanding in Mikelle's eyes and he felt reassured that she wouldn't confide in Frank about his interest in becoming a father.

Greg was filled with conflicting emotions. By having such a personal conversation with Mikelle, one that he didn't wish to have shared with anyone else, they had forged a sort of bond. They'd shared a secret. But the secret was based on dangerous half-truths, and the real secret behind it all—that he was already a father and that Jamie was his son—could cause an instant rift between them. Suddenly Greg felt exhausted.

"Sorry to hold things up," he said to Frank while Mikelle gently laid Jamie in the reclined seat of the stroller. "I'm going to head back to the Gray Lady. See you later."

After this abrupt goodbye, Greg turned and strode quickly away. But he didn't go straight to the inn. He was mentally exhausted, but his body was filled with restless energy. He walked all over town, up and down shady streets lined with historic houses and small, neat yards, till the glow-in-the-dark hands of his watch indicated that it was half past eleven.

The hours had gone swiftly by as he'd examined his thoughts and feelings over and over again. Raw feelings prevailed over practical reasoning most of the time. And when he did manage to think, it was to admit to himself how Mikelle and Jamie made him want something more in his life than just another romantic fling.

He hated thinking and feeling this way. It went against everything he'd based his life on so far and he was fervently hoping these strange yearnings would go away. He decided that a few hours a day away from Mikelle and Jamie might make him more objective. Tomorrow he'd start scouting the island for his fictitious client's building site.

He headed back to the inn, hopeful of finding no one up when he got there. He was relieved to see no lights on downstairs and just a dim glow coming from a tiny porthole window upstairs, which was possibly a night-light in the hall. Mikelle had given him a key to the kitchen entrance so he could let himself in without rousing anyone to unlock the door. There was an outside light over the small porch and Greg was soon inside the warm kitchen that still held delectable aromas from Rose's baking.

He carefully relocked the door from the inside, turned around and came smack up against a pair of soft breasts.

"Greg?"

Greg stepped back and leaned against the wall, running his fingers through his hair. Bumping into Mikelle was the last thing he needed right now. "Hell, where did you come from?" She was in the dark, but the faint moonlight that shone through the filmy curtains made her white robe stand out.

"Did I scare you?" Mikelle's voice held a trace of amusement.

She'd scared him, all right, but not in the usual way. He was scared to death he was going to pull her into his arms. He could feel himself growing rigid just from the idea of her being dressed for bed. A clean, lightly soapy scent emanated from her that made his groin ache even more. She was like the Ivory girl, but a hell of a lot sexier.

He answered indirectly. "Do you go skulking around the dark kitchen every night at the witching hour?"

She laughed, low and throaty. "I just hadn't had the chance yet to turn on the light. The switch is in an inconvenient spot, which sometimes happens in these old houses." She advanced, reaching just past him to flick on the light. She leaned so close he had to grit his teeth to keep from grabbing her.

As soft light flooded the room, Greg's heart tripped into a fast and erratic rhythm. Mikelle stood barely out of arm's reach and was dressed in a white chenille bathrobe. The belt was tied loosely, but it still accentuated her slender waist and the feminine swell of her hips. The hem stopped just short of her knees, showing off Mikelle's shapely legs right down to bare feet and pink-polished toenails.

Her hair looked freshly washed and shone like glossy mahogany. He imagined how sweet it would smell up close, how it would feel like silk sifting through his fingers. Her face was scrubbed clean of the small amount of makeup she'd had on earlier and the effect was as fundamentally appealing as Mom's apple pie. How could someone look so wholesome, yet at the same time make him want to untie that pristine white robe and slide his hands inside....

The heaviness in his groin was too distracting. He hoped his arousal wasn't obvious. He cleared his throat. "You weren't waiting for me, were you? I'm a big boy."

She smiled, but he noted a nervous tick at the corner of her mouth. "Actually I didn't think you'd make it back at all tonight." She turned, walked to the fridge and opened the door.

"Why wouldn't I come back tonight? I paid in advance," he joked. But he already knew what she'd meant.

She didn't turn around, but stared into the fridge like an indecisive teenager scrounging for a snack. "Well, I figured you and Brenda would...you know...have plans."

Greg sighed, his arousal diminished by this confirmation of what he'd suspected all along. Mikelle had pegged him as a playboy. His past seemed to trail him like toilet paper stuck to his shoe. He slumped into a chair by the table.

"Brenda and I aren't involved anymore," he offered tiredly.

Mikelle turned then, her expression a mix of surprise and apology. "I'm sorry. I shouldn't have assumed... It's none of my business anyway. Do you want some milk?"

Greg laughed at the abrupt turn of conversation. "I should have known milk would be your beverage of choice."

She cocked her head to the side, looking demure as all get-out. "Why?"

"It's pure and wholesome... like you."

A wicked gleam shone from those Gray Lady eyes. "Like me? Oh, I have a few sinful little indulgences."

While Greg's imagination played havoc with his self-control, Mikelle poured two tall glasses of milk, then stood on tiptoe to pull a small, silver canister from a top shelf. He should have offered to help, but Greg was busy enjoying the view. She tucked the canister under her chin and carried the glasses to the table.

Greg finally roused himself and tried to be useful. He held out his hands and she lifted her chin, allowing the canister to drop. Greg caught it and placed it on the table between them.

He tapped the lid with a forefinger. "So, what's inside? Wheat germ? Organically grown dried prunes?"

Mikelle removed the canister lid and dumped out a handful of miniature candy bars. Her eyes lit up like stars. "These little bite-size pieces of heaven are the only thing that should be consumed with milk at midnight." She unwrapped one and popped it into her mouth. "Mmmmm... It's my secret store. I love chocolate as much as Jamie does. Maybe more. You see, Greg, I'm not such a food prude as you think."

Greg couldn't help grinning. He unwrapped one of the small bars, too. "There's probably a lot about you that would surprise me."

She grinned back, already unwrapping another candy. "You certainly surprised *me* today."

"I did? How so?"

"You know... the fatherhood thing. I never dreamed you were thinking about adopting a child."

Greg talked around the gooey chocolate. "Especially not after Brenda defamed me."

"But you admitted yourself that you weren't the marrying kind. I admire your honesty, Greg."

The chocolate suddenly stuck in his throat, but that wasn't what kept Greg from replying.

"Actually, I'm kind of glad we got this opportunity to talk," she continued. "Our conversation at the café was interrupted and I wanted you to know I'm open to discussion anytime. Adoption is a big step and there's lots to consider. As you now know, I've been through it from start to finish. Were you surprised when I told you Jamie's adopted?"

He was getting good at hedging. "Well, you and Jamie certainly look like you belong together."

She beamed. "We do belong together. I don't know how anyone could have given him up in the first place, but I'm so grateful they did. All the adoption hassles were worth it. Jamie is the most important thing in my life.''

"I can tell. Jamie obviously adores you.''

"The feeling is mutual.''

"And you think he'll do fine without a father around?''

She shrugged. "I'll try to make sure he never feels deprived. And, who knows, maybe some great guy will come along and we'll just have to 'make room for daddy.' But I'm not holding my breath. Jim is a hard act to follow.''

Greg felt a surge of jealousy, but he was beginning to think Frank didn't stand a chance. It was selfish of him, but somehow he was glad Frank would probably never graduate from uncle to dad. Still not satisfied, though, Greg was about to risk asking more questions when Mikelle suddenly reached over and laid her hand on top of his. She sat very still. "Shhh . . . I think I hear something.''

Greg couldn't hear anything except the increased beating of his heart as it echoed in his ears. If he could be this flustered by a casual touch, what would happen if he actually kissed Mikelle?

"What do you think you hear?''

"Jamie.'' She stood up. "He's whimpering. He might be having a bad dream and if I rub his back it seems to soothe him back to sleep.''

Greg was impressed. "I can't believe you can hear him clear down here.''

"I've got a mother's ears.'' As Greg started to stand up, Mikelle motioned for him to stay seated. "Finish your milk. I'll just run up and check on him.'' As she started toward the door, Greg racked his brain for a good excuse to follow her, coming up with nothing reasonable enough to pass muster.

She stopped at the door leading to the back stairs and turned. "Before I go up, I just wanted to tell you how relieved I am to learn about your adoption plans. Now that I understand your interest in Jamie, I can relax. I couldn't help but feel that you represented some sort of danger to me and Jamie, and now I feel so silly that I let my imagination get the best of me like that. I'm just sort of overprotective. You understand, don't you?"

Greg understood only too well. "I know exactly how you feel about Jamie," he assured her. And he understood why she'd seen him as dangerous. What he couldn't understand was why she wasn't still worried. She'd swallowed his adoption story hook, line and sinker. She was too damned trusting.

She smiled and guilt tore through him like scissors through tissue paper. "Good night, then. See you tomorrow."

"Good night," he returned. But he wasn't too sure about that see-you-tomorrow part. If he was smart, he'd catch the first flight back to New York. Every day he spent in Nantucket increased his confusion and multiplied the potential for disaster. He didn't know how to reconcile his desire to stay and his desire to leave.

He wanted his old life.

He wanted Jamie... but Jamie was in wonderful hands with Mikelle.

He wanted Mikelle... but he wasn't sure for how long.

His checkered past was thumbing its nose at him, taunting him, telling him he could only want a woman for a few weeks, a few months at most. He didn't want to hurt anyone. Not Jamie, not Mikelle. But he was hurting inside all the time now, and he didn't know what to do to make the pain go away.

He finished his milk, the cold creamy drink something he hadn't enjoyed in years. Then he went up to bed, too tired to think another minute. That night he dreamed he was flipping burgers on a backyard barbecue grill, wearing a comically large chef's hat and sporting an apron with the words World's Greatest Dad emblazoned on the front. Mikelle was there, all decked out in pearls and a fifties-style dress, arranging cookies on a plate and pouring gallon-size glasses of milk. About a dozen kids with milk mustaches were tearing through the house and yard.

Greg woke up in a cold sweat.

"I HAVEN'T SEEN Mr. Chandler in two days, Mikelle. Where's he been?"

Mikelle was putting on a denim jacket over a blouse and corduroy skirt as she prepared to leave the house for her monthly bingo night. She'd already bundled Jamie in a red parka. She wasn't that crazy about bingo, but she considered it part of her social and civic duty to support an event that was sponsored by the neighborhood church.

She shrugged, hoping to look unconcerned by Rose's question. "I don't know. He leaves before I'm up in the morning and doesn't come back till I'm in bed. I guess he's working hard." Or playing hard. Mikelle couldn't help but wonder if Brenda had stayed on the island and had enticed Greg back into a relationship, however fleeting.

Rose harrumphed and shifted Jamie to her other hip. "I expected to see more of him."

Mikelle took Jamie from Rose. "I told you he wasn't interested in me. Now maybe you'll believe me."

"I saw the way he looked at you that first day," Rose insisted with a firm nod of her head. "He's interested. Maybe he's just shy."

Mikelle smiled and shook her head. "Get real, Rose. If you'd seen the woman he used to date hanging all over him at the fair, you'd know the man doesn't have a shy bone in his body. He's just not interested."

Rose looked unconvinced. "When do you want me to pick up Jamie?"

"The usual time. When the nursery closes, about eight. But I don't think I'll stay much later. I'm tired."

"No, you're sulky, that's all," stated Rose. "Mr. Chandler being here has reminded you of everything you've missed since Mr. Bennet died."

Mikelle hated the uncanny way Rose had of hitting things right on the nose. "Don't be ridiculous, Rose," she said, more sternly than she intended. She opened the kitchen door and a cool breeze blew in. Remnants of a storm on the mainland had lowered the temperatures for the past two days, making it much cooler than usual for October. When the storm passed, temperatures would rise again. "When you put Jamie to bed, Rose, maybe you should put another blanket in the crib."

Rose, offended by Mikelle's earlier tone of voice, grunted in reply. Mikelle sighed and turned to go, but her way was blocked by six feet, four inches of New York male.

"Hey, pardner," said Greg, chucking a grinning Jamie under the chin. "Goin' out?"

Mikelle wasn't sure whether to smile or throw a frying pan. She was glad to see Greg, but, even though she had no right or business feeling neglected, she resented his absence. So she compromised. She didn't throw a frying pan, but she didn't smile, either. "We're going to play bingo."

Greg's sandy eyebrows lifted. "Friday-night bingo, eh? You're teaching the kid to gamble already, are you?"

Greg's obvious good mood did nothing to sweeten Mikelle's sour one. She kept imagining Brenda prancing around a hot tub in the Executive Inn, wearing nothing but zebra-striped bikini underwear. Playful sex always lifted a man's mood, didn't it?

"We're going to be late if we don't leave right away, and I still have to warm up the car." Mikelle tried to sidle past Greg, but he wouldn't budge. He had on his brown suede jacket and tan slacks. He looked as good to Mikelle as chocolate invariably did around midnight. She hated such a knee-jerk reaction to the man's charm, and she tried to suppress it. She'd been ridiculous to think they'd become friends that first night when he asked her about adoption. Maybe he routinely confided his deepest desires to every woman he met.

"Frank doesn't play bingo?"

"Not tonight. He has work to do."

"That's too bad.... Say, why don't I drive you over in my Cherokee? It's already warmed up."

"You just got home. I wouldn't dream of putting you out."

"I don't mind. I have to stop at the store and get some razors anyway."

And some condoms? wondered Mikelle. "Really, Greg, this isn't necessary."

"Jamie won't have to shiver for a second. He'll be toasty warm as soon as he gets in the car."

He knew her weakness, all right. "That would be nice, but Jamie needs a car seat."

"The Cherokee came with one. Isn't that handy?"

And highly unusual, thought Mikelle. "I've run out of excuses. You're determined to play Sir Galahad, aren't you?"

He swung his arm toward the driveway. "Right this way to the white charger, my lady."

She found herself smiling against her will. But what the heck, she reasoned, he hadn't been neglecting her. He owed her nothing. They meant exactly nothing to each other. He was only a guest in the inn, she told herself. No one special. Then why did her heart thump wildly as he lightly cupped her elbow and led her to the car?

"So where do the Nantucketers play bingo?" Greg asked after Mikelle tucked Jamie into the car seat. "Maybe I'll come in for a few minutes." He slid into the seat and arranged his long legs under the steering wheel. Mikelle resisted the urge to put her hand on his knee, the way she used to do with Jim.

"At that brownstone church a few blocks from here. I'll show you the way."

He started the ignition. "The brownstone church," he repeated, and for the first time since he'd showed up at the back door, the cheerful tone of his voice wavered.

Mikelle chuckled. "Don't worry. No one will try to convert you."

"Does the reverend hang out with the congregation at these bingo parties?"

"Very seldom. Why?"

He pulled out of the driveway and headed down the road before replying. "No reason. I just wondered. So, Mikelle, what have you and Jamie been doing while I scoured the island from top to bottom for a likely spot for my Texas client to build his own East Coast Ponderosa?"

Mikelle's resentment melted away. Greg had obviously been busy doing what he'd come to Nantucket to do, and now he was interested in catching up on their activities in the interim. His sincerity was hard to resist. They chatted in a lively, friendly manner as they drove the few short blocks to the church.

Once inside the social hall, Mikelle was in complete charity with Greg and trying to keep herself from smiling too broadly. Heads turned as they removed their coats and hung them on the hooks by the front double doors. They were in full view of the entire room.

It took about thirty seconds for them to be approached by none other than the balding, benevolent Reverend Holden himself. Mikelle liked the grandfatherly reverend even though, with his old-fashioned views and manners, he sometimes came across as downright corny. He walked straight up to Greg and extended his hand.

"Well, hello, young man. Fancy seeing you again."

Mikelle blinked in confusion. "You two know each other?"

"Sort of," said Greg, looking like a cornered rabbit in a fox's den.

Chapter Five

As they shook hands, Reverend Holden remarked, "I thought you said you lived in New York?"

Greg could feel Mikelle's curious gaze. He should have known better than to come to the church, no matter how small the chance was that he'd run into the reverend. Next to a total collapse of the roof on his sinner's head, this was the worst thing that could have happened. Now he just hoped he could somehow squeak through this predicament without losing Mikelle's trust again. "I do. I'm only on the island for a few days to take care of some business."

The reverend nodded and smiled broadly, looking uncannily like a cherub. His warm gaze shifted to Mikelle. "Staying at the Gray Lady?"

"Yes. It came highly recommended," Greg replied, wishing fervently for angelic intervention before the kindly reverend spilled the beans in front of Mikelle.

"Speaking of recommendations—"

Too late, thought Greg. *Here it comes.*

"I wouldn't hesitate to recommend Greg as a tenant, Mikelle. Anyone who makes such generous contributions to the church certainly isn't the type to skip town without paying his bill."

Mikelle's eyebrows lifted as she gave Greg an inquiring look. She simply appeared to be politely interested, but Greg knew better. She was absolutely intrigued.

"I had no idea you were such a philanthropist, Greg."

Embarrassed, Greg said, "I'm not. I only made the one contribution. The reverend is being too kind."

"And you're being too humble," said the reverend, clapping Greg on the back. "It isn't every day someone brings us almost two hundred dollars' worth of groceries to be distributed to the needy. And I don't believe for one minute that story about buying too many groceries while trailing a pretty girl at the store, hoping for an introduction. Rocky Road ice cream and Lucky Charms could only have been bought as treats for deprived children."

"I don't know, Reverend Holden," said Mikelle wryly, as she shifted a squirming Jamie to her other hip. "A man once told me that gourmet cooks sometimes eat sugary cereal like Lucky Charms while they're creating culinary masterpieces. Gives them energy."

"Someone's been pulling your pretty leg, Mikelle," said the reverend, laughing. "My friendly advice to you is to steer clear of men who tease you with such outlandish stories, and concentrate on men of good solid character . . . like Greg here."

The reverend beamed on Greg, making him feel even more like a heel. How was he going to explain his way out of this mess?

Luckily, at that moment Jamie decided he was tired of staying still while grown-ups droned on about incomprehensible subjects. The squawk he put up diverted the reverend's attention.

"Jamie, my boy," he said, holding out his arms. "Why don't I deposit you in the nursery while your mom sits down at the bingo table? I think the games are about to begin."

Jamie perked up at the word "nursery" and was only too eager to cooperate. As the reverend carted Jamie away, he turned back and said, "I'm glad I ran into you, Greg. I hope you enjoy your stay on Nantucket. You two young folks have a good time tonight." Then he winked and disappeared down a narrow hallway.

In the next few minutes, Greg was saved from a confrontation with Mikelle as several people approached to exchange friendly greetings and small talk. He was introduced to everyone—but immediately forgot their names in the hubbub—and was given a thorough once-over by two elderly women.

He supposed he was being sized up by the locals as Frank's competition. Even the saintly reverend's parting wink had been suggestive. Judging by the tension Greg felt seething beneath Mikelle's relaxed facade, tonight Frank had the lead on him in the romance race by more than a nose.

Finally they were seated with bingo cards in front of them, a pile of bingo chips between them, and a blue-haired lady on each side.

"O-32," called a man seated behind a table set in the middle of the room.

"Why did you lie to me?"

She'd only whispered the accusatory words, but to Greg they sounded like claps of thunder. He pretended to be searching his card for O-32, although it would take a person of average intelligence less than three seconds to see it wasn't there. "I'm sorry. I didn't think it was that important."

"A lie is a lie," she said matter-of-factly.

"I-13."

"If I'd told you the truth, that I'd actually been following you around the store, what would you have thought?"

He darted a glance her way. She kept her eyes trained on her bingo card. "I'd have thought my first instincts about you were right on the mark."

"What? That I'm a child snatcher?"

She sighed. "All I know is that you haven't been honest with me from the beginning."

"G-20."

"So I was following you.... Is that a crime? No, don't answer that. But can you blame a guy for being interested in a cute kid and his equally cute mom?"

"B-15."

"Are you really here on business, Greg, or is that just another lie?"

"Do you actually think I'd make up some bogus business trip just to put the moves on you, Mikelle? There are women in New York, you know."

She was silenced, and he realized how insulting he'd sounded. But how else was he supposed to divert her from the truth?

"I didn't mean you weren't worth a little extra effort," he modified, "but staging a phony business trip is a bit excessive, don't you think? And Jamie's cute, but it's hardly worth several days away from the office just to interact with the kid. I have friends in New York with children they're only too willing to let me baby-sit while they do *Cats* and the Rainbow Room for a few hours.''

"G-45."

He heard her sigh, long and low. "God, now you really think I'm paranoid, don't you?"

"You're not paranoid."

"It's just that I hate lies, no matter how small."

"I should have admitted that I was following you that day at the store. Well, now you know. I'm sorry."

"Is that the only lie, Greg? Can I trust you?"

Hell, no, you can't trust me, Greg thought. "I should be finishing my business in a few days, Mikelle, then I'll be long gone. In a couple of weeks you and Jamie won't even remember I was here."

At least that was the plan. That's what he'd been gearing up to do for the past couple of days. But Greg's heart ached already from the idea of never seeing Jamie again...or Jamie's mother. Was he strong enough, honorable enough, to do the right thing for everyone concerned?

"So what's your point?" asked Mikelle. "You won't be here long enough for me to worry about trusting you?"

"That's the plan," said Greg, repeating his own grim thoughts.

"Great," said Mikelle with sarcasm and a trace of humor. She shook her head, looking at him for the first time since they'd sat down. "Well, if your little white lies only go so far as covering up grocery-store flirtations, and since this particular white lie actually

resulted in food for the poor, I guess I ought to forgive you.''

"I'm sure you should," said Greg, silently promising he'd give her nothing more serious to forgive. He
smiled down at her. "Honest, I'll try to live up to the
reverend's good opinion of me."

She smiled back and he breathed a sigh of relief.
Another hurdle barely cleared, and with no room to
spare—no room for another mistake.

"N-12."

"Bingo!" shouted the lady on Greg's right.

AN HOUR LATER, Rose arrived to pick up Jamie. An
hour after that, Greg walked Mikelle out to the Jeep
with a thermos of hot punch under his arm that had
been handed to him by one of the blue-haired ladies
as a welcoming gift. She'd become quite friendly in
the course of the evening, and he'd not only found
out her name was Gertie Coffin—one of Frank's
many distant cousins— but was told her entire life
story.

Greg consoled himself with the knowledge that the
evening hadn't been a total washout with the ladies.
Mikelle had gotten more and more quiet, but Gertie
took up the slack with her constant chatter. At least
she seemed to like him.

He and Mikelle headed back to the inn through
gathering fog. Seeing only as far as the length of the
headlight beam made the inside of the Cherokee seem
quite cozy. Greg struggled with the urge to pull Mikelle against his side and cuddle all the way home...if
she'd let him. But thankfully there were two obsta-
cles in the way of this dangerous impulse—the gear-

shift and Greg's own conscience, which continued to nag him like a fishwife.

"You're quiet," he said to Mikelle after several moments of total silence. "Are you sorry you agreed to forgive me for lying about the grocery-store fiasco?"

She answered indirectly. "I suppose you can't even grill a cheese sandwich," she said dryly.

"Take-out Chinese is my specialty."

"That's just what I would have guessed."

"So, you've suspected my motives from the beginning, eh?"

"You're going to think this sounds crazy, but you've...well...frightened me a little, ever since I first laid eyes on you. And now I think I've finally figured out why."

He tensed. "Why?"

Before Mikelle could answer, a loud pop sounded at the rear of the Jeep, followed by the telltale thump of a blown-out tire.

"Hell," said Greg, pulling over to the curb. He turned to Mikelle. "Hold that thought till I change the tire. You'll have to get out, but bring Gertie's punch. That'll keep you warm."

Mikelle took Greg's advice and stood to the side, drinking Gertie's punch, while she watched him change the tire. Greg found himself wondering what she was thinking while he accomplished the stereotypical male task. Did she think he was strong and capable, or was she just as adept at tire changing? Would she be okay if she and Jamie were caught with a flat tire on a deserted road one night?

"You ever change a tire?" he asked her, throwing the question over his shoulder while he tightened lug nuts.

"Yes," she answered. "But I'm not nearly as fast as you."

He supposed he would have to be satisfied with her answer. Doing it slowly was better than not being able to do it at all. Then it occurred to him that any male worth his salt, or any man with an eye for a pretty female, would stop on a dime to help Mikelle change her tire. Two cars had stopped to ask them if they needed assistance even with Greg doing the changing. But somehow the idea wasn't reassuring. Any jerk could force himself on her while she was stranded on a lonely road....

"Greg? What's the matter?"

Greg realized he was staring at the last lug nut, his wrench suspended over it, brooding. "Nothing. I'm almost done. In just a second you can get back inside the car."

"No hurry," she said. "I'm plenty warm." Then she hiccuped and excused herself with a giggle.

Greg stood up and turned to observe Mikelle suspiciously. They stood directly under the streetlight and he had no trouble detecting the rosy flush on her cheeks. "Gertie's punch is spiked, right?"

Mikelle gazed back at him, round eyed. "I never touch the stuff. S'not healthy."

Mikelle's words were ever-so-slightly slurred and he had to bite his lip to keep from laughing. "Then you probably wouldn't recognize the alcohol hidden under Gertie's punch spices." He stretched out his hand. "Let me see the thermos."

Mikelle frowned and handed him the thermos, which Greg immediately noted was over half-empty. He sniffed the rim, then took a swallow. The liquor warmed his gullet right down to his stomach. Along with the apple and cranberry juices, cinnamon and cloves, was a generous lacing of gin.

"Gert sure knows how to welcome a guy to town," he commented. "And she sure as hell knows how to keep a body warm on a cold, foggy night. This punch has bite."

"Don't be ridiculous," said Mikelle with a jut of her chin. "Gertie's the lead soprano in the church choir. She has eight grandchildren."

Greg laughed. "What's your point?"

"The bite in the punch . . . it's the cinnamon."

She'd had difficulty pronouncing *cinnamon*, the word coming out more like "cimmammon."

He grabbed her elbow and guided her toward the Jeep. "If such an innocent household spice were behind the power packed by this punch, you'd have drunks hanging out at candy stores, eating cinnamon bears out of brown paper sacks. Come on, Mikelle, get inside while I put the tools away."

Mikelle looked perplexed, but she got inside. Greg wondered how much the booze had affected her. If she really never drank liquor, she could be half-snockered—or at least extremely relaxed.

Finding a rag with the tools—ironically, an old cloth diaper—he wiped the small amount of grease from his hands, then slid into the Jeep, closed the door and started the engine before turning to look at Mikelle. She was making use of the headrest, her eyes closed. The line of her slender neck, so exposed by the reclining angle of her head, looked damned kissable.

He cursed silently and shifted into gear, then noticed that Mikelle wasn't belted.

"Put on your seat belt, Mikelle."

There was no response.

"Look, I know we're almost home, but you still need to wear your seat belt."

Still no response.

"Damn, don't tell me you're asleep."

He gritted his teeth and defied temptation by reaching across her to grab the belt himself and lock it into place. He could smell her perfume, that dewy rose stuff. His chest grazed her breasts and he gritted his teeth harder than ever. When he was finished with the seat belt, he straightened up and found her staring straight at him, her lips slightly parted. Their faces were separated by a mere six inches.

He swallowed hard. "I thought you were asleep," he explained.

"I think I was," she admitted. "I guess you were right. The punch was spiked."

"Are you all right?"

"Yes." She smiled, the curve of her lips a tantalizing invitation. "Actually I feel kind of good. You know...relaxed."

They stared at each other another long moment, then Greg abruptly turned and faced the steering wheel. "I need to get you home."

In five minutes, Greg pulled into the gravel driveway of the Gray Lady and shut off the engine and the lights. He reached for the door handle, but froze when he felt Mikelle grab his arm.

"We were having a conversation before the tire blew," she reminded him. "Don't you want to finish it?"

Greg took a steadying breath. He turned and looked at Mikelle. The porch light illuminated the interior of the Cherokee to a soft, shadowed lucency. The atmosphere was as seductive as candlelight. "Don't you just want to go to bed?" he suggested, then inwardly cringed at the possibility that she might attach a double meaning to his innocently posed question.

She chose to ignore the faux pas. "I'm not tired or sick." She shrugged her shoulders and grinned. "Like I said, I'm just relaxed."

He was tempted to tell her that sometimes being "relaxed" was more of a handicap than being tired or sick. "So what was it you wanted to tell me?" he said, resigned to a few more minutes of torture while he tried to keep his mitts off Mikelle.

"Remember I said that you frightened me ever since I first saw you in the store that day?"

"Yes," he said cautiously. "But you later told me that it was because I seemed too smitten by Jamie. And I've explained that, so—"

"No, it was more than that. I was attracted to you."

Greg's heart flip-flopped. He was getting aroused. Hell, he'd been in a state of semi-arousal since the moment he'd picked her up at the inn. Maybe he wouldn't be such a cad if he just kissed her. In fact, maybe if he kissed her, he'd get the woman out of his system. He'd realize she was no different, no more special than any other woman he'd kissed. She'd be—

She interrupted his rationalizing. "And I'm still attracted to you . . . damn it."

"Why 'damn it'?"

"Because I don't want to be attracted to anyone. I avoid men I'm attracted to."

Well, that said loads about her relationship with Frank, didn't it? "Why, Mikelle?"

"I guess because it makes me feel guilty. I loved Jim a lot. Sometimes I feel like he's just away on some business trip, you know? And if I got involved with someone else, it would be like cheating."

"Judging by what I've gathered about Jim, he wouldn't want you to feel guilty about getting on with your life."

"I know." She sighed softly. "But you're the last person in the world I should be kissing."

"Kissing?" He laughed uneasily. "You're relaxed, all right. That sounded like an invitation."

"I know you're not the marrying kind, Greg," she continued, gazing at him with a soft, serious, sensual look in her gray eyes. "But kissing doesn't have to mean commitment, does it?"

"It never has to me," he admitted sheepishly. "You're right about the marriage thing. I've seldom seen it work for very long, and I don't see much point in setting myself up for failure. I'm attracted to you, too, Mikelle. But, as you said, I'm probably the last guy in the world you should be kissing."

"For some reason, right now I don't feel like being cautious."

"It's the punch."

"No, it's not."

"Yes, it is."

"Kiss me, Greg." She lifted her chin, closed her eyes and scooted as close as the bucket seats would permit.

Greg thought of all the reasons why he shouldn't kiss her. Then he mentally replayed all the rationalizations he'd come up with just minutes before. In the end, like Mikelle, he threw caution to the wind. Bending over the gears, he kissed her. It took about half a second to realize that Mikelle was nothing like any of the women he'd kissed before. But by then it was too late to turn back.

Mikelle felt absolutely giddy, but not because of Gertie's punch. At first Greg had simply leaned toward her and touched his lips to hers. If he'd meant to keep the kiss on a chaste and friendly level, he'd failed miserably. The connection between them was electrifying and soon they both parted their lips. Then Greg eased his tongue into her mouth.

It had been a long time since she'd felt passion with a man, and not because Greg was the first man to kiss her since Jim. There had been a couple of good-night porch kisses with dates before Frank. And Frank had frequently tried to light a fire in Mikelle, but there had never been an answering spark. Till now, that is... with Greg.

Mikelle felt intoxicated by the smell of Greg—fresh night air mixed with a subtle tangy after-shave. She loved the feel of his mouth on hers, the taste of cinnamon on his tongue, the thrilling sensation of his strong hands as they cupped her shoulders. Her own hands had been braced against his chest, but now they wandered over his wide shoulders, up the back of his neck and into his thick hair.

On a gasp, Greg broke contact with her mouth and trailed kisses down Mikelle's throat. "For a vegetarian, you're one sexy lady," he murmured, his breath tickling her skin and sending a thrill down her spine.

She chuckled. "I have to confess, though, I don't wear zebra-striped underwear. I'm pure white cotton and lace all the way."

He groaned. "Talking about underwear is strictly forbidden."

"Why?"

"Because we're only kissing."

"Then shut up and kiss me, why don't you?"

Greg took a deep breath, then eased Mikelle back to her side of the car. At her pouty look, he said, "You'll thank me tomorrow. This was an even worse idea than I initially thought."

"Do you want to go on a picnic tomorrow?"

Greg looked surprised. Mikelle had even surprised herself, abruptly changing the topic of conversation and coming out with an impulsive invitation. Maybe it *was* the punch. "I have to go to a remote part of the island to visit Annabelle. You know, the pink lady at the grocery store? She has some new Jack Russell terrier puppies and I'm trading her one of my paintings for a pet for Jamie. You can help us decide which mutt's the best."

"A remote part of the island, eh?"

"Yes, why?"

Greg appeared to be considering his answer. "Will Jamie be going, too?"

"I know you like Jamie, Greg, but it is rather demoralizing to have to bargain for your company by bribing you with my son," she said dryly. "Especially after we've just shared a few pleasant kisses."

He arched a brow. "Pleasant?"

"All right, not pleasant. Passionate."

"The passion between us is precisely why I want Jamie's company," he said, grinning roguishly. "We obviously need a chaperon."

"Some chaperon," said Mikelle. "He'll be crawling after sand crabs and making mud pies and won't even know we're alive." Mikelle opened the car door and stepped out, surprised to find she was a little dizzy. Was it really the punch that was making her so impulsive and devil-may-care?

Greg got out, too, took her arm and escorted her to the door. "If you still want me to go out to Annabelle's with you tomorrow, after all that punch has worked itself out of your system, I'll go. But if you have misgivings in the morning, I'll know that your behavior tonight—and all the invitations you were so generous with—were direct consequences of drinking too much of Gertie's punch."

Concentrating on not falling on her face, Mikelle merely nodded.

Inside, he followed closely behind as she slowly ascended the stairs. She knew he was afraid she'd keel over, but despite the leaden feel of her legs and the tendency of the room to tilt, she was quite sure she was capable of putting herself to bed. However, she entertained a brief fantasy of being helped into her pajamas. She frowned. Or was that *out* of her pajamas?

Rose met them in the upstairs hallway, looking a little startled and more than a little dismayed by Mikelle's tipsy behavior. She threw Greg a questioning look, but he shook his head and made a quick retreat to his own room. Mikelle could explain as well as he could, and he was anxious to get away from the sexy, playful, lethal side of Mikelle that had been let loose by Gertie's punch.

Just as he opened the door and was about to go inside, he heard Mikelle call softly across the hall, "It's not the punch, Greg. It's not the punch."

Chapter Six

It was the punch, Mikelle told herself. Gertie's "secret sauce" was the only possible explanation for her behavior last night and her dull headache this morning. She scowled at herself in the bathroom mirror as she downed two extra-strength Tylenol with a half can of V-8. She couldn't believe she'd let Greg kiss her....

Who was she kidding? She'd been the one to pucker up first, and if Greg hadn't been gentlemanly enough to nip their ardor in the bud before things had gone too far, she'd probably have made love with him in the cramped back seat of the Cherokee like some love-struck teenager with raging hormones after the prom.

She glanced into her adjoining bedroom, where Jamie played on the carpet with a Fisher-Price garage, complete with tow truck, Little People mechanics and brightly colored cars. They were both already dressed for their trip to Annabelle's house in Wauwinet, a small village on the north end of the island. She'd packed a basket of food and gathered up a blanket, a bucket, a shovel and Jamie's favorite ball for a picnic on the beach that afternoon. Now all she had to do was sneak out the back door, load up the Volvo wagon and she'd be home free.

Mikelle frowned. No, that was the coward's way out. While she was under the influence her thinking may have been a tad fuzzy, but this morning she distinctly remembered everything she'd said and done last night. She had invited Greg to go to Annabelle's with her and Jamie.

It was a beautiful morning and the weatherman on the early news had predicted seventy-three degrees by noon. She couldn't use inclement weather as an excuse to weasel out of her invitation.

Greg had gallantly suggested that she rethink her invitation this morning after the gin had evaporated from her brain cells. But if she went to Annabelle's without him, he'd think she was afraid of spending more time with him. He'd be right, of course, but she didn't want him to know how powerfully she was attracted to him. She wanted him to think last night's wanton behavior was all Gertie Coffin's fault and had nothing to do with Mikelle's own runaway desires.

The only way to pull off that colossal lie would be to behave today as if last night was a fluke. She'd laugh it off. She'd be breezy and sheepishly apologetic. She'd insist they go on as if nothing had happened and return to being friendly strangers.

And she'd never, *ever* let him touch her again. He'd agreed that he was the last guy on earth she should be kissing. She was an old-fashioned kind of girl, still cherishing the fantasy of a picket-fence marriage and lots more children. Greg might be thinking seriously of adoption, but he sure as shootin' wasn't thinking seriously about anything vaguely matrimonial.

"Come on, Jamie," said Mikelle, as she picked him up and smiled into his bright eyes. "We're going to see Annabelle and get you a puppy."

Jamie knew all about puppies because one of his favorite books was a story about a mother dog and her babies. He repeated his version of the word *puppy* and clapped his hands, his eyes brightening even more.

Mikelle kissed his forehead and admired the odd color of his eyes, wondering for the umpteenth time whether they'd end up being green or gray. They seemed to switch back and forth, depending on the light. Or maybe they'd always be changeable. Her brow furrowed for a moment as she recalled where she'd seen someone with eyes of a similar chameleon nature.

Greg. Greg had eyes that sometimes seemed gray, sometimes green, just like Jamie's. Well, she thought, perhaps Jamie's eyes weren't so unique, after all.

She carried Jamie downstairs and into the kitchen. He'd already had breakfast, but she got him a bottle of apple juice from the fridge for a snack on the road. He popped it into his mouth while Mikelle rechecked the contents of the picnic basket and filled the small cooler with drinks. She put in a couple of beers for Greg. She hoped he liked cheese sandwiches.

Rose, in a fresh white apron and with her gray hair brushed back from her flushed face, stood over a sink full of suds. Mikelle could feel the woman's eyes following her as she moved about the kitchen.

"Are you feeling more yourself this morning, dear?" she asked.

"Much more myself, thank you, Rose," Mikelle answered briskly. "Has Mr. Chandler had breakfast yet this morning?"

Rose frowned. "That's it? Aren't you going to tell me what happened last night?"

Mikelle tried to appear nonchalant. It was good practice for later when she faced Greg. "Sure, if you're interested."

"'If I'm interested,' she says," grumbled Rose, scrubbing a copper pot with energy.

"I'll take that as a yes," said Mikelle. "It's really very simple. Gertie Coffin gave Greg a thermos of hot punch. We got a flat on the way home from bingo, and I drank a bunch of the stuff while Greg changed the tire. I didn't know it was spiked. I got tipsy. And, as Paul Harvey says, 'that's the rest of the story.'"

"It's such a short story, you could have told me last night."

"Sorry, I was practically asleep on my feet."

"I was worried. I thought maybe..."

Mikelle raised her brows. "You thought maybe Greg had plied me with drink, then tried to have his wicked way with me?"

Rose looked offended, then turned serious. "I was hoping I hadn't made a mistake by encouraging you to spend time with him. I was hoping he hadn't done something to change my good opinion of him."

"He didn't do anything you'd object to," she admitted reluctantly.

"Good," said Rose with a satisfied nod of her head. "But I'm not surprised."

"You and the reverend barely know him, but you both act as though he's some kind of saint," Mikelle said dryly.

Rose shrugged, smiled. "He's not?"

Mikelle was about to reply that although Greg looked like a Greek god, no, he was not a saint. But neither was she. She reminded herself that he hadn't taken advantage of her last night when many men would have jumped at the opportunity. She decided to keep her mouth shut, except to ask again, "Now will you tell me if *Saint* Greg has eaten his breakfast?"

"Yes. A good one, too. He loves my cooking, that one. It's always a pleasure to cook for a hearty-eatin' man. He's still drinking coffee." Rose nodded toward the door to the dining room. "Go on. Go in and talk to him."

Mikelle did as she was urged to do, although she was beginning to see her friend and housekeeper in a new light these days. It was almost as though Rose had given up on her longtime favorite, Frank, and, like a pragmatic matchmaker, was intent on getting Mikelle married off to the first available hapless male. That would be Greg...although no one could ever describe Greg as hapless. Male, yes. Hapless, no.

She left the kitchen through a swinging door, passed through a short hallway and into the dining room. Greg sat at the end of the table, one hand cupping a mug of coffee and the other supporting his chin as he stared out the window. He had beautiful hands, long and slender and big. He was wearing a light blue shirt with just a thin border of white undershirt showing at the open collar. He looked casual, relaxed...and devastatingly sexy. He turned and smiled.

"Hi."

"Hi." Mikelle shifted Jamie to her other hip and leaned to one side for balance.

"You're still speaking to me?"

"Why wouldn't I?" she said, hoping she sounded breezy. She could feel her cheeks flaming pink, which didn't exactly fit the attitude of nonchalance she was striving so hard to project.

A glimmer of amused understanding registered briefly in Greg's eyes, then politely disappeared. "Then the invitation still stands?"

She shrugged, then smiled. "Of course. I don't blame you for what happened. It was—"

"The punch," he finished for her.

"And I can promise you that I won't try to seduce you again."

"Well, now you've ruined my whole day."

She pretended to ignore this comment, although she was sure her cheeks got even pinker. "I'm only drinking spring water and juice today. I'll stay stone-cold sober."

He raised a brow. "I gather you don't think our kisses last night were the wisest course of action."

"Admit it, you don't think it was wise, either. You said it yourself, Greg. You're the—"

"Yeah, I know. I'm the last guy you should be kissing."

"Still want to come?"

He stood up, all six feet and more of him. His blue shirt was tucked into snug stone-washed jeans. He was one tall, cool drink of water, and boy, was she ever thirsty.

"Where's the picnic gear?" he asked.

She swallowed past her dry throat. "In the kitchen."

He nodded, then walked toward her with his arms extended. Was that ever an inviting picture. Just as she was tempted to forget all her good intentions and step mindlessly into his embrace, he said, "Hi, pardner. That's a jazzy red sweat suit you've got on this morning. Want to hitch a ride to the kitchen?"

Of course he was talking to Jamie. Mikelle labeled herself an idiot for jumping to conclusions about those outstretched arms. Jamie smiled around the nipple of his bottle, a drop of juice winding down his chin. He went willingly to Greg and Mikelle followed them into the kitchen feeling like a kicked dog.

As they packed the Cherokee and stowed Jamie in the car seat, Greg talked to her son just the way Michelle did, assuming the little boy understood just about everything said. He joked in his deep voice, teasing and tickling. Jamie responded with smiles, giggles, squirms and frequent use of his limited vocabulary. He obviously liked Greg as much as Rose did, as much as the reverend did, as much as she did...damn it.

Mikelle sighed as they backed out of the driveway. Maybe she'd given herself too much credit. Maybe Greg wasn't as attracted to her as she was to him. Maybe she had nothing to worry about when it came to a repeat of last night's kisses. Suddenly the sunny autumn day didn't seem so bright.

Greg was grateful for the diversion of the passing scenery. Mikelle looked great today in a green plaid shirt tucked into jeans. She looked as shapely as a Barbie doll, but a hell of a lot more real. She smelled real, too. It was her usual scent of rain-washed roses—the same scent that had drifted through his dreams all night.

He'd backed off last night when Mikelle wanted to keep on kissing, but it had been tough as hell. Lying in his bed afterward, aching for her, he'd decided that he didn't dare stay on Nantucket Island past the weekend. He'd indulge himself in this last day with Jamie, then he'd go back to New York and leave his son in Mikelle's capable hands.

He was through kidding himself. He knew Jamie was safe, happy and loved. He had no excuse to stay. But the thought of leaving crushed his spirit. Today's fun would definitely be bittersweet.

As per Mikelle's directions, they traveled the road that bordered the harbor. Greg watched a ferry churn across the sound and enter the harbor between the arms of two long breakwaters. Big and small houses lined the shore, stacked in uneven rows clear down to the water's edge. Sailboats and powerboats of every description were tied up or riding at anchor. Wharves that used to berth huge whaling vessels stood in line to accommodate the modern-day ferry services.

At least Jamie would have a beautiful place to grow up, Greg thought, but not without remorse that he wouldn't be around to watch the process.

Jamie had been lulled to sleep by the motion of the Jeep and silence wedged uncomfortably between Greg and Mikelle. Apparently neither of them was in the best of spirits. Greg chalked her moodiness up to embarrassment and regret about last night.

Presently they were passing moors covered with patches of deep red autumn huckleberry and dusky bell heather. A sign for Wauwinet appeared, and as they turned onto the quaint main street of the tiny town, Mikelle said, "Annabelle lives just down this road on the left."

Greg nodded.

"Annabelle's a bit eccentric. She's sharp as a tack, but she sometimes gets odd ideas. And she doesn't mince words."

Greg smiled. "I've already met the lady, remember? I know how blunt she can be."

Greg turned down the road Mikelle indicated and soon they pulled up in front of Annabelle's historic lean-to, surrounded by tall hollyhocks. The silver-gray shingles of the steep roof shimmered softly in the morning sun.

Annabelle came out of her house just as Greg killed the engine. Mikelle hopped out of the Jeep, seeming relieved for some other company besides his. Greg couldn't say he blamed her.

"Mikelle, how you doing, honey?" crooned Annabelle in that scratchy, singsong voice of hers that reminded Greg of a rusty gate in the wind. Today she was dressed in a lime green sweat suit and a floppy sun hat, decorated by a wide, polka-dot band. Two bright spots of rouge shone on her wrinkled cheeks and her sharp blue eyes sparkled with intelligence. Greg wondered if she would remember him from the grocery store.

"I couldn't be better, Annabelle," Greg heard Mikelle reply, but he thought she said it a little too brightly, as if she was trying to convince herself as well as both of them. Greg got out of the car and opened the back door to take Jamie out of the infant carrier. Holding Jamie against his chest with the little guy facing forward, he walked around the front of the Jeep to where the two women stood. Mikelle started to introduce him. "This is—"

"No need to tell me who this big fella is," said Annabelle, her eyes widening. "What I want to know is how the heck did you find him?"

"You must remember me from the store," said Greg.

"Store? What store? I don't think we've ever met, son, but it's plain to see you're Jamie's dad."

Greg's smile froze on his face. His heart skipped a beat, then started again with one hard thump he felt right down to his toes. He couldn't speak. He didn't dare look away from Annabelle to see Mikelle's reaction. Was she staring at him? Was she tracing his features in Jamie's face?

Was the jig up?"

"Annabelle," said Mikelle, her voice soft and tactful. "Greg is just on the island for business. He and Jamie may both be big and blond, but they're not related. Don't you remember? Jamie's birth mother made it quite clear that she didn't know who the father was. That's what the certificate said...'father unknown.'"

Greg gave an inward sigh of relief. Because she didn't think it was possible, Mikelle was blind to the truth. Obviously she assumed that Annabelle's advanced age and eccentricity were misleading her. He slid a look her way, astonished that she could be so suspicious one minute and totally unsuspicious the next. Apparently she couldn't conceive of anything as wildly unlikely as Jamie's birth father being identified, much less showing up on the scene.

Annabelle continued to stare with a frown at Greg and Jamie, however, as if she didn't buy Mikelle's story. "Humph!" she finally said. "I've never seen two people who looked more like they were related. Are you sure you aren't this little fellow's dad?"

Greg forced a laugh and said, "Do you think I could possibly give up a kid like this if he were mine?"

The irony of the statement made his heart ache bitterly, though of course he'd been given no choice in the matter. He handed Jamie to Mikelle, trying to lessen the opportunity for comparison by putting distance between him and his son.

"In fact," said Mikelle, "Greg is thinking of adopting a child himself."

"Why don't you just get married?" said Annabelle bluntly. "Or are you shootin' blanks?"

Greg heard Mikelle gasp at Annabelle's audacity. But he simply ignored the bluntly phrased question about his fertility and said, "As for marriage, I've never met a woman I've felt like taking that kind of serious plunge with."

"Come from a broken home, eh?"

"Annabelle," said Mikelle, darting Greg an apologetic look. "You're getting awfully personal with a man you've just met."

"I'm just curious, that's all. Besides, he's no stranger. I remember him now. He's the fellow who was always just a couple of feet behind you at the store a few weeks ago. Stood over the artichokes till I thought he'd turned to stone. Usually a man who's got the jeebies about marriage," she continued, returning to her original subject, "comes from a broken home."

"You're right," admitted Greg, willing to pursue any subject that diverted Annabelle from Jamie's paternity. "My mother left when I was five. I was raised by my dad. And maybe that has got something to do with my reluctance to tie the knot. I don't analyze it, Annabelle. I just go with the flow."

Annabelle raised her brows. Greg could tell she was tempted to say more, but she had apparently decided to cut him a little slack. "Did you bring my painting?" she asked Mikelle.

"I did," answered Mikelle. She dropped Jamie gently onto the soft grass at her feet, then reached into the back seat of the Cherokee and pulled out her painting. It was wrapped in brown paper and tied with string. Greg hadn't even noticed her putting it in the Jeep.

"Untie it," ordered Annabelle, an eager edge to her voice. "I want to see it in the sunshine." Greg found himself just as eager to see Mikelle's new creation. He'd been thoroughly impressed with the paintings on display at the Gray Lady.

Mikelle looked a little embarrassed as she unwrapped the painting. "I still don't know why you wanted this particular subject matter," she said, "but here it is."

She turned the unframed painting over and held it out for Annabelle to get a good view. Greg's heart skipped another beat. He'd give his soul for Mikelle's latest painting. It was a beach scene with the central focus a small, towheaded toddler playing with his bucket and shovel in the sand. It was Jamie. It was his son.

"Oh, Mikelle, honey, you've outdone yourself," praised Annabelle. "I love it. Hell, you can have all five of the puppies for this little gem."

Mikelle beamed with an artist's gratified pride. "I'm so glad you like it, but I don't think Jamie needs five terrier pups, even though they *are* small."

"Can I see it?" asked Greg, trying to keep the yearning out of his voice.

"Sure," said Annabelle, handing him the painting. "Besides, I haven't said hello yet to the real thing." She stooped to pick up Jamie. "Lordy," she exclaimed with a groan, "I think he's grown two inches and gained about five pounds since the last time I picked him up."

While Mikelle and Annabelle cooed over Jamie, who was still groggy from the motion of the car, Greg drank in the beauty of Mikelle's painting. The colors were exquisite, the brush strokes loose and light, the mood they evoked one of freshness and innocence. The sun glinted off Jamie's hair, his toes curled in the wet sand, and the concentrated, content look on his face was definitely worth a thousand words.

If he'd known he could trade a puppy for such a lasting, beautiful reminder of his son, Greg would have happily bought out the local pet store.

"Are you ready to pick out your puppy, Jamie?" asked Annabelle, recalling Greg to the matters at hand. He looked up and saw Mikelle watching him intently.

"This is great work," he told her sincerely, alarmed by the unexpected touch of gruffness in his voice.

"You like it because Jamie's in it, don't you?"

He forced himself to sound objective. "It would be a great beach scene by itself, but Jamie brings it to life."

"That's what kids do, Greg," said Mikelle. "They bring everything to life." While Annabelle carried

Jamie toward the house, Mikelle leaned close to say, "The more I see you interact with Jamie, the more convinced I am that you should go ahead with your adoption plans. It's obvious you want a child in your life."

As they fell in step behind Annabelle, Greg said, "You've got that right." But if she knew which child he wanted, she'd have him measured for cement shoes and thrown into the harbor.

The day turned out to be one Kodak moment after another... and Greg with no camera. He had considered bringing one along on his trip to Nantucket, but was worried that Mikelle would question why he wanted pictures of Jamie. Now, especially after seeing that painting, he was dying for a picture of his son to take home to Manhattan.

Not that he could ever forget a giggling Jamie in the middle of a rough-and-tumble pack of spotted puppies, being playfully licked and mauled. Not that there was any danger of misplacing in his memory file the sight of his son, joyful and possessive, hugging the runt of the litter they'd chosen to take home.

Greg would replay in his mind the picnic on the beach till his dying day. He'd remember every color, from the bright red of Jamie's sweat suit, to the highlights of Mikelle's hair shining in the sun. He'd remember the gentle sound of the surf, the cawing of the gulls, and Jamie's laughter.

He'd remember the smell of sea breezes, rose-scented perfume, and puppy's breath. He'd remember the feel of the wet, cold sand between his toes as he walked along the beach. But most of all, he'd remember Jamie's little arms around his neck as he piggybacked him up and down the shore.

He'd remember it all because he was storing up for the empty days ahead without his son. He'd remember this day with all the poignancy of "the last time."

He acknowledged to himself that he loved his son. And that he loved him enough to let him go.

As the afternoon waned and the breeze got nippy, they loaded up the Cherokee and headed back toward town. Jamie went immediately to sleep in the infant carrier and Mikelle leaned against the headrest, her eyes closed, the puppy snuggled in her lap.

They'd talked comfortably and companionably all day, but they had focused their attention on Jamie, both of them delighted by his obvious enjoyment of everything. Besides, it was safer that way. Jamie really did prove to be an effective chaperon.

Greg thought he'd felt Mikelle's thoughtful gaze on him more than once, and he wondered if she was reconsidering the farfetched possibility that he could be Jamie's father. If she was having suspicions, she hid them well. But Annabelle's comments had made it absolutely expedient that he leave tomorrow. Then Mikelle and Jamie could go on with their lives and, probably sooner than he cared to admit, they'd forget all about him.

Greg reached toward the radio to tune in some music to divert him from depressing thoughts. His eyes were away from the road for no more than a second, but when he looked up again he was staring into the grill of a semi truck. He was still on his side of the road, but so was the truck.

There was no time to panic, only to react. Instinctively he braked and veered sharply to the right, avoiding a head-on collision, but skidding completely off the highway and into an open field.

Greg's head hit the roof of the Jeep and he heard Mikelle exclaim and Jamie cry out as the car bumped and careered over the rough ground. He prayed they'd come to a safe stop before hitting something big enough to tip the car and start rolling. His prayer was answered and the Cherokee shuddered to a final halt.

Two stunned seconds later, reaction set in. Jamie set up a wail that could raise the dead. Adrenaline jetted through Greg's bloodstream as he quickly made sure Mikelle was all right. She was shaken but unhurt, and she had miraculously held on to the puppy during the entire episode.

Then he ripped off his seat belt and jumped out of the car, rushing around to the back and flinging open the door. Mikelle was right behind him, whispering under her breath over and over again, "Oh, my God, Jamie. Oh, my God, Jamie."

Jamie was okay. He was still strapped firmly in his infant carrier and, except for being jerked around a bit, he seemed to have sustained no injuries. But he was scared and startled by the abrupt way he'd been roused from his nap. Mikelle held him and rocked him and tried to soothe him. Greg held the puppy and watched, helpless and frustrated. At first he was relieved that they'd got through the ordeal without serious injuries, but now he was mad as hell.

As people from the highway started to jog their way down to the car, Greg wondered which one was the truck driver. Up the road a bit, he could see the truck parked, every wheel neatly aligned. This indicated to Greg that the driver was okay, and—by hell—he wanted an explanation for what had just happened! Nothing short of a heart attack would be reason enough for that truck driver to have swerved so far into the wrong lane!

A middle-aged man in jeans and a denim shirt got there first, winded and sweating. "Hell, man, I'm sorry! Is everyone okay?"

"No, everyone's not okay," said Greg tersely. "Can't you hear the kid crying?"

Just then the puppy started whining and he wet all over the front of Greg's shirt. This just added to Greg's anger toward the trucker. It was *his* fault, not the pup's, that Greg was covered in puppy pee.

"He's not hurt, is he?" said the truck driver, referring to Jamie. "I radioed for an ambulance before I left the cab. They'll be here any minute."

"How did it happen?" asked Greg, stepping up to the man till they were practically nose to nose. He sniffed the air, checking for alcohol on the man's breath. There didn't seem to be any indication that he'd been drinking, but Greg would make sure the man was given a Breathalyzer test when the police showed up.

The man could tell what Greg was thinking and his flushed face got redder. His tone got a little belligerent as he answered, "I said I was sorry. It was an accident, man."

"But I want to know how it happened. You're driving a ten-ton truck. You've got no business making mistakes."

"My arm got a cramp—"

Greg handed the puppy to a lady standing nearby and grabbed the truck driver's shirtfront. He could barely contain the rage he felt. "Do you realize you could have killed my—"

He'd nearly said "family." But that's exactly what they'd become. His *family!*

"Hey, lay off! It wasn't my fault! I dropped my cigarette! It was burning a hole in my pants, man. It hurt like hell!"

"I don't think you understand. You could have killed them," he repeated with deadly calm.

A few more people had gathered, but Greg didn't care. All he knew was that because of this man's carelessness, his son might never have seen his first birthday. And Mikelle might never have had another chance to get tipsy and silly and sexy, like she had last night.

A fierce protectiveness surged through him.

"You think a few cigarette ashes hurt, do you?" he asked. "Well, maybe you don't know what real pain is."

Then he pulled back his fist and punched the guy square on the nose.

Chapter Seven

Pandemonium broke out. Greg heard Mikelle calling his name, Jamie crying, people shouting as hands grabbed at him, trying to pull him away from the truck driver. In the distance there was a police siren and the singsong of an ambulance.

But Greg was beyond control. One punch on the nose didn't seem nearly enough punishment for the man who'd nearly snuffed out two lives as near and dear to him as his own. No... *more* dear. Because without them, what would he have to live for?

He was finally subdued by two policemen who dragged him unceremoniously away, his heels digging trenches in the soft ground. Later, calmer and feeling slightly dazed, he leaned against the police car and watched as paramedics examined Jamie and Mikelle at the rear of the vehicle. The truck driver, the front of his shirt spotted with blood from the broken nose Greg had given him, was being treated, too.

"You're lucky. He's not pressing charges," said the older of the two policemen, a man who looked to be in his early forties.

"*He's* lucky," said Greg. "I could sue him for negligent driving. He doesn't dare rile me any more than he already has."

"The country's litigation crazy," said the officer, scratching away on his notepad. "Can't say I'd blame you if you did sue the pants off the guy, though. I'm a family man, myself. If some jerk came that close to turning my wife and kid into crash dummies, I'd want to flatten the guy, too."

Greg rubbed the bridge of his nose with thumb and forefinger. "They're not—"

"Your wife's a doll, if you don't mind my saying so," he continued without looking up. "A rock, too. Most women would have passed out cold when they saw that truck coming at them head-on. And that kid... Anyone ever tell you he's the spittin' image of his old man?"

"You don't understand, officer. They're not my—"

"Family life's great, ain't it? I've been married nearly twenty years, myself. Got a wonderful wife and four kids. You think they're a worry at this age, just wait till that kid of yours is driving. Hell, when you see all the crap that I do, it makes you want to keep them under lock and key till they're thirty-five."

Greg raked a tremulous hand through his hair. "Do you want my driver's license, officer?"

"Yeah, yeah. Just a minute." It appeared that the officer wasn't through philosophizing. "Nearly broke up with my wife a few years back. But we worked it out, and I'm glad we did... for our sakes and the kids'. It's not easy raising kids alone these days, and I didn't like the idea of being away from them, you know? I guess I'm just an overprotective dad." He looked up from his scribbling and grinned. "Kind of like you, mister."

Greg gave a halfhearted grin in return. "Yeah," he agreed with a sigh. "Kind of like me."

BY THE TIME they were back on the road, it was dark. The paramedics had seen no reason to take any of them in for treatment or observation, so they were allowed to return home on their own. The police car did, however, follow them till they reached the outskirts of town. The Cherokee, which had been built for rugged terrain, was no worse for wear after bouncing across the field, but Mikelle could tell that Greg's nerves were as taut as a banjo string.

It had been difficult for her to put Jamie back in his seat for the remainder of the trip. He was still scared and she wanted to hold and cuddle him, but she knew that wasn't safe. Thankfully, as soon as the Jeep started moving, his weary little eyes closed and he fell fast asleep.

"Thank God," said Mikelle, turning back in her seat and facing forward. "I was afraid he'd start crying again. Even though he doesn't really understand what happened, along with the shock of waking up so suddenly, I'm sure he sensed the danger. All the noise and confusion and strange people frightened him, too."

"It was all so unnecessary," said Greg in a grim voice. His profile in the passing car lights was hard and unyielding. "That idiot driver shouldn't be allowed to get behind the wheel of something as lethal as several tons of steel and a tank full of combustible fuel. I was so angry, I could have killed him."

"I know," said Mikelle softly. "I'm glad you didn't."

"All he got was a citation. He deserves to be jailed for about ten years."

Mikelle chuckled softly, feeling a slight release of tension. "If you'd killed him, you'd be the one behind bars. Even he doesn't deserve a death sentence because he made a mistake."

"A damned dangerous mistake."

"But we're all fine." She reached across and laid her hand on his arm. "Thanks to you."

"I just did what anyone would do. We were lucky there was an open field we could use as a landing strip after we flew off that highway."

She rubbed his arm, trying to soothe away some of the tension. "I don't think I know a half-dozen people who could have acted with as much presence of mind as you did." She thought of Frank and wondered if, under the same circumstances, he'd have been so adept at avoiding tragedy. Greg made her feel safe and protected. And once Rose found out what he'd done, there'd be no end to her singing his praises.

He turned to look at her. "You're amazingly calm, all things considered."

Mikelle shook her head, her eyes filling with involuntary tears. "Don't let this facade fool you. I'm right on the edge, Greg. If anything had happened to Jamie, you'd have had to pull *me* off the truck driver."

His gaze returned to the road. "You're a strong lady. After losing your husband last Labor Day in that boating accident, this must have been especially frightening to you."

"Yes," she said thoughtfully. Her hand fell away from Greg's arm and she stroked the sleeping puppy in her lap. "Yes, I was more frightened than you'll ever know. I couldn't bear to lose Jamie...under the circumstances."

They were just blocks from home now, and they both fell silent. Mikelle was thinking about what Greg had just said about Jim's death. She was sure she'd never told him the details of that horrible day last September when Jim's boat capsized in turbulent waters. It was too painful, too personal, to talk about.

Of course he could have heard about it from some of the local people, but Nantucket folk were notoriously reticent about discussing their neighbors' personal lives. They were especially sensitive about intruding on someone else's grief. She counted most of the population of the small island as friends, and she knew they wouldn't discuss her willingly with a stranger. How did Greg know that Jim died at sea? He even knew the exact day....

Mikelle was filled with a sudden sense of dread. Maybe it was a delayed reaction to the accident, but with Jamie fast asleep and safe in the back seat, she didn't think so. It was the same feeling she'd had off and on ever since she'd first encountered Greg in the grocery store. The odd part was, one minute he made her feel safe and the next minute he seemed the very embodiment of danger.

She thought she'd figured that out. She thought she was simply afraid of her attraction to him. But, she realized now, it was really more than that. He'd explained his interest in Jamie, but there were still times when she found his reactions, his emotions, a little too strong for someone who had no vested interest in her son. He'd been ready to kill that truck driver for endangering them. Or was that protective gesture done with only Jamie in mind?

And more than once, he'd seemed to know things about her and Jamie that she couldn't remember telling him. Almost as if he had access to some other source.

Then Annabelle had complicated the issue with that silly outburst about Greg being Jamie's father. Mikelle could almost smile at such a ridiculous idea....

Or was it such a ridiculous idea? Suddenly Mikelle had absolutely no desire to smile. She felt frozen, as if her heart had quit beating about an hour ago. As if the earth had quit revolving and everything on it had come to a screeching halt.

Was it possible? Could Greg Chandler somehow be the "Father unknown" on Jamie's birth certificate?

Jamie's birth mother wanted her name kept confidential, but the lawyer had told Mikelle a few things about her just so she'd know the sort of environment Jamie came from. She remembered now, and with a growing sense of terror, that Jamie's mom was a beautiful jet-setter who kept an apartment in Manhattan. She was probably just the type of glamorous female a guy like Greg would attract.

Greg and Jamie both had changeable gray-green eyes. They were both tall and blond.

Mikelle felt sick to her stomach. The whole idea seemed too farfetched, like something out of a soap opera. But if by some crazy chance Greg *was* Jamie's dad, what was he doing on Nantucket Island? What did he want?

Any fool knew the answer to that question, thought Mikelle. *He wanted her son.*

They pulled into the driveway of the Little Gray Lady. After Greg turned off the engine and lights, he said, "You're awfully quiet suddenly."

Mikelle didn't answer at first and Greg reached over and touched her shoulder. She couldn't help it; she flinched.

"Hey, what's that about?" he said, surprise in his voice.

Mikelle forced herself to act as normal as possible. She turned and stared into eyes that looked silvery gray in the light from the back porch. Eyes like Jamie's. "Sorry. I'm still jumpy, I guess," she said, managing a smile. "What time is it, Greg?"

He glanced at his watch. "Almost six-thirty. Just in time for dinner on Steamboat Wharf. Will you go with me?"

"I can't—" she began.

"We can shower and change first, of course," he said, smiling with such seeming sincerity and charm Mikelle's heart fluttered despite her alarming suspicions. "I've got to change out of this shirt Jamie's new pet baptized with puppy pee."

"Greg, it's not that. I—"

"I know. You don't want to leave Jamie. But I'm sure he'll sleep like a rock once he's tucked into his crib. Kids are resilient, much more so than adults. You're the one that needs a little T.L.C., and I'm just the guy to give it to you, starting with a hot bowl of chowder and some fried clams."

"Greg, I know Jamie will be fine. And so will I. I've got a date tonight with Frank."

There was a pause, then he repeated in a flat voice, "A date with Frank?"

"Yes. And he's picking me up at seven, so I've got to hurry," said Mikelle in a rush of words. "I have to get Jamie down and settle this pup somewhere for the night. Do you think you could help me by carrying—"

"Sure, I'll carry Jamie upstairs."

"No!" she said, too fast. Greg gave her an odd look. She quickly covered, saying, "I want to carry Jamie in case he wakes up and feels disoriented. If you could carry the puppy, then bring in the ice chest and picnic basket, I'd be eternally grateful."

"Sure," said Greg in a clipped voice. Mikelle could tell he thought little of her expressions of gratitude. Just minutes ago she'd been thanking him for saving their lives. Now she was acting as skittish as water on a hot griddle. But considering the frightening possibilities she'd come up with in the last ten minutes, he was lucky she hadn't wrapped one of his glow-in-the-dark condoms around his neck and tied it in a tight bow.

Mikelle carried a still-sleeping Jamie upstairs while Greg did the grunt work in the kitchen. Rose walked in just as Mikelle walked out. If Greg told Rose about the accident, Mikelle sincerely hoped he'd downplay the seriousness of it so Rose wouldn't fuss and worry.

Mikelle was in no mood to placate Rose. After what happened today, she had no desire to leave Jamie, either. But she was anxious to keep her date with Frank because she was going to confide in him her suspicions about Greg. And then together they'd make a few phone calls and do a little investigating.

Hopefully she'd soon know who Greg Chandler really was and what he really wanted.

FROM HIS BEDROOM WINDOW facing the front of the house, Greg watched Mikelle step into Frank's conservative white sedan. The moon was nearly full and the sky clear, with no trace of the fog that crept up on the island so frequently.

It was much warmer tonight than last night, and it looked as if Mikelle was wearing a dress made out of some sort of semisheer material. The breeze fluttered the skirt around her legs, pale colors in the flowery print winking silver in the moonlight. She was wearing high heels, too, making her long legs look all that much longer. She only had a flimsy little shawl thrown over her shoulders, and Greg frowned, wondering if she'd stay warm in such a getup.

Worse still, he wondered why she looked so dressy. Her style was usually quite casual. Tonight it appeared as though she'd gussied up for Frank. Greg's frown deepened. Maybe Frank had more of a chance with Mikelle than he'd lately come to believe.

At one time Greg had been prepared to accept the possibility that Frank could marry Mikelle and adopt Jamie. But not anymore. Not after today.

It took a near tragedy to open his eyes, but now that they were open, Greg knew he didn't want Jamie calling anyone Dad but him. He had to be part of Jamie's life. He couldn't just walk away. He couldn't just go back to New York as he'd planned and forget he had a son. Forgetting Jamie was an impossibility. Wanting to be part of his life, watching him grow, had become absolutely necessary to Greg.

Today he'd had a frightening preview of the pain he would experience by losing Jamie, and Greg wasn't up for that kind of lifelong misery and regret. After the accident, the resulting surge of protectiveness, the overwhelming reality of his love for his son, made it quite clear to Greg what he wanted.

He wanted to be there for Jamie's first step.

He wanted to watch him blow out the birthday candles on his first birthday, his tenth and his twenty-first.

He wanted to teach him to play ball.

He wanted to teach him to drive.

He wanted to sit up till midnight waiting for him to come home from his first date.

He wanted to be . . . a father.

As Frank's car pulled away from the curb, Greg let the curtain he'd been holding to the side fall back into place. He started pacing. His mind was in turmoil. He knew what he wanted as far as Jamie was concerned, but his feelings for Mikelle were much less clear and far more complicated.

He'd felt just as much concern for Mikelle as he had for Jamie when that truck had nearly hit them head-on. He'd felt the same strong urge to protect her.

But did he love her? Even if he did, was love all it took to keep a marriage together? He sure as hell didn't know. But marriage would be one way to get Jamie without taking him away from Mikelle.

Greg stopped in midpace and dug his fingers into the deep furrows all this worrying and fretting was carving into his forehead. He couldn't believe he was thinking what he was thinking! How could he even consider marrying Mikelle just to get Jamie?

And why should he have to? No one had asked him if he'd wanted to give up his son in the first place. No one had given him the choice that was his God-given right.

There was a knock at the door. Greg was instantly alert. Had Mikelle come back?

"Who is it?" he called.

"It's Rose, Mr. Chandler. I'm sorry to disturb you, but I need your help."

Greg glanced quickly down at his boxer shorts and grabbed a green flannel robe off the end of the bed and slipped into it. As he tied the robe at the waist with one hand, he opened the door with the other. "What is it, Rose? Is Jamie all right?"

Rose didn't answer immediately. Wearing a light jacket over her dress and clutching a purse to her chest, she just stared at him.

Greg self-consciously pulled together the edges of his robe and threaded his fingers through his hair, which was still damp from a shower. "Rose?"

Rose seemed to recall her scattered thoughts. "Jamie's fine, Mr. Chandler," she said, a smile tilting her lips. "Thanks to you. Mikelle told me what happened and I can't tell you how much I appreciate you getting them out of that mess without so much as a scratch."

"If you came to thank me, Rose..." Greg began, not too eager to be thanked for saving Mikelle and Jamie when his heart and mind were full of thoughts and feelings that, if acted on, could still hurt them very much.

"No, I came for something else, as well," she returned briskly, seeming to recognize his reluctance to accept praise. "There's an emergency. A friend of mine is sick and needs to be taken to the hospital. I might be gone several hours and I need a baby-sitter for Jamie. Will you do it?''

It finally registered in Greg's befuddled brain that Rose was dressed to go out. "Of course I'll baby-sit," he answered automatically.

Her smile widened. "I knew I could count on you." She turned and headed toward Jamie and Mikelle's room, seeming to assume Greg would follow. He did. "There's no time to call around, and since Mikelle seemed to think it important to support Frank and some local artist at an exhibit at the gallery tonight, I don't think she'd appreciate it if I called her and asked her to come home."

"So that's why she was so dressed up?"

She cast him an inquiring look over her shoulder. "You saw her?"

"Through the window," he admitted, hoping he didn't look sheepish.

Rose nodded, a knowing look in her eye. "I don't think she wanted to go, but she'd promised. She was very anxious about Jamie. I guess she's afraid he'll have nightmares. Made me promise to watch him extra well tonight, as if I don't always watch him like his very own grandmother would! I know Mikelle would approve of you standing in for me."

They'd reached the door to Mikelle and Jamie's shared bedroom. She lowered her voice to a whisper. "I don't think he'll wake up, but I thought I'd better show you where the diapers are." She walked on tiptoe into the room, which was softly lit by moonlight coming in through the sheer drapes at the window and a Barney night-light near Jamie's crib. She pointed to a top drawer of a combination chest and changing table. Greg nodded from the door.

Rose came back and stepped into the hall. "There are bottles of juice in the fridge. If he's hungry you can always give him some milk from a cup with a cookie, or Cheerios, or something. I'm sure you can handle it. Just keep your door open so you can hear him. I may be a while, but I'll bet Mikelle is home in a couple of hours."

"It doesn't matter. We'll be fine. You'd better go," Greg advised her. "I don't know how sick your friend is, but—"

"It's her gallstones," said Rose, headed for the stairs. "They won't kill her, but they're painful as the dickens."

"Goodbye. Good luck," he called as Rose headed toward the kitchen and the back door. She waved and smiled.

Greg stood at the top of the stairs and waited till he heard the back door close behind Rose. Then he listened to the silence for a minute before walking back to Mikelle and Jamie's bedroom.

He stood over the crib and looked down at his son. Greg couldn't believe it; he and Jamie were alone. He was completely in charge of taking care of one eleven-month-old toddler who just happened to be his son. Two months ago he'd never have believed that he'd prefer a Barney light to candlelight, or sharing a bottle of juice with a toddler instead of a bottle of champagne with another kind of babe.

Tenderness swept over Greg like a tidal wave as he continued to stare at Jamie. The little guy was sleeping on his stomach with his rump in the air. He was wearing a white sleeper that was covered with small red and blue balloons. He'd kicked off his blanket and Greg reached down to recover him.

Jamie's head was turned to the side toward Greg, his thumb in his mouth. Greg hadn't known that Jamie sucked his thumb. He'd never seen him do it during the day. But there were a lot of things he didn't know about his son, he realized with a twinge of pain. He'd lost eleven precious months of this child's life, but he had no intention of losing any more.

Just how he was going to arrange to be a real dad...well, the details were definitely fuzzy.

Greg was reaching out to touch a curl of hair that had fallen over onto Jamie's forehead, when his hand froze. There was a sound coming from downstairs; the most pitiful wailing Greg had ever heard. It was coming from the laundry room directly under Jamie's bedroom. They'd covered the floor with newspapers and put the puppy in there for the night.

Greg cursed gently under his breath. He didn't want Jamie disturbed. After today's trauma the poor kid might not want to settle for anyone besides his mom. Judging by the way Jamie suddenly began to suck his thumb vigorously, and the way a tiny line appeared between his brows, it looked as though he was just about ready to wake up and wail as loudly and pitifully as the pup.

Greg knew he had to do something. He left the room and went downstairs, flipping on lights as he went. He walked through the kitchen and directly to the laundry room. He opened the door and found the small room in total darkness, but the light from the kitchen flooded in and revealed one small puppy sitting in the middle of a pile of chewed-up newspaper, its snout aimed at the ceiling as it continued to howl bloody murder.

"Good grief, what's your problem, fella?"

As soon as the puppy opened his eyes and realized that rescue was at hand, he scurried across the floor toward Greg. He was a comical sight, with his tail wagging so hard his entire rear end was in nonstop motion.

Greg stooped and picked up the dog, carefully sidestepping four small circles of wet on the newspapers that were still spread out on the floor. As he hugged the puppy's wiggly little body against his chest, Greg's face was immediately covered with licks of gratitude. "Whoa there, fella. I like you, but I'd just as soon leave off with the kisses."

Greg thought he heard ticking, so he flicked on the light and saw a windup alarm clock lying facedown on the floor. "The old clock trick, eh?" said Greg, addressing the puppy. "But the ticking obviously didn't lull you to sleep like it was supposed to."

Then he saw a stuffed hippopotamus of an improbable shade of green pushed up against the dryer, and picked that up, too. "And you're way too smart to mistake this monstrosity for your mother or one of your siblings, aren't you?" He put the hippo's face close to the puppy's, but the dog looked away as if he was ignoring the impostor. Greg tossed the toy onto the dryer.

"I know you're missing your mother," he said, stroking the puppy's fuzzy head. "But you'll get used to your new home and I promise you'll like it. Jamie's a sweet kid, and once he's learned not to pull your ears and sit on you, he'll be a great friend."

By now the puppy had settled down and was staring solemnly at Greg with huge chocolate brown eyes. "You just want some company, don't you? Well, since I'm baby-sitting, you'll have to come upstairs with me. And since you obviously aren't housebroken, we're going to have to think of a way to keep you from making a mess of Mikelle's carpet or my robe."

He started opening kitchen drawers till he found what he needed.

Chapter Eight

Frank hung up the phone. "That's it. I've called every Realtor on the island. Not one of them has done a lick of business with Greg Chandler."

Mikelle sat on the edge of Frank's desk, cradling a mug of tea in both hands. Beyond the door to his small office in the Impressions Art Gallery was the buzz of conversation. The exhibit of paintings by a local artist had been quite successful and patrons were still milling about in the front of the store.

Mikelle took a sip of tea, trying to think logically. Trying not to panic. "Maybe he wanted to look over the island himself before getting Realtors involved."

Frank crossed his arms and leaned against the wall opposite Mikelle. "He's been here a week, Mikkie. He's had more than enough time to make several trips around the island. I know you don't want to jump to wrong conclusions, but you have to admit it's odd that he's here to procure property for a client, yet he hasn't contacted even one Realtor. If he'd seen some land he liked, he would have at least made inquiries about prices."

"You'd think so, wouldn't you?" Mikelle admitted grimly.

"This shoots holes in his supposed reason for being on the island. And if it's not you he's after, then—"

Mikelle held up a hand and squeezed her eyes shut. "Don't even say it. I don't want to believe that Greg could be Jamie's father." She opened her eyes and looked pleadingly at Frank. "The mother said she didn't know who the father was. That's what she put on the birth certificate."

Frank shrugged. "Maybe she lied."

"But if the mom wasn't talking, how did Greg find out about the baby?"

"Maybe she had an attack of conscience and decided he had a right to know."

"Why would she keep something like that to herself in the first place? It makes me wonder if she had a specific reason for keeping the baby away from his natural father."

"Only she could tell you that, Mikkie."

"If he *is* Jamie's father, and he came here to claim rights, he would have said something by now. Wouldn't he, Frank?"

Frank shook his head. "Hell, I don't know. I haven't trusted the guy from the beginning."

"Me, neither." Mikelle got up and started pacing the floor. "I've had an odd feeling about Greg Chandler since I first laid eyes on him." She didn't add that she had almost concluded that her odd feeling was a too-powerful attraction. "Certain things he's said and done have been suspicious, but I could be totally out in left field on this."

"He and Jamie do look alike."

"Just because they're both tall and blond? So are Marla Maples and Ivana Trump, but The Donald obviously noticed a difference."

Frank raised a brow. "Glad to see you've still got a sense of humor. But it sounds to me like you're trying to convince yourself that you're wrong about this paternity thing, not me."

"I know, but I'm desperate. Greg wasn't there when Jamie was born, but if his DNA happens to match my son's, he could have more right to him than I do. To say it isn't fair is a colossal understatement."

She turned and faced Frank. She could feel the day taking its toll as tears began to gather in her eyes. "The point is, Frank, *I'm* Jamie's mother. I picked him up at the hospital when he was just a few hours old. I've loved him as if he were my own baby." She shook her head vigorously. "No, I take that back. He *is* my own baby. I can't lose him, especially to some guy who thinks marriage is a joke and goes around carelessly impregnating women." She set down her tea and rubbed her temples.

"You're all tensed up, hon," said Frank. "Come here." He held out his arms.

Mikelle stepped into his comforting embrace. She leaned her hot cheek against his cool shirtfront while Frank kneaded the tight muscles in her back. It would have been a great pleasure and a definite release of tension just to let herself cry. But she wouldn't allow it. She had to stay calm and focused.

"I wish we could get in touch with my lawyer tonight."

Frank chuckled. "Lawyers don't work weekends, Mikkie. We left a message on his machine. I think it was a good idea giving him my number instead of yours. Maybe if he checks in before Monday, he'll call tomorrow. But don't depend too much on getting the definitive word on Jamie's paternity from him. First he's got to get Jamie's biological mother to fess up and give him a name.''

Mikelle sighed. ''Thanks for your help tonight, Frank. I'm sorry I dragged you away from the exhibition for so long.'' She pulled back and gave his shoulder a sisterly pat. ''You'd better get back out there.''

''Won't you come with me?''

''Just long enough to say goodbye. Rose is with Jamie, but I'm still anxious to get back to him. I'll take a cab.''

''Are you going to be okay at the inn with this guy? Are there other guests?''

Mikelle made a slight grimace. ''Since the Montana couple left on Wednesday, Greg's been the only guest. But he's not dangerous, Frank.''

''How do you know?''

''I just know.'' Her tone brooked no argument.

''Well, then, try not to worry.''

''I'll try.'' Mikelle smiled and began to pull away, but Frank didn't let go. In fact, it looked as if he intended to kiss her. Mikelle was in no mood for smooching, and she was surprised Frank wasn't sensitive enough to understand that. Besides, after Greg's kisses last night, kissing Frank would definitely pale in comparison. She didn't need to be reminded how wonderful Greg's lips felt against hers.

''Frank—''

He let her go reluctantly, a chagrined smile on his face. "I know. You've got to go." He turned to the desk and picked up the phone. "I'll call a cab."

GREG PUT THE PUPPY up on Jamie's changing table and pinned a white dinner napkin on him like a diaper. Corralling the wagging tail proved a bit of a problem, but it was short enough to stuff inside the diaper without causing the dog discomfort. Jamie sat in the crib, sucking on a bottle of juice, watching.

"That oughta do ya, mister," said Greg in his best John Wayne imitation. He glanced over and winked at Jamie. "You're next, big guy."

When Greg had come back upstairs and discovered Jamie wide-awake, but thankfully not crying, he'd hurried downstairs and got a bottle of juice out of the fridge. Since Jamie's bottom was already secured against leaks, Greg diapered the puppy first. Jamie didn't appear to mind. In fact he seemed fascinated by the proceedings. At least he wasn't having nightmares about the accident.

Greg put the puppy on the floor and shut the bedroom door so he wouldn't wander. He needn't have worried; the pup trailed Greg from changing table to crib, right under his feet.

"Watch out, Gus," he said to the pup as he lifted Jamie. "Don't trip me up. I've got precious cargo here."

He laid Jamie on the table. Jamie continued to suck his bottle and look up at Greg with wide, curious eyes. "I've never done this before on a baby," Greg confessed. "The only practice I've had with diapers is that slipshod job I just did on Gus."

Jamie blinked.

Greg undid the snaps on Jamie's sleeper. "You know, Jamie my boy, Gus is a good name for a pup. You think we ought to call him that?"

Jamie burped.

"I'll take that as a yes." Greg proceeded with the diaper change. He decided he was pretty good at it. "It's all a matter of physics, Jamie," explained Greg. "I guess if you can figure out how to build skyscrapers, it's not impossible to master the dynamics of diaper changing. In fact, if given half a chance, I think I'd be one heck of a dad."

Greg frowned. But Connie hadn't given him that chance. She'd decided on her own to give their son to strangers to raise.

He glanced at the clock on the wall, the face shaped like a football. "I wonder what your mom's doing right now, Jamie. I gotta tell ya, I was real surprised that she decided to go on a date with that yawner, Frank, instead of staying here with you. Well, son—" Greg smiled. He liked the sound of that. He'd never dared call Jamie "son" before, but it felt so good, he decided to try it again.

"As I was saying, *son,* you've got to admit Uncle Frank's a bit of a snooze act. And after what happened today, I didn't think your mom would want to leave you tonight even for a few minutes."

Greg resnapped the sleeper and picked Jamie up, carrying him to the rocking chair near the long, narrow window that looked out over the driveway. He sat down, settling Jamie comfortably in the crook of his arm, with Jamie's bottom on his thigh. Gus stretched up on his back legs and put his front paws on Greg's shin, so he picked up the puppy, too. "She probably won't be back for hours. And neither will Rose. It's you and me, son. Just you and me and Gus.''

Then it hit Greg. *Mikelle and Rose would be gone for hours. He and Jamie were all alone. If he wanted to pack up his and Jamie's things, they could probably catch a late plane off the island and be in Manhattan by midnight.*

"How could they arrest me for kidnapping, Jamie? You're *my* kid. Since I was never told about you, since I never even knew you existed till two months ago, no judge on earth could say I willingly gave you up for adoption. The criminal here is Connie. She's the one that ought to be jailed.''

Jamie had been watching and listening and sucking away on his juice. Now his eyes began to droop sleepily. Greg softened his voice to a whisper. "You probably think I'm a mean old coot, wanting both Connie *and* the truck driver behind bars. But I'm just crazy about you, son. I want to be part of your life, but I don't see how that's possible without doing something drastic. When your mom finds out I've been lying through my teeth all this time, she won't trust me as far as you can throw Hoover Dam. She thinks I'm a worthless playboy and she'd fight like hell in court to keep me away from you. What choice do I have, Jamie? What choice do I have?''

He eased Jamie into a more reclined position and started to rock. As Jamie and Gus drifted to sleep, Greg's mind raced. He listed everything he'd have to pack to keep Jamie comfortable till he could do some shopping in New York. He wondered if his secretary, Ms. Barnes, who was a grandmother, could advise him on finding an agency that hired out nannies with impeccable résumés.

He'd want a nanny who was patient—like Mikelle was when Jamie broke the pickles at the grocery store.

He'd want someone with a low, melodic voice for storytelling and lullabies—like Mikelle's.

He'd want someone who could hear Jamie rooms away—like Mikelle could.

He'd want someone who smelled like roses, and had eyes like gray mist....

He shook his head, dislodging those last inappropriate thoughts. He had a lot to do, but first he'd let Jamie sleep for a while. He closed his own eyes, but continued to plan their escape.

WHEN THE CAB dropped Mikelle off at the curb, she was surprised to see no lights on in the house. When Rose baby-sat, she usually sat up in the kitchen, watching TV or doing needlework. And when Mikelle jiggled the back doorknob, there was no response. She got out her key and let herself in, a growing sense of dread making her shake inside and out.

"Rose?" she called softly. Then louder, "Rose, where are you?" No one answered.

Mikelle headed for the stairs. She couldn't remember seeing Greg's car in the driveway. Had he moved it after he'd unpacked their picnic things? He usually parked out front, but she'd been so preoccupied she hadn't noticed where he had parked the Jeep when she left with Frank, nor had she noticed it just now when she got out of the cab.

But she wasn't going to take the time to check. She had to see Jamie. She had to make sure he was all right. And where was Rose? Had she taken Jamie to her apartment above the garage? But there had been no lights on there, either.

By the time Mikelle reached the top of the stairs, her heart was hammering. "Rose?" she called again. She turned and headed straight for the room she shared with Jamie. Even before she flicked on the light, she could see the crib was empty.

Empty.

Mikelle's stomach bottomed out. Her legs got weak as water and she leaned against the doorframe for support.

She gazed in disbelief around the room. Several drawers were open. Some of Jamie's clothes were on the floor by the dresser. She could no longer deny what she dreaded above every tragic possibility.

He'd taken Jamie! Greg Chandler had taken her son. Somehow he'd tricked Rose and gotten away without her knowledge.

A surge of adrenaline rushed through Mikelle's veins. She turned and headed toward Greg's room. She'd check there before she went to Rose's apartment. Maybe he'd left clues that would give her an idea when he'd left. Maybe there was a chance of catching him at the airport.

The door was ajar. It was dark inside, but as she pushed through, the hall light flooded the room. What she saw stopped her in her tracks.

Greg and Jamie and the new pup were asleep on the bed. All three of them. Mikelle thought she might pass out from relief. Again she supported herself against the first available doorframe, swallowing hard against a dry throat. She felt giddy as love for her son surged through her. Jamie wasn't halfway to New York, he was here with her, safe and sound.

She couldn't wait to hear Greg's explanation. But until she got one, she'd enjoy the picture. And what a picture it was. There was enough warmth and human interest in this one little scene to inspire a modern-day Norman Rockwell.

Greg slept on his side, both long, bare legs stretched out over the entire bottom half of the antique bed. He had a robe on over boxer shorts, but the robe was open and the hem pushed up to midthigh. She could glimpse his bare chest, seeing just enough to make her want to see more. The pup, who woke up and was staring at her, was cuddled against Greg's back.

Greg and Jamie shared a pillow. Jamie was sucking his thumb. He was curled up in a comfortable ball, facing Greg.

Mikelle didn't know what to think. A minute ago she had been convinced that Greg had kidnapped her son. Now it looked as though he'd simply been babysitting. Without Rose around to stop him, he could have walked out the door with Jamie. But he hadn't. Did that mean he wasn't Jamie's father? Or did it just mean he had no intention of kidnapping Jamie, but would go about stealing him through proper legal channels?

The bottom line was this: Mikelle had no more idea than before about who Greg Chandler was and what his motives were concerning her and her son. And complicating the issue most of all was what the scene before her was making her feel.

Tenderness. Yearning. Love.

And these feelings weren't just for Jamie, they were for Greg, too. But how could she go from one minute wanting to kill Greg, to wanting to crawl into bed with him and cuddle right along with Jamie and the pup? She was on an emotional seesaw, with love and desire on the up side, anger and distrust on the down. At the moment she was up, somewhere far above the clouds.

Suddenly Greg stirred, propped on his elbow and looked at her. His hair was tousled and his eyes were droopy from sleep. He looked sexy as all get-out.

She quickly decided to keep her suspicions to herself. They could be total hogwash. She *wanted* them to be total hogwash. And maybe, by staying cool, listening and watching like a hawk, she'd find out the truth about Greg Chandler.

"You're a heavy sleeper," she said with a smile that had an irritating tendency to quiver at the corners. "I was beginning to think it would take a marching band playing John Philip Sousa to wake you up."

"I haven't been asleep long. I must have been under pretty deep." Deep, like his voice. And a little husky from sleeping, too. It was very appealing.

"Where's Rose?" She made a determined effort not to sound the least bit worried.

"She had to take a friend to the hospital. Something about gallstones."

"Ah, Mrs. Kirby," said Mikelle, understanding Rose's desertion. "She's a widow and has no family on the island. Rose is her best friend."

"She was in a hurry. She was sure you wouldn't mind if I watched Jamie."

"Of course I don't mind," Mikelle lied breezily. "It looks like you had your hands full." Suddenly she noticed the diaper on the dog. "What have you put on the pup?"

Greg sat up carefully, so he wouldn't disturb Jamie. He pulled his robe together in the front, but not before Mikelle got a heart-stopping view of his wonderfully sculpted chest. She imagined threading her fingers through the light furring of dark blond hair that grew in a triangle, then narrowed to a thin line that disappeared under the waistband of his boxer shorts. She wet her lips and forced herself to look away.

"I have a feeling you're not going to appreciate my resourcefulness, but since Jamie's diapers were too big, I—"

Mikelle looked harder at the dog. "You pinned one of my good dinner napkins on that pup's rump," she accused. She could see his tail trying to wag beneath the napkin.

"Well, actually, that's the third. He's not exactly housebroken yet."

"That's why I put him in the laundry room with all the newspapers," Mikelle reminded him, folding her arms across her chest and trying not to smile.

"He was making a racket down there and I was afraid he'd wake up Jamie. Besides, I think he was lonely. You can't just take a pup away from its mom, give it an alarm clock and a green hippopotamus for company, and expect it to be happy. I decided to keep him with us. Diapering him seemed the only way to do that without causing permanent damage to your carpets."

You can't just take a pup away from its mom and expect it to be happy. Mikelle was busy assimilating that simple statement and using it to reassure and convince herself that even if Greg was Jamie's father, he'd never take him away from her. A man who had compassion for a lonely puppy couldn't possible be hateful enough to inflict the same kind of pain on a human being. But she was jumping to conclusions, she reminded herself. There was still no proof—no real proof at all—that Greg was in any way related to her son.

"Mikelle? Are you upset?"

"Upset?"

"You know, about the napkins. I'm sure you'll have to replace them, so add the price for a new set to my bill when I leave tomorrow."

"You're leaving tomorrow?" Mikelle's knee-jerk reaction of overwhelming disappointment surprised her. She ought to be jumping up and down for joy. His leaving so soon supported the probability that he wasn't Jamie's father. But if he wasn't Jamie's father, there was no harm if he stayed longer, was there? "Did you find a building site for your client?"

Greg swung his long legs over the side of the bed and stood up. He was so tall, so damned sexy.... "I saw several possible sites that were listed for sale, but I need to talk to my client before going any further."

"Were the prices right?" she asked. She held her breath, waiting for his answer. If he lied to her about meeting with Realtors, she'd have every reason to distrust him.

He ran both hands through his hair, the long fingers making little impact on the appealing disorder of blond waves. "My client is so rich, he doesn't care about prices."

"Didn't you even meet with Realtors?"

He gave her a keen look, then smiled crookedly. "Not once. I don't like being hustled and given the hard-sell routine. I'll get in touch with a Realtor when I need one."

Mikelle was relieved and happy that she hadn't caught him in a lie. She was truly beginning to believe she'd exaggerated all her suspicions about Greg. Now that he was leaving, they seemed paranoid and ludicrous.

Now that he was leaving, she wanted nothing more than to put her arms around him and make him stay....

"I'll carry Jamie to his bed," he offered, and Mikelle merely nodded as she watched him pick up Jamie. Suddenly there was a desperate ache in her heart and she didn't trust herself to speak. He was so gentle. As he lifted him, he brushed his lips over Jamie's hair. She followed Greg to the crib and watched as he carefully laid Jamie down and covered him up.

"Sorry about the mess in here," Greg whispered over his shoulder. "Jamie dribbled a bunch of juice down the front of his sleeper and I was looking for another one. With Jamie in one arm and the pup trying to trip me up, I wasn't very tidy about the whole thing."

"That's okay," she mumbled around a throat tight with emotion.

He straightened up, stared down at Jamie for a long moment, then walked out of the room. Mikelle was wondering if he was even going to say good-night before disappearing into his room and shutting the door. But halfway across the hall he turned, smiled wryly, hooked a thumb over his shoulder and said, "What about Gus?"

"Who's Gus?" asked Mikelle, walking toward him, thrilled to have a few more minutes with him before they each went to their separate bedrooms... alone. "You mean the pup?"

"That's what we named him."

Mikelle raised a brow. "You and Jamie?"

"When I suggested the name, he made a sound—"

"A sound?"

"Well, okay, he burped. I took that as a yes, and I've been calling the pup Gus ever since."

Mikelle chuckled. "I guess it's as good a name as any."

"So, what are we going to do about him tonight?"

Mikelle liked the way he said "we." She pretended for a minute that they were a family and trying to decide what to do with the new canine member of it.

"I suppose I could find a large box—one that he couldn't crawl out of—line it with papers and put him in my room for the night. Maybe then he wouldn't feel so alone."

"Sounds like a plan. But throw a blanket or something in the box, too. Something he can snuggle up to." A ghost of a smile flitted briefly over Greg's lips. "Everyone sleeps better snuggled up to something."

Mikelle could feel color flooding her cheeks. She ducked her head and turned to go. "I'll see what I can find in the garage."

He moved to stand between her and the stairs. Her downcast gaze climbed the mountain of man that stood as a barricade to her escape. She knew her limit and she'd reached it about ten minutes ago. Through the V of his open robe she could see a tantalizing glimpse of heaven. Her fingers itched to explore what promised to be a tactile paradise.

"Do you need some help?"

Psychiatric, yes. To find a box, no.

She allowed her gaze to continue up along the column of his throat, fascinated by the slight bulge of his adam's apple and the beard stubble under his chin. She examined the angle of his jaw, admiring the masculine definition of it. She looked at his mouth and remembered again how delicious those lips had tasted.

"You aren't dressed to go outside," she said, swallowing hard.

"Then I'll wait here with Gus."

Mikelle thought that was an excellent idea. And while she was gone, could he please transform into something repulsive? Dr. Jekyll did it, why couldn't he?

Mikelle nodded and left without meeting his gaze. That would truly have been her undoing. He probably had hypnotic powers along with all his other talents. But hypnotism wasn't necessary; Mikelle was already mesmerized.

She welcomed the cool air that greeted her as she opened the back door and headed for the garage. A cold shower would have even been better.

She found a box, then found Rose in the kitchen when she returned. Rose reported that her friend, Mrs. Kirby, had been hospitalized and was scheduled for surgery in the morning.

The cool air, the musty garage and Rose's description of Mrs. Kirby's upcoming surgery, all helped sober Mikelle. If she wanted to stay sober and thinking straight, it wouldn't be wise to see Greg again tonight. So she sent Rose up for the puppy, instructing her to tell Greg that she was going to take Gus outside for a potty stop. She hoped in the interim that Greg would do her self-control a favor and go to bed.

An hour later Rose had gone to her apartment, and Jamie and Gus were fast asleep. Mikelle had taken a shower and put on a white cotton nightgown. She slathered lotion over her arms and legs and brushed her hair. Not in the least sleepy, she stood at the window and looked longingly outside.

It was stuffy in the room, so she opened the window a crack. But the in-flowing air felt and smelled so refreshing, Mikelle impulsively decided to go up on the widow's walk and enjoy for a few brief minutes what could be the last relatively balmy night of the season. She wouldn't be gone long enough for Jamie to wake up, and perhaps the fresh air would make her drowsy. Right now she couldn't imagine being able to spend the night doing anything other than think, and yearn, and regret.

Greg was leaving tomorrow. She should be relieved, but she wasn't. She shouldn't be already missing him, but she was.

Sighing deeply, she put on her white chenille robe and a pair of slippers and went downstairs, out the back door and up the narrow stairs to the widow's walk. After Jim's death, the widow's walk had been like a sanctuary, a place to sort out her thoughts, a place to be alone.

But tonight she wasn't alone.

"Hi, Mikelle," came Greg's voice out of the darkness.

Chapter Nine

Still dressed in a green flannel robe over boxer shorts, Greg sat on a low bench at the back of the narrow widow's walk. He was surprised to see Mikelle, but no more surprised than she was to see him.

Her eyes grew enormous, and her hands clutched the front of her robe, as if to assure herself that she was decently covered. But as far as Greg was concerned, Mikelle could be wearing an ankle-length muumuu and she'd still be sexier than any bikini-clad beach bunny he'd ever seen.

"I didn't know you were up here," she told him, setting the record straight.

"It's okay, isn't it? Or is the widow's walk off-limits to guests?" He wondered what she had on under that pristine robe. His guess was that it was something white and lacy and as sexy-wholesome as Doris Day.

She folded her arms in a self-conscious gesture over her chest, as if she'd read his thoughts. "Of course the widow's walk isn't off-limits. It's just that it's past midnight. After your stint of baby-sitting—both human and canine—I thought you'd be out for the count."

"I wasn't sleepy."

"Neither was I."

There was a pause and Greg waited for her to make some kind of lame excuse and hurry down the stairs and into the house. If she was smart, that's exactly what she'd do.

"You probably came up here to be alone," he said, giving her an out. "I'll leave." He leaned forward to stand up.

"No, don't go," she said, too quickly and too earnestly for him to believe she was simply being polite.

He leaned back again and stared at her. He felt excitement mixed with alarm. To avoid temptation, one of them needed to hightail it out of there, but it appeared that neither of them intended to go anywhere. Temptation was about to have a heyday.

"All right," he heard himself saying. "I'll stay if you're sure you don't mind."

She uncrossed her arms, backed away and braced herself against the railing that faced the front of the house. "I don't mind. Besides, I'll bet this is the first time you've visited the widow's walk. It's beautiful up here on a night like this, and since you're leaving tomorrow..." Her brows dipped in a troubled frown. "Are you really leaving tomorrow?"

He couldn't help the thrill that raced through him. She was actually sorry he was going. But tonight's temporary fit of insanity during his time alone with Jamie had convinced him that a hasty exit was absolutely necessary.

That wasn't to say he wouldn't be coming back. He'd be back, all right, but he'd be armed with blood-test results and legal papers that would guarantee him visiting privileges with his son.

Tonight he'd ransacked Jamie's chest of drawers for clothes suitable for strolling Central Park, and had even packed a diaper bag. But in the midst of mania, a solid, sober truth materialized. He'd finally, irrevocably realized that he couldn't take Jamie away from Mikelle. He just couldn't do it.

But he couldn't give up his right to play some small part in Jamie's life, either. He wasn't that generous and noble. Damn it, he was no saint.

"Greg?"

Greg stirred himself. "Yeah, I'm really leaving tomorrow."

"Your business is done?"

"I've done everything I can do at this point." If he stayed any longer, he'd end up doing something crazy, like taking Jamie for a walk...straight to the airport. Or like taking Mikelle for a walk...straight to bed. Gazing at her now, an absolute knockout even in a plain robe and no makeup, he realized the latter was the more dangerous possibility.

He felt her gaze on him. The sexual tension was palpable. Any doubts Greg had about their attraction being mutual completely disappeared. And he was afraid she had as little willpower as he did at the moment.

To toy with this attraction between them was dangerous. To give in to it was certifiable madness. In a few days she'd hate him for disrupting their lives, for forcing her to share Jamie for a few hours each week and alternate holidays. She'd be furious with him for lying to her all this time.

If he were a truly honorable man, he'd tell her now. He'd tell her he was Jamie's father. But then everything would change. She'd look at him differently.

There would be no attraction. Hell, she wouldn't even like him and might even try to drop-kick him over the railing. Was he total scum to want this last night at the Gray Lady to end on a more positive note than that?

But he was fooling himself. He wanted more. He wanted Mikelle, but Mikelle wanted a white picket fence and he couldn't give her one.

He should leave. He should leave that very instant. But he didn't. He couldn't.

"It's a clear night. Would you like to do a little stargazing?" She made an awkward, nervous motion toward the telescope tucked in the far, outside corner of the widow's walk and shrouded in some sort of canvas covering.

She was always surprising him with spontaneously issued invitations. This one sounded innocent enough, and was probably offered out of desperation for anything to do besides gawk at each other. If he had something to think about other than what Mikelle might be wearing under her robe, maybe he could trust himself to enjoy her company a little longer. Then he'd leave. But he had to have just a few more minutes with her before everything changed between them.

"Sure," he said as casually as he could. He stood up and joined Mikelle at the railing. He felt his stomach tighten, every nerve seeming to quiver with the impact of her nearness. He stared out over the sleeping neighborhood below instead of at her. "What stars are we going to gaze at? Clint Eastwood? Tom Cruise? Personally I vote for Michelle Pfeiffer."

She laughed. "That was the corniest joke I've heard since the third grade."

"Yeah, but it broke the tension, didn't it?" he suggested daringly.

She scooted away a few inches. "With the accident and all, it's no wonder we're both tense."

That's not the kind of tension I'm talking about, Mikelle, and you know it, he thought to himself.

"Have you ever really looked at the sky, Greg?" Her chin tilted upward and her hair fell in a heavy, dark mass against her shoulders.

"Sure." But for the moment, he couldn't tear his gaze away from her. She, on the other hand, kept her face averted. Was she trying to pretend that there was no heat between them?

"I mean *really* looked at it? It's incredible." She moved to the telescope, untied the covering and laid it over the railing. He thought he noticed her hands trembling a little.

"You're well equipped for galaxy surfing," he commented, trying to sound interested, but really just aching to hold her, to make her tremble all over, from head to toe. "That telescope is a pretty nice piece of machinery. What size lens is it?"

"Six inches. It was Jim's hobby, you know. Have you ever tried one out?" She positioned the telescope in a northerly direction, then finally turned and looked at him. The expression in her eyes was uncertain, shy. The soft moonlight made her skin look like satin. He was dying to touch her. Pretending there was no heat between them was impossible. Even Mikelle's mention of Jim did nothing to lesson Greg's desire for her.

He swallowed hard and tried to keep up his end of the forced conversation. "When I was in the sixth grade, my friend Paul Pitcher had one. We used to scope out all kinds of heavenly bodies."

"Which kind?" asked Mikelle with a tiny smile. "The celestial or the neighborhood variety?"

He grinned. "I was no Peeping Tom, but there was a time or two when Peggy Dodd, all decked out in her baby-doll pajamas, 'eclipsed' our view of Mars. But she knew we were watching," he added.

"Girls were making themselves available to you clear back in the sixth grade?"

Greg shrugged and moved to stand next to her at the telescope. Her light rose scent enveloped him. "Aren't the brightest stars actually planets?"

"You and Paul must have learned a little bit about astronomy, despite the distractions," she said ruefully.

"A *very* little bit," he admitted. "Actually, I think I've impressed you with everything I know. From now on it's amateur hour."

Mikelle believed him when he said he was an amateur at astronomy, but she knew he was an old hand at anything that had to do with women. His devastating effect on the opposite sex probably even predated Peggy Dodd. And she was the latest to fall victim to his lethal charm, because despite his Don Juan reputation, despite the suspicions she still harbored about why he was on the island, Mikelle couldn't resist the chance to be near him. Like an idiot, she'd chosen to remain in his company on the widow's walk.

He'd offered to leave, but she'd asked him to stay. Was she crazy or what?

But he was going back to New York tomorrow, and these were the last few private minutes they'd be able to share....

He stood so close, she could feel the heat from his body. A pleasant queasiness came over her, blood rushed to every secret corner of her body, and her heart slammed against her ribs like a stir-crazy prisoner against the bars of his cell.

She hid her agitation behind a schoolmarmish facade, saying, "Tonight would be a good night to see the star formation called Cassiopeia. Here, you can find it yourself. I'll just direct you." She stepped away and pivoted the telescope toward Greg. "Turn it north. Find the Big Dipper, just to your left a little."

Greg pointed the telescope toward the Big Dipper, which stood out clearly despite the bright moonlight.

"Look into the telescope and follow a line connecting the two Pointers—"

"The two what?" asked Greg. As he bent his tall frame to fit his eye against the narrow end of the telescope, Mikelle fought the urge to run her fingers through his hair. The moonlight made it gleam like spun gold.

"The two stars at the end of the bowl," she explained, swallowing past a tightness in her throat. "Follow the line connecting them across the sky to the first bright star. That will be the North Star."

"Okay. That star looks pretty bright. Now what?"

"Continue the same arc to the right and a little farther down till you come to a *W* in the sky, lying on its left side. There are five stars in the *W* which are especially bright, and all of them of about the same intensity. Do you see it?"

"Yeah. I do. That's Cassiopeia? Interesting... And that kind of splotchy band extending upward from it is the Milky Way, right?"

"Right. You're a quick study, Greg," murmured Mikelle.

He straightened up and turned around, bumping into her. The impact was fleeting but electrifying. He caught her arms and steadied her. As if he'd made a sudden and desperate decision, he bent his head, and with his warm breath spilling over her cheek he said gruffly, "I may be a quick study, Mikelle, but I'm not very smart. And neither are you."

"Wh-what do you mean?" she stuttered.

"You know exactly what I mean," he challenged, still holding her arms. "If we were smart, we wouldn't be out here alone."

"I don't know what you—"

He gave her a tiny shake. "Why don't we be completely honest for once?" he said fiercely. "I'm dying to make love to you. And I don't think you're so naive that you think you can stand there, looking sexy as all get-out, and not be asking for trouble."

"I'm not naive," she said breathlessly. "Maybe I want trouble. Maybe I want to make love, too."

He squeezed his eyes shut. "Why would anyone want trouble?"

"Trouble can be exciting."

Greg opened his eyes. Mikelle looked so desirable, so vulnerable. "You don't strike me as a thrill seeker, Mikelle. But even if you were, you're too level-headed to want *my* kind of trouble," he said with what he thought was commendable self-control. "The kind of trouble you want comes with marriage. You want the quarrels over toothpaste caps left off and toilet seats left up. You want the trouble of getting reservations for a candlelight dinner at your favorite restaurant on your silver anniversary. Hell, you want commitment, and I can't give you that!''

"Have I asked for a commitment?'' She shook her head and with a ghost of a sad smile said, ''I'd be a fool if I didn't know you're a hopeless case when it comes to commitment. I've had plenty of evidence to convince me that picket fences are like barbed wire to you—just another form of confinement.''

He sighed. ''You've got me pegged, all right, so what's a nice girl like you doing with a guy like me?''

''You may not want something permanent, Greg, but there are lots of things about you that a nice girl like me finds very attractive. I loved our time together at the beach. And the kind way you've treated Jamie and me, and even Jamie's new pup, proves you're a man of strong feeling and passion. I want to tap into that passion, Greg. Just for tonight. Just for *now*. I want you to make love to me.'' Her chin thrust out stubbornly, adorably. ''And I don't give a damn about tomorrow.''

His grip tightened as he searched her face. ''Do you realize what you're asking, Mikelle?''

''Of course I do,'' she said, her voice soft but her tone insistent. ''I didn't come up here with the intention of seducing you.'' Her lips curved in amusement. ''But now I realize that that's what I've wanted to do since the first day we met. And believe me, that's saying something.''

She grew serious again. ''I haven't made love with another man since my husband died, or even had the slightest desire to. Lovemaking is not something I take lightly.''

Her words humbled him, inflamed him. He knew he was on the verge of surrendering to the strength of their combined desires. He made one last token attempt at resistance. "But I'm leaving tomorrow."

"You said you still had business on the island—"

He hesitated, then said in the most deadly serious tone he could manage, "Things will be different when I see you again."

Mikelle shrugged, making a show at nonchalance. "All the more reason why we should take advantage of this moment when we both want the same thing." Mikelle reached up and laced her arms around Greg's neck. Her upturned face was beautiful, sensual, and damned persuasive. "Or am I wrong? Don't you want me?"

He released a shaky sigh. "You're not wrong. There's no denying how much I want you." If she wanted proof, all he'd have to do is take her in his arms. The evidence of his arousal would be hard to miss.

"Then make love to me, Greg. And let me make love to you."

Who could resist such a plea? Greg was not made of stone. Despite the screaming objections of his better judgment, he gave in to what he wanted most in the world. He drew her into his arms.

Too late he remembered the strongest argument of all against making love to Mikelle. She was different. She was special. She wasn't like any other woman he'd ever been with. Holding her was like coming home. . . .

He embraced her for a long moment without kissing her, experiencing the wonder of new feelings. It felt so right holding her, so exhilarating. Then he pulled away slightly and reached down to cup her chin. He lowered his head and reverently touched his lips to hers.

Reverence gave way immediately to a physical and emotional hunger Greg had never felt before. Not even yesterday, when he'd first kissed Mikelle, had he felt such an overpowering urge to possess someone—heart, soul and body. He crushed her against his chest and deepened the kiss, probing the sweetness of her mouth with his tongue. She was moist and warm and responsive, and she trembled in his arms.

Desire thrummed through his veins with an increasing urgency. Her soft, pliant body against his made his thoughts run wild.

He slipped a hand between them and untied her robe with one efficient tug, the captured warmth from her body enveloping him. He slipped his hands around her waist and felt the slick, cool cotton of her nightgown. He glanced down; it was white, just the way he imagined it would be.

He kissed her neck, from ear to collarbone, while his hands wended their way up her back, then around to the front. He cupped both firm breasts at once, gently taking the hard nipples between thumb and forefinger. When she moaned and arched into his palms, he exulted in her response. She wanted him as much as he wanted her.

But he was setting them both up for heartache, because in a few days Mikelle would find out who he really was. She'd be furious, and this night of intimacy would turn from beautiful memory to bitter regret. He could never give her what she deserved. She deserved a husband, a till-death-do-us-part commitment, a backyard barbecue with all the fixin's....

But then why did it feel so right holding her? Why did he feel as if he'd be crazy to ever let her go?

Mikelle knew now that she'd been crazy to think she could make love with Greg tonight and forget about tomorrow and the rest of her life. Tonight was a revelation. She'd found someone who made her feel just as fulfilled, just as womanly as Jim had. *More* than Jim had, she admitted despite the loyal side of her that resisted such an idea. No matter what happened in the foreseeable future, she'd never forget this night.

It was a daunting, frightening thought, but Mikelle realized she was falling in love with Greg Chandler. And if tonight was all she'd ever have of him, she'd take it gladly and save her regrets for another day.

She was weak from the havoc his kisses and his warm, demanding hands had made of her senses, but she wasn't too weak to give back as good as she got. From day one she'd had a secret fantasy that involved her hands on Greg's chest. She was not as adept as he was at untying robes, but she got the soft flannel parted and her hands inside in record time.

Touching his chest was even better than in her fantasy. The springy hair tickled her palms. The smooth, hard muscles of his torso glided under her fingers as she stroked him from his shoulders to his taut stomach. Following the same tantalizing path, she kissed him. She nuzzled her face against his warm chest, finding and teasing the small, hard nipples with her mouth and tongue and teeth.

Greg groaned with pleasure as his hands grasped Mikelle's shoulders. Then his fingers slid around her neck and caught in her hair. He gently tugged on the silky mass till she tilted her head and looked up at him. Her face was radiant and etched with passion. "Mikelle," he whispered, "you're driving me nuts. If you keep this up, I'm going to have my wicked way with you right here on the widow's walk."

She stretched on her toes and playfully nipped his ear. "Why not?"

Suddenly, Greg remembered Jamie. "What about Jamie? What if he wakes up and needs you?"

By the chagrined look on Mikelle's face, she'd forgotten Jamie, too. "Oh, you're right," she said, pulling away. "I was only planning to be up here a minute or two, just long enough to cool off—" She stopped short and smiled ruefully. "I did anything but cool off, didn't I?" She caught his hand and tugged him toward the stairs. "Come on. I'll check on Jamie and meet you in your room in five minutes. Deal?"

FIVE MINUTES LATER, Greg was still waiting. He had taken off his robe and slid between the cool sheets of his bed. An antique Tiffany lamp on the bedside table cast soft prisms of light on the wood floor. The window opposite the bed was pushed up about three inches, and sea breezes belled the gauzy curtains. The vase of flowers Rose brought fresh to his bedroom every afternoon gave the air a faint, sweet, outdoorsy smell.

Greg wondered if Mikelle was having second thoughts. He sure as hell was. Despite the aching arousal of his body, Greg was half hoping Mikelle would realize what a mistake she was making by sleeping with the enemy. She didn't know he was the enemy yet, but in a few days they'd be digging trenches on opposite sides of a battlefield.

Thirty seconds later, Greg's door opened. As Mikelle closed the door quietly behind her and padded barefoot across the floor, Greg's second thoughts were forgotten. By the time she stood by the bed, dressed in a creamy white silk teddy and nothing else, he'd almost forgotten his name.

"You look beautiful," he told her, then enjoyed the pleased blush that tinted her cheeks. "What happened to that demure little cotton thing you were wearing?"

"I *sleep* in cotton," she said with a coy smile. "For seducing my male guests, I always wear silk."

"It doesn't really matter what you wear, Mikelle," Greg informed her with a teasing leer, "because you won't be wearing it for long."

She laughed and he reached for her. Then, in the space of a frenzied heartbeat, he had lowered her to the bed and followed her down.

Despite his warning to the contrary, Greg took his time undressing Mikelle. He was going to make sure she enjoyed to the fullest each and every moment they had together.

Mikelle thought she was going to die from the exquisite torture of anticipation. Greg inched the straps of her teddy off her shoulders with slow deliberation, each bared increment of flesh welcomed with a lingering kiss. Once the straps were down he worked the silky material of the teddy over the swell of her breasts. His tongue made circles of pleasure against her exposed flesh while her nipples strained against the fabric, pouting and hard with expectation.

Mikelle was almost too caught up in the sensations Greg was creating in her own body to enjoy the pleasure of creating similar responses in him. When she'd walked into the room, he'd been sitting up in bed, his chest and broad shoulders bare and brown in the muted lamplight. Her hands were on those shoulders now, the lean muscle feeling so incredibly good against the tender skin of her palms. But she wanted to do more, feel more of him before he made her too drunk with pleasure to know her own mind.

She pushed him till he rolled onto his back, then she straddled his hips. She could feel his hard erection through the thin fabric of his boxer shorts and she felt a corresponding heat and wetness between her legs.

"This is a dangerous position, Mikelle," Greg told her. He lay very still beneath her, but he was like a latent volcano, brimming with a fire and force that was barely held in check. His eyes were half-closed, but heat simmered under the fringe of tawny lashes. His facial muscles were taut with controlled passion, his lips curved in a slight, almost mocking smile that seemed to say *I dare you.*

"Dangerous for who? You or me?" she taunted.

"I'm not worried," he bragged, folding his hands over his chest in a relaxed pose. "I like women who take the upper hand."

Mikelle smiled. "You *should* be worried. I haven't been with a man for a long time." He responded to her playful threat with a lazy smile.

She shimmied out of her teddy till the fabric fell in soft folds around her hips. As he watched, Greg's jaw clenched a little tighter, his smile disappeared and an intensely determined expression radiated from his eyes. Judging by the white knuckles of his hands as they remained folded over his chest, he was fighting the urge to grab her. Mikelle understood that he was holding back so she could wield her own feminine powers for their mutual enjoyment.

Mikelle leaned forward and kissed him. Her breasts brushed against his chest and his arms circled her back and held her lightly. The kiss was long, deep, savoring. Then she kissed him along the line of his jaw, down his neck and across the strong ridge of his collarbone.

Scooting down and easing herself between his legs, she placed her hands, palms down, on his chest and bent to kiss him there, circling with her tongue the hard nub of each brown nipple. Then she brushed her breasts across his chest and stomach, back and forth rhythmically. She went lower and lower, alternately nuzzling him with her open mouth and brushing his body with her breasts.

She kissed his flat, tightly muscled stomach, then curled her fingers under the elastic band of his boxer shorts. Suddenly Greg reached down and cupped her shoulders, pulling her up to face him.

They were both breathing fast and shallow. "Now it's my turn," he informed her hoarsely. He rolled her onto her side and made short work of removing her teddy, then tossed it carelessly onto the floor. He slid his hand up her calf, behind her knee and over her hip. He pulled her close and nudged her knees apart, then positioned one long leg between them. They lay side by side, his weight shifted onto her, his arousal pressed against her stomach.

Mikelle was already weak with need, but he took her to the very edge of madness as he expertly, lovingly caressed and kissed her breasts, then slipped his hand between her thighs and gently probed and stroked her damp heat.

She lifted her hips and clutched his arms. "Greg," she moaned, surprised by the edge of desperation she recognized in her voice. "Greg, please..."

Greg knew Mikelle was ready, as ready as he'd been for some time. He helped her remove his boxer shorts and then they were both naked. She lay back on the pillows and drew him urgently to her, opening to him with the kind of eagerness a man dreams of. He was as eager as Mikelle, so Greg eased himself inside her.

Pleasure washed over him like a tidal wave, but he braced himself above her, savoring the moment. Something was building inside him, something even stronger than the searing intensity of his physical need. As he gazed down at Mikelle's face, at her parted, slightly swollen lips, at her luminous eyes and flushed skin, he was overwhelmed with a feeling of tenderness and protectiveness. If he didn't know better, if he didn't mistrust his own emotions, he'd say he was feeling...love.

"Greg." She sighed. She moaned softly and again lifted her hips, leaving no doubt of her readiness, and leaving Greg no time or inclination for self-analysis. He began to move. They looked into each other's eyes, their gazes never wavering as Mikelle rose to meet each of Greg's thrusts.

Then the aching demand of their bodies took over and Greg moved faster. Moments later, Greg felt Mikelle tense. He watched her neck arch and her head press back into the pillow as she climaxed. It thrilled and humbled him to watch her shuddering release. She was beautiful, natural, so damned honest and open. Then, like the awesome force of a volcano, he experienced his own release.

Only when it was over, when he'd pulled her close against his side and she'd nestled her head against his shoulder, did Greg think about birth control. His passion for Mikelle had completely distracted him. Given his history, given the fact that he'd already fathered a son unintentionally, he was amazed at his own carelessness. But his feelings were ambivalent. He could never think of Jamie as a mistake.

One arm cradled Mikelle's shoulders, and he was lightly stroking the bare skin above her elbow, getting drowsy, feeling more complete and content than he'd ever imagined possible. With considerable surprise, it occurred to him that he wouldn't mind if Mikelle *did* get pregnant. The possibility of another baby, especially with this woman, was damned appealing.

According to Smith's report, Jim Bennet had been the infertile partner in the marriage. But Greg obviously was not infertile and he could give Mikelle a baby of her own, a precious gift that her husband had never been able to provide. The idea filled him with guilty pride and pleasure. He bent and kissed her forehead.

She shifted in his arms and looked up at him.

"You were so quiet, I thought you were asleep," he said with a tender smile.

"I was rendered speechless," she returned playfully.

"Me, too," he admitted.

She pushed up in the bed and propped herself against his chest, her breasts teasing him with their smooth roundness. Her lips were very close to his. He was immediately aroused. "You know what they say, don't you?" she asked him.

"What?"

"One kiss is worth a thousand words."

About a million words later, Greg succumbed to sated, happy exhaustion. With his arm wrapped around Mikelle's shoulders and with her head tucked under his chin, he dreamed of backyard barbecues and smiled in his sleep.

Chapter Ten

From sheer force of will, Mikelle carefully eased herself out of Greg's warm embrace and hurriedly slipped into her teddy. It was morning, time to face reality. But before leaving the room she took one last lingering look at the man she'd just spent the last several hours with, making incredible love.

He was as gorgeous asleep as he was awake. The harsh gray light of earliest morning flattered few people, but Greg looked just as good now as he had last night in the moonlight, and yesterday at the beach in the bright sunshine. Instead of looking messy, his hair looked great scattered on the pillow. Instead of looking grubby, the stubble on his jaw only emphasized his masculinity. And—to cinch the whole thing—he didn't even snore.

He appeared completely content; she could almost imagine she saw a hint of a smile on his lips.

Mikelle couldn't help smiling, too. Greg Chandler might have lots of experience with women, but last night he'd been hers alone. She hadn't wasted the opportunity, either; she had stored up lots of memories for the lonely nights ahead.

Her smile faltered. She wouldn't think about the lonely nights. There was still the morning ahead before Greg had to leave for the airport. They could breakfast together. And maybe, just maybe, when business brought him back to the island he'd be as eager to see her as she'd be to see him.

Mikelle was convinced now that Greg had been telling the truth about why he was on the island. Obviously she'd blown a lot of small incidents out of proportion to come up with the harebrained idea that Greg could be Jamie's biological father. Jamie and Greg's similarity in looks was coincidental, and the few times Greg seemed to know things about her he shouldn't could be logically explained.

But the main argument against Greg being Jamie's dad was Mikelle's heartfelt conviction that there was no way Greg could have been so dishonest with her. After last night, she was beginning to think Rose and the reverend were right about Greg. He was just about perfect . . . and if given half a chance, she could fall deeply in love with the man.

As Mikelle tiptoed across the hall, she could smell coffee brewing in the kitchen and heard Rose banging pots and pans. It was just barely six-thirty, and despite the fact that they had no other guests besides Greg, Rose was up bright and early. Mikelle was grateful she hadn't slept in and been caught in Greg's room. Rose might like Greg, but it still would have given her a shock to see them tangled up in the same bed.

Jamie was still asleep with his thumb in his mouth and his diapered fanny stuck in the air, and Gus seemed content to stay a while longer in his box, so Mikelle took a shower. While she got dressed—

choosing a pale yellow sweater, soft well-worn jeans and loafers—she caught herself whistling.

It was amazing, she thought, how good it made you feel to be loved passionately, then held tenderly. She could almost convince herself that Greg felt something more for her than a passing attraction. But she forced herself to be realistic and consider the man's reputation. She'd just have to settle for short-term bliss with Greg and forget all that picket-fence nonsense. But she couldn't help but wish things were different, and that Greg were a different sort of man. A man who could commit.

When Jamie woke up, Mikelle chatted happily with the hands-down most important man in her life as she bathed and changed him into a pair of blue corduroy overalls and a soft white turtleneck.

"Shall we go downstairs and rustle you up some breakfast?" she said as she lifted Jamie and hefted him onto her hip.

Jamie nodded, smiled and said, "Egg!" quite clearly, leaving no doubt in Mikelle's mind what her son was in the mood for. She picked up Gus on her way out the door. Jamie squealed with delight, patting the dog rather roughly on the head while Mikelle whispered instructions on how to be careful and gentle with the new puppy.

She walked quickly through the kitchen to the door, took Gus around to the enclosed backyard and set him down just inside the gate. He whimpered a little as Mikelle walked away, but quickly seemed to get interested in the unexplored territory around him and tottered away on his stubby legs, his blunt nose pressed to the ground.

As Mikelle and Jamie reentered the kitchen, Rose looked up from her work at the counter to say, "Good morning," turned back to her mixing bowl, then immediately turned around again to stare over her bifocals at Mikelle.

Mikelle pretended at first not to notice Rose's scrutiny. She put Jamie in his high chair, washed her hands, then moved to the refrigerator. She poured juice into Jamie's trainer cup, gave it to him, then took an egg out for scrambling. Finally Mikelle could stand it no longer. She faced Rose.

"What?" she said with a laugh in her voice, lifting her hands in an innocent gesture. "I haven't had breakfast yet, so I can't have food on my face. What is it, Rose? Why are you staring at me?"

"You look like the cat that ate the canary, that's why," said Rose with a decided nod. "Smug and cleaning her whiskers, too, I'd say."

Mikelle felt herself blushing. Was it so obvious she'd made mad, passionate love last night? She turned away and cracked the egg in a bowl, allowing her hair to fall forward and hide her face. "I haven't been snacking on birds lately, so I don't know what you're talking about," she said lightly. "And if I ever grew whiskers, you can be darn sure I'd have them waxed off by now."

Rose spread one hand flat against an ample hip and with her other hand she shook her mixing spoon at Mikelle. "You know exactly what I'm talking about. You're blushing like a June bride. Did you and Mr. Chandler get a chance last night to get to know each other better?"

"I guess you could say that."

Rose smiled broadly. "That's good. I knew you two would hit it off if you half tried."

They'd more than half tried. Mikelle got delicious shivers down her spine just thinking about their lovemaking.

"Don't get too excited, Rose," Mikelle warned her as she beat Jamie's egg with a fork and forced herself to put last night's memories away till she could savor them in private. "Greg's leaving today."

Rose's smile fell. "Leaving? So soon?"

"His business is done for now. He's going back to New York."

"Is he coming back?"

"Probably. Maybe. He says he is."

"When?"

"I don't know, Rose. Why don't you ask him?"

"Maybe I will," said Rose with a sniff as she turned back to her muffin batter. "He hasn't been here long enough to make a good decision about where to build."

Mikelle sighed. "Apparently he disagrees."

"He's been too hasty," she argued. "My sainted mother used to say—"

The dining room door swung open and Greg stepped into the kitchen. "What did your sainted mother used to say, Rose?"

Everyone in the room smiled. Greg was wearing a sage green sweater and khaki pants, was freshly shaven and glowing with health and vitality. His eyes connected with Mikelle's, conveying intimacy without saying a word. After a charged moment, he tore his gaze away from hers and turned smiling eyes to Jamie, then back to Rose.

"You're up early, Mr. Chandler."

"Nothing to stay in bed for," he said, sliding a quick but meaningful glance toward Mikelle. "Now, Rose, back to your mother...?"

"Well, my mother used to say that breakfast was the most important meal of the day," she improvised, beaming at Greg as she dropped huge spoonfuls of batter into a muffin pan. "And for a big man like you, I'd say that goes double, Mr. Chandler."

"Rose, when are you going to stop all this formality and start calling me Greg?"

Mikelle watched Rose turn "rose"...positively pink with pleasure. Apparently there were no age barriers to the far-reaching effects of Greg's charm. "I'll have your plate ready in twenty minutes...er...*Greg*. Do you want eggs?"

"Yes, Rose. At least two, maybe three. I'm hungry as a horse this morning." He threw Mikelle another suggestive look and she almost dropped the piece of toast she was buttering for Jamie.

"I like a man with a good appetite," said Rose, bending over the oven to put the filled muffin pan inside. "How about some coffee while you wait?"

"Don't mind if I do," said Greg, striding across the room toward the coffeepot, which just happened to be very near where Mikelle was standing. Rose, who ordinarily bristled when guests strayed into her kitchen and made themselves at home, didn't seem to mind Greg helping himself at all. She got him a cup out of the cupboard and handed it to him, still smiling from ear to ear.

"Cat got your tongue, Mikelle?" asked Greg as he poured his coffee.

"Funny you should mention cats..."

"What?"

"Never mind," said Mikelle, hoping she didn't look as flustered as she felt. She could smell his after-shave. Just being near him gave her goose bumps. Bits and pieces from last night kept intruding into her thoughts. "When I'm done, I'll join you in the dining room for breakfast. That is, if you'd like me to."

"I'd like that a lot," he assured her with a smile that warmed Mikelle down to her toes.

As he took a sip of coffee, he swiveled slowly and looked around the room. Lowering his cup, he said, "Where's Gus?"

"In the backyard," said Mikelle, taking down a copper skillet from a hook above the counter. "I've got to do some serious housebreaking today. If he wants to sleep inside at night, he has to learn the difference between grass and carpet."

"Why don't I go out there and give the little rascal a lecture on potty training right now," said Greg.

Mikelle smiled. "I'll call you when breakfast is ready."

WHEN GREG FIRST STEPPED into the backyard, Gus had initially been thrilled for company. He had rolled onto his back for a belly rub and, shortly after, a little playful wrestling. But now the curious pup was engrossed in sniffing out the far back corner of the yard by the neighbor's fence, where Greg suspected another dog had recently visited.

So Greg just sat on the grass and soaked up the sun. A famous author had once written that the ultimate luxury was sitting on a lawn, all by yourself, waiting for someone you love. You're alone but you know you won't be for long.

That's how Greg felt this morning. Waiting for Mikelle to fetch him for breakfast was as peaceful and pleasant as anything he'd ever experienced. And seeing her now as she opened the gate and walked toward him was just another notch up on the happiness meter. That she had Jamie with her was a wonderful bonus.

Did this contentment mean he loved her? When he woke up that morning he'd been acutely disappointed not to find Mikelle still in his arms. But he'd quickly shifted his focus to the exciting prospect of seeing her later in the kitchen, or in the dining room, or just running into her in the hall. He felt more than passion for Mikelle, but he wasn't sure how much of what he felt was because of Jamie.

He refused to analyze feelings this morning. There were other things to consider. He still intended to pursue joint custody of Jamie. But instead of returning to New York and arming himself with legal support first, he planned to confess everything to Mikelle before leaving the island.

After last night, there could be no secrets between them. He had to be as honest and open with her as she'd been with him. She'd forgiven him before, and surely after everything that had happened between them last night, she'd forgive him again and be reasonable about sharing Jamie with him.

"Breakfast isn't quite ready," said Mikelle, setting Jamie on the grass, then easing down to sit crosslegged beside him. "Rose is making something special for your last day."

"I'm in no hurry," said Greg, watching Jamie crawl away after the puppy. "It's a great day. But how could it be otherwise after such a great night."

Mikelle smiled uncertainly and Greg reached over and took her hand. "About last night, Mikelle—"

"Mikelle?"

They both looked up and saw Rose at the gate, looking irritated. "What is it, Rose?"

"There's a phone call for you."

"Would you tell whoever it is that I'll call back?"

"I tried, but he insisted it was important."

"He?"

"It's Frank Coffin."

Greg felt Mikelle's fingers tighten momentarily around his. It wasn't an intentional squeeze, it was more like an involuntary reaction. And the expression on her face was tense, distressed.

"What's the matter, Mikelle?" asked Greg. "If you don't want to talk to Frank, just have Rose tell him you—"

"No, I'd better take the call," she said, slipping her hand out of his and rising. "He said it was important." She threw him a weak smile. "I'm sure I'll be right back."

Frowning, Greg watched her go. He wondered if or how Mikelle's relationship with Frank would change after last night. He knew he had no right to demand any kind of exclusive relationship with Mikelle when he couldn't promise her anything concrete in return.

To add to Greg's irritation, Frank's call had interrupted an important conversation with Mikelle. He was leading up to telling her about being Jamie's father. Now it would have to wait.

He turned his attention to Jamie. He was at the back fence with Gus, who had found a knothole in the wood and had stuck his nose through the opening. Jamie had pulled himself to a standing position and was reaching down to touch Gus on the back. He was supporting himself with just one hand on the fence. This gave Greg an idea.

He stood up and walked toward Jamie, stopping about six feet away. Then he squatted down and rested his elbows on the tops of his knees.

"Jamie. Hey, big guy, what are you doing?"

Jamie turned his attention away from the dog and looked at Greg. He smiled. "Puppy," he said, tapping Gus on the rear.

Greg's heart swelled with pride. "You're a quick learner, Jamie. You can say puppy really well, just after a couple of days' practice. I bet you can walk, too."

Jamie continued to watch Greg, the big smile still intact.

"I know you had a bit of a scare a few weeks ago, bumping your head on that table and all, but there are no tables out here, sport. There's just you and me and a lot of nice soft grass." He ran his open palm over the lawn. "If you fell down, you'd just land on your Pampers-padded rear end. If you fell forward, I'd catch you." Greg held up his fingers in a Scout salute. "Scout's honor, Jamie."

Jamie looked with interest at Greg's upheld hand, then lifted his own hand in an attempt at imitation. He was so engrossed in Greg and the one-sided conversation, he quit using the fence for support. He was standing entirely on his own now.

"That's right, Jamie. You can stand on your own. You've been able to do that for a long time, I'll bet. Now, if you'll just give it a try, I know you can walk, too." He stretched out his arms. "Come right over here to me, Jamie."

Jamie looked uncertain. Greg wiggled his fingers. "Come on, Jamie," he said with a big, encouraging smile. "Come to Daddy."

Gus pulled his nose out of the knothole just then and streaked across the lawn, yapping. Jamie was distracted and Greg was afraid he'd lost the moment. But the child just wobbled for a couple of seconds, then turned his attention back to Greg.

"You want to walk, don't you, Jamie? You want to give that rascal Gus a run for his money. Well, you can. Come here, son. Just come to Daddy."

Jamie took a step, then another. His face glowed with excitement. He took another step and giggled with the sheer joy of independent movement.

Greg thought his heart would burst. He was so proud. He felt so much love. "That's right, son. Just a few more steps. Come on, Jamie," he coaxed. "Come to Daddy."

Jamie took three more steps, stretched out his arms and scrambled the rest of the way. Greg caught him just as he keeled over going forward. Laughing, he lifted Jamie up and twirled him in a circle. Jamie's legs flew out behind him as he squealed with delight.

"Wait till we show your mom," said Greg, holding Jamie against his hip and heading toward the gate. "Wait till she sees what you can do!"

"That's all right," said Mikelle from the other side of the low gate. "I've seen—and *heard*—plenty."

Greg was stopped cold in his tracks, more from the tone of Mikelle's voice than her actual words. He looked up and knew he was in trouble. He'd never seen Mikelle so angry, or so intensely determined. Rose stood behind her, her eyes trained to the ground, tight-lipped and worried.

The jig was up.

Mikelle opened the gate. "Give Jamie to Rose."

"I can take him in—"

"Just give my son to Rose, Greg," Mikelle said in a fierce undertone. "We have some talking to do and you're not stepping inside my house again except to pack."

Greg handed Jamie over the gate to Rose. Rose walked hurriedly away to the back door, never once looking Greg in the eye.

"I guess that 'something special' Rose was cooking for me is going to end up in Gus's doggy dish," he said with desperate humor.

"How can you make jokes?" asked Mikelle, crossing her arms over her chest and standing with her legs slightly spread. It was a belligerent pose. "But then, everything's a joke to you, isn't it, *Daddy?*"

Greg sighed and stared at the ground, rubbing the back of his neck. "You've got me all wrong, Mikelle. I don't think everything's a joke. I sure as hell don't think this is a joke. I never meant for you to find out this way." He looked up and met her eyes squarely, hoping for some small sign of compassion or understanding. There was none.

Mikelle laughed harshly. "We both know the joke's on me. You've been lying to me from the start. I thought there was something shifty going on, but I kept telling myself I was making a big deal out of nothing. Turns out I wasn't. Turns out I've made just as big a fool of myself over you as Peggy Dodd did. Or was that nostalgic little anecdote just another story you made up? It played well on the widow's walk last night." She walked past him into the center of the yard and kept her back turned.

Greg followed and stood behind her. "I hated lying to you, Mikelle. I was going to tell you I was Jamie's father this morning...just a few minutes ago, in fact. Then you got that phone call and—"

She turned abruptly. "Save it, Greg. Can you really expect me to believe anything you say now?" Her lips curled in a sneer. "How convenient," she said mockingly. "You were going to tell me just a few minutes ago but we unfortunately got interrupted. I know I've given you plenty of reason to think I'm naive to the point of stupidity, but I'm not *that* naive. You've had all week to tell me."

"When I first came to the island, I wasn't intending to tell you at all. I only wanted to see my son and make sure he was in a good home."

"You must have had me investigated or you'd never have found us in the first place. Wasn't sticking your nose into every private corner of my life enough to convince you that I'd make a decent parent? Or didn't my résumé impress you?"

Greg felt himself flushing. "I had a right to know something about the people who were raising my son. I knew his mother couldn't be trusted to—"

"*I'm* Jamie's mother," she said tersely, unshed tears glistening in her eyes. "And don't you ever forget that."

Greg raised his hands in a placating gesture. "I know you are. And you're a damned good mother. No one could ever replace you for Jamie."

"Quit shoveling the bull, Greg."

"I mean it, Mikelle. You and Jamie were meant to be together. I can see that. But after spending time with him, being with him this last week, I've realized that *I* was meant to be part of Jamie's life, too."

"Don't flatter yourself. Jamie will forget you the minute you drive down that road. Which can't be too soon for me!"

Greg felt that dig cut deep to his heart. He was afraid she was right.

"You're not taking him away from me, Greg. I won't let you. You gave him up. You have no business coming here and claiming rights."

She brushed past him and started walking toward the gate. He grabbed her arm, yanking her around to face him. "I *never* gave him up. I was never given a choice, Mikelle. Connie never told me about Jamie. I didn't even know she was pregnant. I had no clue I was a father till Connie's sister paid me a visit in August and spilled her guts to ease her conscience."

Their eyes locked for an emotion-charged moment, then Mikelle's gaze dropped to his hand, which was still clutching her arm. He sighed deeply and let her go. When she didn't immediately run off, he was hopeful she was finally willing to listen to his side of the story.

Greg stuffed one hand into his pocket and distractedly rubbed his chest with the other. "When I heard about the adoption, I admit I was initially relieved."

"I'm sure you were," she said coolly. "You wouldn't want to be bothered with anything or anybody that might cramp your style."

"You don't understand," he said, totally exasperated. "I was never around children. I was an only child. My mother basically deserted me when I was five and my dad made it abundantly clear that I was an unfortunate by-product of the biggest mistake of his life."

"What's your dysfunctional childhood got to do with this?"

"I'm trying to explain why the idea of being a father never appealed to me. But when I saw Jamie... when I held him for the first time, everything changed for me."

Greg could swear Mikelle's eyes softened for a second, but only for a second. The militant gleam was back in full force as she marched past him and through the gate. "You're too late, Greg. Jamie belongs to me."

"No court in the country would deny me rights to my own son," Greg yelled, fast behind her.

She opened the door to the kitchen and turned around. "They deny rights to *unfit* parents all the time."

She tried to shut the door in his face, but he pushed through. "For Christ's sake, Mikelle, you don't really believe I'm unfit, do you?"

Halfway across the room, Mikelle turned on her heel. "I don't know anything about you. For all I know, everything you've ever told me about yourself is a lie. *I* didn't hire a private detective. But from what I've heard—"

Rose was at the sink, but she turned and watched the scene with eyes as round as the dish she was washing. Jamie was in the high chair pounding a set of keys on the tray when they came in, but now he was motionless, too, seemingly mesmerized by the strange behavior of the big people.

Greg made a dismissive gesture. "If you mean Brenda—"

"I mean Brenda, who was pretty up-front about the two of you. She corroborated everything you freely admitted. You're a playboy and a cynic about marriage. Do you think I want my son growing up with those kinds of values?''

"I would never—"

"My lawyer didn't mince words about you, either. Frank and I left a message with him yesterday and he—"

"Frank, eh?" said Greg sarcastically. "Well, we know *his* motives are pure as the driven snow. He's jealous. He'd be thrilled to help you dig up dirt about me."

"There was so much of it I needed another shovel," she shot back.

Greg suddenly realized that they were probably upsetting Jamie. He turned to look at him and noticed the poor kid's bottom lip quivering. He grabbed Mikelle's arm and, this time gently, urged her in front of him and through the short passageway to the dining room and on to the parlor. Once inside, he closed the double doors.

When he turned back around, Mikelle had assumed her militant pose again. "When my lawyer learned that I had suspicions about you, he called your ex-girlfriend, explained the situation in part and asked her point-blank if you were Jamie's father. She admitted it was true, but flipped out when she heard you were hanging around here. She had nothing nice to say about you."

"Why don't you ask *me* about *her?*"

"Is that how you talk about all the women you sleep with? Is that how you'll talk about me someday?"

Greg rubbed his throbbing temples and paced the floor. "Of course not, Mikelle! Connie was bad news." He stopped pacing and faced her. His look and voice were imploring. "Please, please believe me when I tell you this.... You're different. Different from any woman I've ever known."

Mikelle closed her eyes and lifted her chin, as if she was fending off the words. "No, I don't believe you," she said carefully. "You've been using me. You've been using me to get close to Jamie. You...made love to me just to soften me up so you could come and go as you please." She opened her eyes and the expression in them was sad and cold and closed. "I think that's despicable."

"I'd agree with you if that's what I'd really intended. I tried *not* to get involved with you, Mikelle, but I couldn't help myself."

"You ought to exercise a little more self-control," she advised him. "I'm surprised you didn't whip out those party condoms last night. They would have really glowed in the dark on the widow's walk. But maybe you'd used them up already."

Greg shook his head, suddenly weary beyond description. "You seem determined to think the worst of me. You're being so unreasonable!"

Mikelle's eyes filled with tears again, but this time she wasn't able to fight them back. They flowed over her lashes and down her cheeks. Greg wanted to take her in his arms and kiss them away. At that moment he hated himself for the grief he'd brought into her life.

"You don't seem to understand," she choked out. "I'm fighting for my son! I love him more than life itself and you want to take him away!"

"If I was going to take him away, I could have done that last night, Mikelle," he said gently, reasonably.

"Hell, I was tempted.... But I decided that I couldn't hurt you or Jamie like that. I realized that I couldn't separate you two."

"Then what do you want, Greg? What kind of parental rights do you think you're entitled to?"

"I was going to talk to you about that this morning when good old Uncle Frank interrupted us. I want visiting privileges—" He saw her eyes light with hope. "But I also want to take him with me to New York now and then. I want occasional holidays, too, and some vacations."

Her jaw tightened, and her lips pressed into a thin line. She wasn't going to cooperate.

"And if you won't work with me on this, Mikelle, I'll just sue for joint custody. Then you won't have a choice. It'll be fifty-fifty all the way."

Mikelle dried her tears with the back of her hand and lifted her chin. "That's out of the question. I won't have Jamie treated like a Ping-Pong ball. He needs security and stability. He shouldn't have to deal with the problems of what would be, for all intents and purposes, a broken home." She walked past him to the door.

"You need a reality check here, sweetheart. Life is not a fairy tale. Kids nowadays deal quite successfully with joint-custody situations."

"What if I remarried?"

He paused. "That's your choice."

"If I marry and have more children—which is what I want more than anything—Jamie will always be the only one with a dad in Manhattan."

"So? I'll be the best damned dad in Manhattan."

Mikelle shook her head. "You don't understand."

"Neither do you," he accused.

"We've reached an impasse. You'd better pack."

"Mikelle?" he said, stopping her just as she was about to step into the hall. She turned. Her expression was hurt, stubborn...painfully touching. "You'll be hearing from my lawyer."

Chapter Eleven

Central Park in late October was beautiful. The trees were golden, the air was crisp. Lately Greg had been spending a lot of time there during the middle of the day when he was supposed to be eating lunch. The wistful mood of fall seemed to suit him. More than once he'd been late getting back to the office for an appointment.

This behavior was definitely out of character. A couple of times he'd caught his secretary, Ms. Barnes, looking at him anxiously. She'd even offered once to call his doctor and schedule a complete checkup. Greg had assured her he was fine.

Yeah, just fine. Physically he was a rock. Emotionally he was mush. He missed Jamie. He missed Mikelle....

It was Halloween today, and he'd been imagining Vestal Street all decked out with pumpkins and scarecrows, and sheets draped over bushes with ghostly faces drawn on with Magic Marker. It would be an old-fashioned holiday in a quaint, safe setting perfect for little Halloweeners. Had Mikelle dressed Jamie up? Was he being carted from door to door for his fair share of sweet loot? He hoped so. He yearned to be there to see for himself.

He yearned to be there after Jamie was worn-out from trick-or-treating and fast asleep, too. He could imagine Mikelle slipping into something in silk, or something in demure cotton, and their having their own session of tricks and treats....

But Greg knew this was nothing but a sweet, sweet dream.

While he sat in the park, Greg had many people share his bench. Bus drivers, waitresses, ad executives, bankers, actors and homeless people all, at one time or another, initiated small talk with Greg. He listened politely—even sympathetically, when sympathy was called for—but he didn't offer much conversation or advice in return. Hell, he was no bartender.

The only one he talked to these days was his lawyer.

Today he was waiting for a call from his attorney, and he'd brought his cellular phone along just in case the call came through while he was slumming in the park. The small flip phone was inside the right pocket of his trench coat. He pulled the collar up around his ears. The north wind that swirled the leaves into eddies at Greg's feet brought more than a nip of cold with it these days.

A girlish figure bundled up in slacks, trendy boots, and a calf-length leather coat approached the bench. Whoever it was was hiding her face and hair inside a pullover rubber mask of Tweety-Pie. This was not the first masked stroller Greg had seen this Halloween. But he tensed a little, prepared to do battle for his wallet if necessary.

The thing was, the girl behind the mask seemed slightly familiar. It was the way she walked, or something. She sat down on the bench and turned to Greg.

"I tawt I taw a puddy tat."

Greg's tension disappeared. He smelled Obsession and smiled. "Woodstock, I presume."

"You dope" came a derisive voice from under the mask. "You've got your birds mixed up. I'm Tweety."

"You're Hayley, if I'm not mistaken."

Off came the mask, revealing Jamie's biological aunt. Greg hadn't seen her since that fateful day two months ago when she'd slam-dunked him with the news that he was a father. She pulled her long blond hair out from under the collar of her coat and shook it free. Greg's heart lifted at the sight of Hayley, despite her uncanny resemblance to Connie.

"I went by your office," she said. "Your secretary said I might find you here."

"Central Park is a big place."

"I figured you wanted to be alone. This is the most remote spot at this end of the park and I just followed my instincts, like a trail of bread crumbs, till I found you."

"You have good instincts."

She smiled. "My instincts also told me that though you *think* you want to be alone, maybe you could use a little friendly company."

Greg sighed. "'Friendly' is the operative word. I've been feeling like a first-class heel lately. If there's anyone on God's green earth who could stand my company for more than a minute and leave without murder on their mind, I'd definitely call them a loyal friend."

"Been brooding, have you?"

"Morning, noon and night."

"Connie told me you went to Nantucket to find your son."

He gave her a concerned look. "Did she put two and two together and figure out that you were the leak, Hayley?"

"My sister has plenty of air between her ears, but since I was the only person she told about you being the kid's father, yeah, she figured out that I blabbed."

"I hope she didn't hassle you."

Hayley shrugged. "A little, but nothing I couldn't handle. I don't regret telling you. You had a right to know."

Greg shook his head. "I don't know what my rights are anymore, Hayley. The bottom line is, maybe my rights don't matter. Maybe the only people who deserve consideration here are Jamie and Mikelle... his *real* mom."

"I heard the kid was adopted by a lady whose husband died a year or so ago."

"Yeah. She's a trooper. She's a great mom, too. The best."

"But she didn't take kindly to you jerking her around for days, letting her think you were just some schnook on the island for business purposes, did she?"

He gave an incredulous chuckle. "How do you know so much?"

Hayley waved a breezy hand in the air. "From the lady's lawyer to Connie's lawyer, to Connie, to me. Connie blamed me for everything, so I got an earful. She got over her tizzy fast, though. She doesn't really give a rat's rear about the kid. She was only ticked off that you might reap a little happiness out of the whole mess. But I get the feeling that by telling you about—Jamie, did you say?—I've only caused you a world of grief."

Greg lifted his hands in a helpless gesture. "A private investigator located Jamie for me and I went up to Nantucket to check things out. It took me about thirty seconds to fall hard for the kid. He's a doll, Hayley. A real doll."

"And his mother?" she asked him shrewdly.

Greg smiled wryly. "I fooled myself into thinking I was only sticking around to assure myself that Jamie was in a good home. But I couldn't tear myself away from either of them. I wanted to be the kid's father in every sense of the word. I knew it would be criminal if I took him away from Mikelle. They adore each other."

"Couldn't a compromise be reached? Couldn't you guys, you know, share Jamie?"

"That's what I thought. That's the kind of legal agreement I had my lawyer working on after the blood tests confirmed that Jamie was mine."

"Mikelle agreed to the blood tests?"

"She had no choice. They were court ordered. The blood was drawn by his pediatrician in Nantucket and sent down here for analysis. As far as I was concerned, the tests were just a technicality. I knew he was my kid from the start." He smiled ruefully, sure a little pride was shining through. "Hell, he looks just like me."

"But Mikelle is only doing what she has to do *legally*, right? I gather she's not willingly working with you on this?"

Greg rubbed his temples. "We only talk through our lawyers. Mikelle blew up when she found out I was Jamie's father. She doesn't think I'm fit to be his part-time guardian. She thinks I'm a third-rate lothario. She thinks I use women to get what I want, then throw them out like yesterday's newspaper."

She raised a brow. "And all this is based on rumor?"

He hesitated, then realized that she probably already guessed what had happened between him and Mikelle. "I slept with her the night before she found out about my relationship to Jamie. The next morning I planned to tell her who I was, but someone beat me to the punch. Now she thinks—"

Hayley leaned back and crossed her legs. "What any woman would think under the same circumstances. What *is* the truth here, Greg? How *do* you feel about Mikelle?"

Greg noticed a woman walking by, pushing a stroller. He stared. She was a leggy brunette...but she wasn't Mikelle. They never were. He sighed. "I've had three weeks to think about that, Hayley. But I wasn't even halfway to the airport the morning I left Nantucket when I realized—" His voice lowered, softened. "When I realized that I love her."

"You've been in love before," she reminded him, just as softly.

"Precisely. Which is why I didn't trust myself to tell her before. And I didn't know what I wanted *then*." He leaned forward and clasped his hands, dangling them between his knees. "Now that I do know what I want, it's too late."

"What do you want?"

Greg was sure he looked sheepish. "Don't faint....
I want to marry her."

"Hold the presses! This is headline news," said
Hayley, her eyes widening. "One of New York's leg-
endary bachelors commits himself!" She paused.
"But are you sure it isn't because...well, you
know..."

Greg nodded his understanding. "Even without
Jamie in the picture, I'd want her. I want to have
more kids with her. God, I never thought I'd hear
myself say this, but I want the picket fence, the backyard barbecues, the whole family scene. Trouble is,
there's no way I could ever convince Mikelle of this."

Hayley clipped him on the shoulder. "So just like
that you're giving up? You meet your 'one and only'
and you're giving up without a fight?"

Greg leaned back against the bench. "You don't
understand. She's hurt and afraid. She doesn't trust
me. I'm a threat to her happiness."

"Because you're suing to share custody of Jamie?"

"Yes...at least, that's what she thinks I'm doing."

"Aren't you?"

"That's what I intended to do, but I've changed my
mind. I don't think I could stand seeing her every time
I picked Jamie up for a visit. I couldn't stand the polite conversations as we discussed Jamie's schooling,
his health, his future, and not want to be more inti-
mate with her...not want to talk about *us.*" His voice
and expression grew grim. "And I sure as hell
couldn't stand to see her married to someone else."

"You've got it bad."

"To say the least."

"Then woo her, damn it!" said Hayley, sounding completely exasperated. "Prove to her that you can be committed! Prove to her that she's different than all the other women you've been with. Don't give up, Greg. Don't flush your chance for happiness down the toilet!"

"Well, I have *considered* making one last stab at it," he admitted, afraid to say too much. Afraid if he talked about it, he'd realize how futile it was and finally and completely give up. "But first I have to settle things for Jamie. His future has to be secure no matter what happens between me and Mikelle."

Hayley frowned. "So, let me get this straight. You're *not* going to sue for joint custody?"

"No."

"What are you going to do, then? Don't tell me you're giving Jamie up, lock, stock and diaper pail? Or are you suing for *full* custody? Tell me, Greg." She caught his arm and squeezed it. "Tell me before I die of curiosity!"

Just then the cellular phone rang. Greg was grateful for the interruption, but he gave Hayley what he hoped was a convincingly apologetic smile, then reached inside his pocket and flipped open the phone. "Hello. Yeah, Dave." There was a pause while he listened. "Yeah, that's what I want to do. Yeah, I'm sure." He glanced at Hayley's expectant face. "The papers are ready to go, then? Good. Send them overnight express. I want Mikelle to know my decision as soon as possible."

MIKELLE WAS SITTING with guests at tea when Rose appeared at the door. She said nothing, but the look on her face made Mikelle's throat go dry with fear.

She quickly excused herself and followed Rose into the kitchen.

With a pained expression, Rose picked up the overnight-express envelope off the counter and handed it to Mikelle. Mikelle stared down at the return address. It was from the law firm Greg had been using. The neatly typed letters blurred and her hands shook.

"I knew this would come eventually, but I guess I kept hoping he'd change his mind."

"Could you give Jamie up if he were legally yours?" asked Rose.

Mikelle gave a huff of exasperation. "Why do you persist in sticking up for him, Rose, when he did nothing but lie and deceive?"

"He went about it all wrong, but you have to admit he's just as much a victim as you are."

Mikelle tapped the envelope against her palm as she stared, unseeing, through the window that faced the front of the house. The lawn was covered with brown and orange leaves. "He isn't stable enough to raise a child," she said.

"So he's sowed a few wild oats! With his looks, it would be hard to resist all the opportunities thrown his way. Even Jim was a bit wild before he settled down with you, wasn't he?"

Mikelle refused to reply. She wasn't about to help Rose defend Greg.

Undaunted by Mikelle's silence, Rose continued. "You know as well as I do that he adores Jamie. You've seen them together. You've said yourself that he worries more than you about Jamie. That's what made you suspicious of him in the first place. Jamie will be perfectly safe and happy while he's with his father."

Mikelle slumped into a chair, still holding the unopened envelope. Her eyes filled with tears. "The point is, he won't be with *me!* Rose, I'm losing him just like I lost Jim!"

Rose put her arm around Mikelle's shoulders. She spoke gently but firmly. "You won't lose him. Greg only wants joint custody, and I'm sure he'll be reasonable and let you keep Jamie on the island most of the year."

"That's damned generous of him," grumbled Mikelle, roughly wiping away a tear that had fallen. She blinked back the rest of her tears, stood up and turned to snatch a letter opener from a basket on the counter.

"If you weren't so stubborn...or so afraid...maybe there could have been a much better solution to this mess."

Mikelle gestured with her letter opener. "Don't start that again. Greg was only interested in me as Jamie's mom. He *used* me."

"How can you know for sure?"

"Has he called? Has he made one attempt to see me?"

"Would you have talked to him? Would you have listened?"

Mikelle inserted the letter opener and ripped the envelope open with one vigorous tug. "I would have listened, but I wouldn't have believed a word he said. Even if he does care for me, there's no future in it. And I want a future with brothers and sisters for Jamie and a man I can love for the rest of my life."

"And you're so sure Greg can't be that man?"

"Oh, he *could* be, all right, but he doesn't want to be. And the proof of that lies inside this envelope. If he wanted Jamie and me as a package, would he be suing for joint custody?"

Rose had no reply. She sat down in a chair with a defeated sigh and watched Mikelle slide the legal papers out of the envelope. Mikelle had only read the first paragraph or so when she had to sit down, too.

"I don't believe it," she said wonderingly, the tears falling unheeded now. "I just don't believe it."

Rose looked stricken. "No, don't tell me.... He didn't file for *full* custody, did he?"

Mikelle lowered the paper and looked at Rose. "No," she said, her voice shaky with astonishment. "He's not suing for custody at all. He's relinquishing all parental claim to Jamie. He's not contesting the adoption. Jamie's...mine, Rose. He's all mine!"

The two women sat in stunned silence, each keeping their gut reactions to themselves. For Mikelle, the first sensation was profound relief and joy. Then guilt set in, threatening to make her happiness short-lived. How could she be completely, totally happy at the considerable expense of another?

Mikelle couldn't help but put herself in Greg's place. Up till now she'd been too angry, too frightened to see his side. Now his side, his suffering, were all too obvious.

Jamie, blissfully asleep upstairs, was hers. And he'd never know he had a father who was prepared to fight for him, then gave him up because, as the paper said, "The biological father deems the welfare of the child to be better served by allowing full custody of the child to remain with the adoptive mother."

By the quiet way Rose stood up and began preparations for the evening meal, her face sober, her movements weary, Mikelle knew Rose was thinking the same things she was. They were both feeling sorry for Greg.

Mikelle slumped in the chair, taking a moment to feel sorry for herself, too. Odds were, she'd never see Greg again. She'd never look into those gray-green eyes, or feel his lips on hers, or those strong arms around her. And in Jamie there would be a constant reminder of what might have been.

She straightened with sudden determination. At least she'd hear his voice once more...because she was going to call him. She was going to call him right away, before she lost her nerve. Clutching the papers, she moved toward the back stairway.

"Where are you going?" asked Rose.

"I'm going to call Greg."

Rose became instantly alert, her eyes bright. "Why?"

"To thank him," said Mikelle. "What else?" She walked up the stairs, hoping she wouldn't run into any of the guests. She had a full house, so the only private phone available was in the bedroom she shared with Jamie. If she spoke softly, she wouldn't wake him.

She moved carefully past his crib and sat down on the edge of her bed. She called directory assistance and got the phone number for Chandler Enterprises, the architectural firm Greg owned. It was nearly three-thirty in the afternoon and she was hoping he'd still be in the office.

The first time she dialed the number, she hung up before the call went through. She sat with her hand on the receiver, her heart beating wildly. What would she say? What would *he* say? She tried to calm herself by envisioning how the conversation might go. She'd say, "Thank you for letting me keep your son, Greg." He'd say, "That's quite all right, Mikelle. I never wanted a kid in the first place."

No, not likely, thought Mikelle. She was sure she couldn't be that simple and straightforward and he wouldn't be that flip. He loved Jamie. She knew he loved Jamie.

Resigned to the fact that the exchange would be awkward, painful and unpredictable, Mikelle dialed the number again. Gripping the receiver, she suffered through four rings before a woman answered. It was a receptionist. She forwarded the call to another line and, five rings later, another woman answered—Greg's secretary.

"Mr. Chandler is in a meeting at the moment. Can I have him call you back?" she asked.

"No," said Mikelle, in a panic. She'd have to talk to him now, or never. "I need to talk to Greg right away."

There was a pause. "May I ask what this call concerns?"

"It's personal. Please just put me through."

"Is this an emergency?"

"Well, not exactly..."

"As I said, Mr. Chandler is with an important client, so if you'll just give me a number—"

"Tell him it's Mikelle," she finally said. "Don't worry, he won't get angry if you interrupt him. Just tell him it's Mikelle."

There was another pause. "All right. Hold the line, please."

Mikelle wondered if she'd overrated her importance by assuming Greg would take the call if he knew it was her, but it was worth a shot. When the line immediately clicked on again she half expected to hear a tactfully phrased excuse from the secretary, but it was Greg's voice, clear as a bell.

"Mikelle?"

Mikelle felt a thrill go through her. She swallowed with difficulty. "Yes," she said softly, partly because Jamie was asleep just a few feet away, but mostly because she was bowled over by her reaction to Greg's voice.

"Is everything all right? Why are you talking so softly?"

She could hear the anxiousness in his tone even across the hundreds of miles that separated them. "I'm all right. Jamie's all right, but he's asleep and I'm using the phone in the bedroom."

"Oh," he said. Then there was silence.

"I—I called to thank you," she stuttered.

More silence followed.

"I don't know what else to say.... I know you care about Jamie, and I know this must have been hard for you."

"I did it *because* I care about him. You and Jamie belong together. I did what I thought would cause you and Jamie the least amount of anguish and hassle."

"I'm more grateful than you'll ever know—"

"I think I know."

"But I'm surprised. I thought you wanted to see him, to spend time with him."

"I did. I still *do*. But I guess that's entirely up to you now. I didn't want to battle with you over custody or visitation rights. I didn't think that would promote happiness for any of us.''

There was another pause, during which Mikelle wanted desperately to explain that she understood better now why he'd lied to her, but there was a knot of emotion in her throat the size of Detroit. She wanted to forgive and forget that part of their experience together and offer Greg the visitation privileges he still wanted. It didn't seem right for him to be shut out completely. But she couldn't get the words past that darn lump...! She prayed he wouldn't hang up. She breathed a sigh of relief when she heard his voice again.

"You were furious with me when I left. You surprised me, too. I never expected you to call."

She forced herself to speak, the words coming out in a whisper. "You understand why I was angry, don't you?"

"Yes. You were scared stiff you might lose Jamie. And you felt betrayed. I hope your fears about Jamie are completely alleviated?"

"I still can't believe you gave him up." Mikelle bit her lip, holding back the tears. *He gave him up.* It sounded so final, so heartless on her part. "I'm sure we can work things out so you can...you know...see him from time to time." *And I can see you, too,* she added to herself.

"I thought you were completely against visits, Mikelle. I thought you considered me an unfit guardian."

Mikelle flinched. "I know that's not true. I was angry. I said a lot of things. Remember, I felt betrayed."

"Let's talk about that—"

Mikelle tensed. "No, I don't want to. I don't expect you to—"

"You felt betrayed because you thought I made love to you just to get close to Jamie's mom. You thought it was just part of my plan, didn't you?"

"Y-yes."

"Well, you were wrong. I care about you, Mikelle. Considering my reputation—which is only half-deserved, I'd like to clarify—I know you think you're just another notch on my bedpost, but you're not. You're special, you're—"

"I'm Jamie's mom," she said dully.

"Christ, Mikelle, I'd care about you even if you were King Kong's mom! Jamie brought us together, but, believe me, the attraction I feel for you has nothing to do with baby bottles and potty training!"

"How can I believe you?"

"Why would I lie? What reason do I have to lie now? Jamie is legally yours."

"I know, but—"

"Trust me. This time I'm telling the truth. Scout's honor."

She envisioned him holding up the three middle fingers of his right hand in the Scout salute, just like that time in the backyard when Jamie took his first steps. Mikelle's heart ached with love for both of the players in that affecting family scene. But the daddy in the scene had the power to hurt her more than any other human being on earth. She'd be crazy to give him the chance to exercise that considerable power.

"Greg, I don't exactly know what you're asking."

"I'm asking you if we can see each other again."

"Just you and me? Not you and me and...Jamie?"

"Just you and me. I want the chance to prove something to you."

"What do you want to prove?"

"Agree to see me and you'll find out."

"Tell me now."

"I'd rather tell you this face-to-face."

"Tell me now, or I won't even consider—"

He gave an exasperated chuckle. "Okay. Okay. It's like this...." There was another pause, then, "I love you, Mikelle."

Mikelle's heart leapt with joy...and fear. "I wish I could believe you."

"Because...?"

"Because...because I love you, too."

She heard him release a long breath, as if he'd been holding it till he heard her answer. "You can believe me," he said.

"Prove it."

THE NEXT DAY, the first bouquet of red roses arrived at the Little Gray Lady, along with a single piece of unpainted wood about four feet long and three inches wide. The wood was decorated with a yellow ribbon. The attached card said, simply, Trust me, it's true.

Mikelle held a rose to her nose and breathed deeply. She picked up the wood and studied it, wondering what it signified. It was all very intriguing, very heady, very exciting. She wanted to believe Greg. She wanted to, but she didn't dare....

Chapter Twelve

By the end of the week, nearly every room in the Little Gray Lady was filled with the sweet fragrance of roses. Vases full of the lush, red blooms graced tables in the parlor, the dining room, the kitchen, and in Mikelle's bedroom.

And by the back door there was a growing pile of wood and a basket full of yellow ribbons.

"Maybe it's material to build a doghouse for Gus," said Mikelle, staring down at the wood pile. "Or a tree house for Jamie."

Mikelle had just taken Jamie out of his high chair and he was toddling across the floor toward the Tupperware cupboard he routinely enjoyed ransacking. It was the only cupboard they hadn't secured with baby-proof latches to keep Jamie safe from cleaning products and items he shouldn't get his curious little hands on. Gus pranced after his cohort in mischief. They were already the best of friends.

"The wood is something for you," said Rose, with a gleam in her eyes that had first appeared when Mikelle confessed she'd made a date with Greg for the weekend.

"For me? What could he possibly be thinking of making for me?" *A hope chest, maybe?*

"Have you asked him?"

"Only about a million times. He's as silent on the subject as he is about where he's taking me tonight."

Rose glanced eagerly at the clock above the sink. "It's nearly seven. He'll be here any minute."

"I think you're as nervous as I am," said Mikelle, but she didn't think it was possible for anyone to be as nervous as she was. She glanced in the mirror that hung on the wall by the door and ran her fingers lightly through her bangs. She'd taken great pains with her appearance tonight and she hoped she'd look half as good to Greg as he would to her.

He'd told her to put on one of her "posh frocks," so she'd dug out from the back of her closet a broomstick-pleated, drop-waisted dress of ivory georgette. The top was embroidered and there were tiny pearl buttons that ran the length of the sheer dress, from scoop neckline to hem. Underneath she wore a silky sheath of the same color. The sleeves were long and see-through. She'd bought the dress months ago but had never worn it. It made her feel feminine and very sexy.

She hoped she wasn't making a mistake by wearing it... or by going out with Greg. But who could resist his charm? He'd called her every night that week, seeming, with the calls and roses, to be determined to sweep her off her feet.

In the back of her mind she knew that while romance was important in a relationship, love and commitment were the foundations that would make it last. But she couldn't help but thoroughly enjoy being wooed with such expertise, even though she still feared he'd end up breaking her heart....

When the doorbell rang, Rose and Mikelle jumped and Gus immediately began barking. He followed Mikelle through the dining room, into the hall, and skidded to a stop in front of the door, barking at full blast the whole time.

"Shh, Gus," said Mikelle, "This one's a friend, not a foe. At least, that's what I'm counting on."

She opened the door. If she had thought her heart was beating too fast before, now it was completely out of control. Greg was wearing a black tuxedo. He was like a glossy ad from *GQ* come to life. He was one tall, polished hunk of sophisticated male.

"Hi, Mikelle." His eyes, shining silvery gray in the porch light, slid approvingly over her. She felt the blood rush to the surface of every square inch of her body. "You look fabulous." She wasn't imagining the warmth in his expression and voice, nor could she deny how truly happy he seemed to see her. And there was something else in his expression, too. Did she dare hope it was...love?

"You're no slouch, either," she managed to say. "Come in." With a nod of her head she indicated Gus, who was still yapping at the top of his lungs, and added, "If you dare."

Greg looked down at Gus and laughed. "So the runt of the litter has delusions of being a Doberman, eh?" He stooped, bracing his hands on his knees. "Don't you remember me, Gus?"

Gus stopped barking, sniffed Greg's outstretched hand and immediately began to wag his tail. Mikelle couldn't help but compare herself to the friendly puppy. She was as easily won over by Greg's charm.

But the pup had a lot less to lose by giving his heart so freely.

Greg was petting an ecstatic Gus when they heard quick footsteps on the wood floor coming from the dining room. It was Jamie, and just behind him, Rose. Greg glanced up and froze. An expression of such unqualified affection came over his face, Mikelle had to fight back a flood of emotion.

Jamie stood, as steady as could be in his high-topped sneakers, and stared at Greg. As recognition dawned, a smile spread slowly over his face. Greg looked quickly, uncertainly, at Mikelle. Mikelle nodded her approval and Greg stretched out his arms to Jamie. "Hi, big guy," he said.

Jamie walked with surefooted haste straight into Greg's embrace. After a hug and some hair tousling, Jamie was ready to get down again. Since he'd learned to walk, he didn't like being held for long.

Greg set him on the ground and Jamie patted the puppy's head. "Gus," he said as clear as day. "Gus," he repeated, looking up at Greg.

"Yeah, pardner. It's Gus, all right," agreed Greg, grinning from ear to ear. "You're walking like a trooper, kid. Way to go."

"It's nice to see you, Mr. Chandler," said Rose, who stood tentatively in the doorway between the hall and the dining room.

"I thought we agreed that you'd call me Greg," said Greg, walking over to Rose to squeeze her hand warmly.

Rose beamed with pleasure. "Would you like a drink or something before you two go?" she offered.

Greg's gaze shifted to Mikelle. Now that he was inside the house, in the mellow light of the hallway, his eyes looked green. And Mikelle thought they radiated a sort of sexy assertiveness. It was as if he'd made up his mind that he wanted something and was prepared to move mountains to get it. Goose bumps erupted on Mikelle's arms. What if *she* was that something?

"Thanks for the offer, Rose," said Greg. "But Mikelle and I have reservations. Maybe another time?"

"I hope so," said Rose with such fervor that Mikelle threw her a cautionary look.

"You need a coat," he said, addressing Mikelle and looking at her with such warm awareness she felt like the only person in the room. Suddenly she was no longer competing with an adorable toddler, a playful pup, and an Irish charmer who could cook like a dream. In less than a minute, he'd helped her into her calf-length, tan wool coat and they'd said their goodbyes.

In another moment, they were driving down the street toward town, inside what had to be the same green Jeep Cherokee he'd rented the last time he was on the island. When she commented on this, he said, "When I find something I really like, I stay with it."

Mikelle told herself that he'd intended no double meaning, but she couldn't be sure. The only thing she knew for sure was that being with Greg again made her feel deliriously happy and . . . uncharacteristically shy. But then, he'd told her over the phone that he loved her. A declaration like that coming from a man like Greg would make most women feel a little flustered at their next meeting.

And, to make it worse, like an idiot she'd admitted to feeling the same for him. Then she'd challenged him to prove his love. But as long as there was doubt in her mind and heart that Greg could truly love her, she could withhold a part of herself and protect her emotions. If he managed to convince her that his love was the real thing, she'd be as vulnerable as one of the delicate roses he'd sent her.

"Where are we going?" she asked him.

"It's a surprise."

"I know every nook and cranny of this island. There aren't too many surprises left."

"Maybe not on the island, but there are plenty of surprises left in our relationship," he told her, turning his gaze from the road to throw her a quick, meaningful smile.

"Our 'relationship,'" she repeated musingly. "I didn't know we had one."

"We could."

But for how long? she wondered. She didn't want another passionate fling with Greg, then have to see him every time he visited Jamie. She'd already decided it was only right that he be able to spend time with his son, but, while they'd briefly discussed it, they hadn't worked out the details for visitation.

She just knew, though, that she'd fall hard for Greg. If they broke up, he'd probably get over her and on to another romance in no time, while she would be carrying the torch for him till her dying day. If that happened, she'd probably never remarry and have those dozen or so kids she wanted.

So what was she *doing* on a date with him?

When Greg turned off the road, Mikelle recognized the ocean-side restaurant called Devereaux's. It was a huge Victorian house that had been transformed into several elegant private dining rooms.

Since it was quite pricey, she had only been there a couple of times with Jim. She was suitably impressed. Obviously Greg had done his homework and found the perfect place for a romantic evening.

While a valet parked the Jeep, Greg escorted Mikelle up a cobbled walkway to the front door of the establishment. Tiny clear lights had been strung in the trees around the house and the effect was enchanting. You could hear the surf breaking on the shore and smell the salty sea.

Inside, a majordomo showed Mikelle and Greg through a plush hallway and up a highly polished cherrywood stairway to an upper room. The room was much larger than Mikelle would have thought necessary for a single couple...but space was needed for the small band and the intimately proportioned dance floor.

A waiter seated them at a table that was covered with beautiful china, sterling and crystal. Two large vases of roses placed on side tables scented the air. To perfect the romantic ambience, the room was illuminated by candles on the dining table and a small chandelier over the dance floor. Two feet away from where they sat was a secluded alcove with a window that overlooked the sea. They consulted the menu and together agreed on what to order.

"I made sure they had vegetarian dishes before I made reservations," said Greg.

"That was thoughtful of you."

"I aim to please," he assured her with a wink.

When the waiter had gone, and with the band playing softly on the other side of the room, Mikelle finally took a steadying breath.

"I feel a little overwhelmed," she admitted in a whisper.

"You don't have to whisper," Greg told her with a smile. "The band has been perfectly placed so that dinner conversations are private."

"Everything about this place is perfect," said Mikelle wryly. "It's not where I usually hang out."

Greg laughed. "The Seaweed Burger Barn and the street-corner accordion player were already booked for the night, so I had to make do."

She laughed. "It's not that I don't absolutely *love* the place, but I'm just wondering if you enjoy this kind of opulence as a steady diet. It might get a little rich for a simple islander like me."

He leaned close, his eyes lighting with humor. "Remember, I'm just a simple islander, too."

"Are you referring to Manhattan?" she questioned with a raised brow.

"It's an island," he insisted. "And I actually prefer more casual dining, too. I love picnics on the beach, for example, complete with sandy cheese sandwiches and warm beer."

She couldn't doubt that he was referring to their picnic on the beach together with Jamie. Her lips curved up at the corners. "Then why did you bring me here?"

"I'm blatantly attempting to impress you."

"Obviously. Well, you're succeeding. I feel like Cinderella at the ball."

"Good. But I hope you're not planning to desert me at the stroke of twelve?"

"As long as you behave like a prince, I guess I'll stick around."

He waggled his brows wickedly. "I can't make promises. How do the princes *you* know behave?"

They don't break your heart, Mikelle thought, but said instead, "They ask a woman to dance when she's dying to."

He acquiesced with a nod and a smile, then stood and helped her to her feet. In three steps they were on the parquet dance floor and he pulled her into his arms. Mikelle had impulsively suggested dancing, but now she questioned her judgment. Being in Greg's arms again was heaven. She remembered in exquisite detail all the passion and intimacy of the night they made love. Her body warmed, her senses became acutely aware of how very attractive, how very male Greg was. He smelled so good. He looked so handsome, so vital.

"I've missed you," he said, looking down at her tenderly. The pressure of his hand at the small of her back increased. He pulled her closer and lightly rested his chin against the top of her head. "I've wanted to hold you like this for weeks."

"I've missed you, too," she admitted. She was desperate to tilt her head back and trail her lips along the angle of his firm jaw, but she resisted the urge. "Things are moving too fast, Greg," she murmured. "I'm confused. Like I said, I'm overwhelmed."

"Overwhelmed, eh? There's that word again." He pulled back and looked down at her with teasing concern. "I thought women liked to be wined and dined. Am I spreading it on too thick?"

"I don't know. It's not that I'm ungrateful, it's just that..." Her voice trailed off. She didn't know how to say what she was feeling.

"It's just that any John Doe can lavish flowers and attention on a woman, but that doesn't prove he loves her, right?"

She made an embarrassed shrug. "I guess so."

Greg sighed and stopped dancing. "When you challenged me to prove my love, Mikelle, I thought this was what you wanted," he began earnestly. "But the bottom line is, when someone tells you he loves you, you have to take a chance on believing him. There are no guarantees in this life. You ought to know that better than anyone."

"Yes, I do know, but you have to admit our short history together has been shaky."

"In other words, I lied to you before to get what I wanted, so why wouldn't I do it again? You don't trust me."

"I want to."

"I don't know how else to convince you I'm telling you the truth. I thought you'd realize how much I care about you when I gave up legal rights to Jamie."

"I thought you did that for Jamie."

"I did, but I did it for you, too. Jamie's young. He could have adjusted if push came to shove. He needs you—there's no denying that, but I think you need him just as much."

"Oh, Greg . . ."

"And *I* need you." He placed his forefinger on her lips. "No, don't talk. Just let me hold you. This evening is just for you and me—no past history and no kids allowed. We both love Jamie, and he'll be there when we get home. I think he can manage without us for just one night."

Mikelle took Greg's advice. Nothing sounded better to her than to forget everything except these precious moments...this magic night with Greg. So, for the first time since they'd met, they talked openly with no secrets between them. They enjoyed each other freely, with the sweet anticipation of what might come later the only tension between them.

After dinner, Greg reached across the table and took Mikelle's hand. "I'm staying at—"

"No, let me guess," said Mikelle with a teasing smile. "You're staying at the Executive Inn, right?"

"It doesn't have the unique amenities of the Little Gray Lady, but my room—like all the rest—does have a hot tub," he returned in the same light tone, but his eyes conveyed serious intent. "Why don't you come back with me and try it out?"

She hesitated for the space of thirty anxious, excited heartbeats, then squeezed his hand. "I'd love to."

GREG THREW his car keys on the dresser in his room at the Executive Inn and turned to face Mikelle. She stood ramrod straight with her back to the door, her arms stiff and her elbows locked as she clutched in her hands a little cream-colored evening bag. As he undid his tie and slowly slid the thin strap of silky material from under his collar, she watched with eyes as big and shiny as silver dollars.

"You look scared to death."

"I am."

"Why?"

She shook her head ruefully, her agitated gaze flitting over him from head to toe, then away to the corner of the room where the hot tub was situated. She looked at that modern monument to sensuality for a wide-eyed moment, then back at him. "I was just thinking that there's nothing sexier than watching a man take off his tie, especially when he's wearing a tux."

He smiled and undid his collar stays. "I can beat that...if you're interested."

"Oh, I'm interested, all right. That's why I'm so scared. I thought I could handle this, but now I don't know...."

He walked over to a table where the bottle of champagne he'd ordered rested in a silver bucket of ice. He lifted the bottle and worked on the cork. "We've been together before, Mikelle. This isn't like a maiden voyage, you know," he teased.

"Then why the champagne?" she fired back with a tremulous smile. "There's no need for a vessel christening."

He chuckled. "It's all part of the traditional seduction." The cork popped and he lined up two long-stemmed glasses. As he poured the frothy wine, he said, "I'm using every clichéd trick in the book, Mikelle, but the methods are tried and true. I'm persistent. I don't plan to let you leave this no-tell hotel without having my wicked way with you."

"Thanks for the warning," she said dryly, but there was an adorable catch in her voice. "But that's the problem, you see. I was counting on your persistence when I agreed to come over here."

She was so honest, so up-front with her feelings. It was a trait he found damned alluring. "Then why haven't you taken off your coat?"

"Because I could get used to this, Greg...." She made a helpless gesture with one hand.

He set down the bottle and walked toward her, stopping just short of pulling her into his arms and passionately kissing away all her fears. His plan was to proceed with caution. He knew she needed time to trust him again.

"I want you to get used to it. I want us to make love so many times that I'll have every freckle on your delectable body kissed, counted and memorized." Her shiver made his pulse leap into a faster rhythm. Good intentions notwithstanding, he wouldn't be able to keep his hands to himself much longer.

"You wouldn't get bored kissing the same old freckles over and over again?"

"Each time I'd just kiss them in a different way. Would you like a demonstration?"

She looked at him for a long, searing moment, the sexual tension between them so strong Greg felt ready to ignite. Then she slipped her shoulder out of one of her coat sleeves and said with her wonderfully uncanny mix of pure Doris Day and lethal Lana Turner, "Then I suppose I'd better take this thing off, hadn't I?"

He took her proper little handbag and put it on a chair by the door, then he stepped behind her and slipped the coat off both shoulders. He kissed her lightly, lingeringly on the back of her neck, then did the same to both shoulders. The warmth of her skin radiated through the sheer material, making him want to kiss every bare square inch of her. He whispered in her ear, "Yes, it will be much easier doing a freckle census if I have access to the entire neighborhood, so to speak."

He took her coat and hung it up, congratulating himself on his remarkable control. He wanted to strip her, fling her onto the first available flat surface and make love with her till sometime next week. She watched him as he walked back from the closet, her gaze frankly appraising, openly admiring, and damned near too arousing for him to be able to maintain further restraint.

"When you look at me like that, I can't—" he growled.

"You can't what?" she taunted.

"I can't be accountable for my actions."

"Don't worry," she said playfully. "I won't hold you accountable. I just want to *hold you.*"

He shook his head, his body aching with desire. "How can you be so shy and unsure one minute, then so seductive and coy the next?"

She suddenly grew serious. "When I'm with you, Greg, a part of me that died with...with my husband, comes alive. I've been a mother twenty-four hours a day for a year now, except for those few hours with you three weeks ago when you made me feel like a woman again. A real flesh-and-blood, passionate woman."

Greg wanted to say something in return, but he was too moved, too humbled to speak. That he wanted to make her feel like a woman for the next sixty years or so would be the most fitting reply, but it was too soon to propose. Instead he smiled and said, "How about those freckles?"

Mikelle smiled flirtatiously and began a slow, deliciously erotic striptease. Greg sank slowly down on the edge of the bed, afraid his legs wouldn't hold him up. First the dress came off, button by button, inch by tantalizing inch. Then the sleek little sheath she wore beneath the dress shimmied past her slim hips to a soft pile at her feet. She deftly kicked the clothes to the side and stood before him in a flesh-colored bra, a scrap of lace panties, a garter belt, and nude hose.

He swallowed hard. "You never fail to surprise me, Mikelle," he said hoarsely. In three strides he reached her, caught her in his arms and carried her to the bed. Bracing himself above her, he bent to kiss her with all the pent-up yearning of three weeks of absence and agony, and three torturous hours of hard-fought self-control.

When the kiss ended, he looked into her hazed eyes and with the little breath he had left, said, "That's one way I'll kiss and count your freckles. Do you want another demonstration?"

"Yes," she said, as out of breath as he.

"I think I see one here," he said, kissing her forehead. "And here," he said, kissing the tip of her nose. "And here...and here...and here..." He feathered a pattern of light kisses across her cheek, along the curve of her jaw, under her chin and down the length of her supple, sweet-scented neck.

"Which of the kisses do you like best?"

"I don't know," she said haltingly. "Maybe I'd better have another demonstration."

"It's only going to get harder and harder to decide, Mikelle," he warned her. "I've got a million of 'em."

A million kisses later, some given, some received, Greg hung on to the fringe of self-control by a frayed thread. He wanted Mikelle more than he wanted his next breath. Sensing his need, matching it, Mikelle urged him onto his back, straddled him and pushed his jacket off his shoulders. "I don't think this occasion calls for anything quite so formal as a tux," she said.

"I couldn't agree more," he murmured, shucking off his jacket and tossing it off the bed.

Mikelle unbuttoned Greg's shirt with trembling fingers, pulled the tail from his pants and folded back the dressy white linen. His chest was even more heavenly than she remembered. She ran her hands up and down the muscled surface, her fingertips buried in a light matting of golden brown hair. She bent and explored his chest with her lips and tongue and teeth, lingering with absorbed delight on the tight nub of each nipple. His moan of pleasure reminded her that there was much more to discover and more gratification to be given.

She took off his cuff links and helped him out of his shirt. He slid to the edge of the bed and Mikelle got on her knees and kissed his bared shoulders from the back while he undid his cummerbund, impatiently toed off his shoes and pulled off his socks. Then he stood up and slipped out of his pants in one fluid movement, turning impatiently back to Mikelle.

As he came to her, Mikelle felt nearly overwhelmed with feelings for this man. He was beautiful, he was tender, he was her lover. And he was the father of her son. She wished he could be the father of the brothers and sisters she wanted to give Jamie.

"I love you, Greg."

She'd said it without conscious thought, without will or intention. It caught him unawares, but his face lit from some inner source, some heartfelt emotion. He didn't say so, but she knew then that he loved her, too. She only wished he loved her enough to marry her....

Bittersweet regret was washed away by the consuming demand of physical need. Greg made short work of removing her bra and panties, but then made the removing of her garter belt and hose a slower, more sensual process. He found more freckles...at the curve of her calf, behind her knee, on the inside of her thigh. He kissed and cataloged them all—"for future reference," he said.

Then Greg pulled himself up to claim her mouth again in a full, deep kiss. Her breasts ached with tender arousal as he cupped them in his warm, demanding hands. He teased the nipples with rhythmic strokes of his thumbs.

Weak and desperate with desire, she twined her arms around his neck, wrapped her legs around his hips and tried to show him with every ounce of her being that she was ready.

So was he. He positioned himself and slipped inside her. At the moment of their closest, deepest connection, he held himself still and looked into her eyes. "I love you, Mikelle," he told her, leaving no doubts, no regrets. She would take his love and cherish it for as long as he was willing to give it.

Then they began to move. She met each thrust of his hips with eager and complete participation. The sensations intensified till ripples of sweet release washed over Mikelle. As Greg cried out his own release, Mikelle clutched him to her chest. They were one, physically and spiritually. They loved each other...and for now that was enough.

LATER, AS THEY SIPPED wine and luxuriated in the hot tub, Mikelle surprised Greg again. Sated and content, feeling like a fat cat in a creamery, he sat in the corner seat and dreamily watched the pulsating water do its magic on Mikelle. Even with her eyes shut as she leaned back in the tub, she looked so relaxed, so happy. And then she issued an invitation.

"Jamie will be a year old tomorrow."

"I know," he admitted a little sheepishly. "I hope you don't think I purposely made my visit coincide with Jamie's birthday."

She opened her eyes. "Even if you did, I'd forgive you. So, why don't you plan on coming to his party? It'll just be a family thing... you, me, Rose and Gus. And Jamie, of course."

A family thing. Greg liked the sound of that. Then he remembered a surprising omission. "What about Uncle Frank?"

"He won't be there," said Mikelle in a voice that revealed nothing.

"Why not, Mikelle?" asked Greg, not satisfied to let it go without an explanation. "Is he out of town or something?"

"I guess he could be. He has a girlfriend in Boston. He spends a lot of time there."

Greg grinned. He couldn't help it. He nudged Mikelle with his foot and she opened her eyes. "What?" she said, responding to his smile with one of her own.

"You told him you wouldn't see him anymore, didn't you?"

"Don't get a swelled head, Chandler."

"You told him to get lost even before I called last week and told you I loved you, didn't you?"

She shrugged. He could just see her shoulders and the edge of a bare breast rising in the water. He immediately felt himself tightening with renewed arousal. "I couldn't lead the guy on. There was no hope. I didn't want to waste any more of his time, and I told him so. He was nice, but—"

"But what?"

"But he wasn't you."

"Come here, Mikelle."

"Why?"

"I see some freckles. . . ."

Chapter Thirteen

Greg was sitting at the kitchen table wearing a shiny, red, cone-shaped party hat secured to his head by a stretched-to-its-limit elastic band.

"It's a bit of a tight fit, but you don't mind, do you?" asked Mikelle, holding back a giggle.

"Why should I mind?" Greg groused with good humor. "I look like a character in a *Saturday Night Live* skit and feel like my throat's being systematically sliced, but other than that, I'm having a great time."

And he really was.

Jamie was in his high chair, banging his spoon against the plastic tray. He didn't look too thrilled about wearing the party hat, either, because he kept grabbing at the elastic. But when he wasn't looking annoyed about the hat, he was looking with wide-eyed eagerness at the cake on the table. It was a bright purple blob with a green stomach, small beady eyes and a big mouth, big feet and a big tail. It was Barney, the dinosaur.

Although it was a perfectly executed replica of the popular kids' icon, Greg eyed the cake with mild distaste. "I don't understand this goofy dinosaur phenomenon."

"Jamie loves Barney," said Mikelle, reaching into a drawer for a pack of birthday candles.

"I'm going to have to have a talk with that boy," Greg murmured, reaching down to rub Gus's head as the dog nosed around under the table.

"I know it's a lot of food coloring, but birthdays only come once a year," said Mikelle. "We'll counteract the effects of all that sugar and junk with plenty of veggies for dinner, right, Jamie?"

Jamie ignored his mother and continued to eye the cake with obvious lust.

"Did you make this cake, Rose?" asked Greg.

Rose was stacking bowls to bring to the table. She turned and smiled. "I'm a good cook, but I'm not much of a decorator. Barney was created by a real artist."

Greg turned to Mikelle. "In other words...you did this?"

"I plead guilty," Mikelle admitted, laughing.

"You're a woman of manifold talents," said Greg with a suggestive wink.

Mikelle pretended to ignore him, but her face turned an alluring shade of pink. "I think it's time we lit the candle on Jamie's cake and got on with the business of eating. What do you think, Jamie?" she asked him. "Are you ready for Barney?"

Jamie bounced his bottom up and down in his seat and kicked his legs energetically. "Barney!" he exclaimed with a big grin and another bang of his spoon.

"We'd better feed him before he bounces out of that chair and takes matters into his own hands," Greg advised dryly. "That's my boy!"

Mikelle lit the candle and pushed the cake to the end of the table, but just out of Jamie's reach. Jamie watched and listened, fascinated, while three adults in silly hats sang "Happy Birthday." When it was over, they clapped, so he clapped. But then he was ready for cake.

"Barney!" he bellowed, a tiny frown appearing on his forehead.

"First blow out the candle, Jamie," said Mikelle, holding the cake in front of him. She showed him how, but when he puckered his lips nothing came out but a couple of dribbles of spit. So Mikelle helped him. With the candle and the usual rituals dispensed with, Mikelle cut the cake and gave Jamie a piece of Barney's tail.

Jamie ate with his fingers and was soon covered with a lot of purple icing. He wasn't adept at using a spoon yet, so he soon got frustrated and used his fingers to eat the chocolate ice cream, too. Full and happy, and rapidly growing sleepy, Jamie slumped in his chair and looked apathetically at the brightly colored birthday packages his mom stacked on the table in front of him.

"I think maybe we should wait till after his nap for the presents," suggested Greg.

"Too much excitement," Rose agreed. She took a soft, wet paper towel and wiped Jamie's sticky face and hands.

"The fact that he's letting you clean him up, and he's not squirming and complaining, proves he's beyond tired," said Mikelle, watching with eyes that radiated affection. Greg loved to watch her watching Jamie. But then, he loved just looking at her for any old reason....

"Speaking of presents," said Greg to Mikelle, "I've got one for you."

She looked surprised, but pleased. "For me? But it's not my birthday. What's the occasion?"

Greg picked up the heavy item he'd hidden behind the table, all wrapped in sunflower-printed paper and tied with a huge yellow bow. "This goes with the wood I've been sending you."

Mikelle's eyes lit up. "You mean I'm finally going to find out what kind of project all that lumber is for?"

Greg nodded.

"Let me take Jamie upstairs, then I'll open it," she said excitedly.

"I'll take Jamie upstairs," offered Rose. "Look, he's already nodding off."

Jamie's head kept drooping, then jerking up again as he tried to stay awake. "All right, Rose. Take the poor kid upstairs," said Greg, laughing. "He's had a full day already."

He stooped over, took off Jamie's hat and gave him a kiss on the top of the head, then gently tousled his hair. Rose beamed approvingly and took Jamie out of his chair and up the stairs to his room, with Gus following just behind. As soon as the others left, Greg and Mikelle took their hats off, too.

"This is an odd-shaped present," said Mikelle, running her fingers around the contoured package. She picked it up and groaned. "And it weighs a ton!"

"Just open it," Greg advised. He was as eager as she was. He wanted to explain how this present, combined with the wood, would make a dream come true. At least he hoped she'd see it that way.

She tore away the paper and stared at a large can of white paint. "Just what I always wanted," she said with a wry smile. "Whatever you're going to build with that wood is going to end up being white, right? But I still don't know what it's all supposed to mean, Greg."

"It really is something you've always wanted," he hinted.

Mikelle just lifted her shoulders in a shrug and said, "Sorry, but I'm clueless."

Greg leaned across the table and took Mikelle's hand. "It's material to build a picket fence, you dunce," he said affectionately.

She frowned. "Now I'm really clueless."

He sighed and gave her a look of loving resignation. Softly he said, "You've always wanted the white-picket-fence scenario, haven't you? You know . . . the complete family with enough kids for a football team and the father of the house as a permanent fixture?"

Her fingers stiffened in his and she pulled her hand out of Greg's loose grip. Her expression was troubled, guarded. "You know I have, but what's a pile of wood and a can of white paint got to do with all that? A fence without the family to go with it won't make my dreams come true."

"It's a start," Greg assured her, disturbed by her reaction. "You don't understand what I'm getting at, do you?" Or maybe she understood but she wasn't ready to play house.

"What *are* you getting at, Greg?"

He took a deep breath. This was a question he'd never asked before... had never expected to ask in a lifetime. But now his entire happiness depended on her favorable answer. "I'm asking you to marry me, Mikelle."

She said nothing. She just sat there and stared at him, her brow still furrowed in a frown.

He laughed uneasily. "I've surprised you."

"To say the least."

"You believe I love you?"

"Yes, I believe you do."

"And you said you loved me."

"I do."

"Then why does this come as such a shock?"

Mikelle shifted in her chair, seeming to try to gather her thoughts, to understand and ultimately express her feelings. "Greg," she began in a reasoning voice, "you've made no secret from the start that you and marriage don't mix. It was the one thing you were totally honest with me about from the beginning."

"I've never wanted to get married before, but now—"

"But now all your reservations are so easily set aside?"

"Not so easily as you think. I've had weeks to think about this. I'm the first person to admit that marriage takes more than love to make it work, but I'm willing to gamble on you. Only I don't think it's much of a gamble. You're incredible, Mikelle. I've never met anyone quite like you before."

Mikelle shook her head and stood up. She crossed her arms and paced the floor. Greg watched with the kind of anxiety he wouldn't wish on his worst enemy.

Finally she stopped and turned to face him. "We've only known each other a month, Greg."

"A month, a year... How long does it take to know someone? I guess you're not ready to gamble on me, though...right?"

"I realize marriage is a gamble no matter how long you know a person, but we've got someone else to consider here."

"Jamie?"

"Of course, Jamie."

"Jamie can only benefit from having both his parents under the same roof."

Mikelle was silent again for several emotion-charged minutes. She stared at him, seeming to try to read his mind, his heart. He wished she did have telepathic powers, because then she'd have no doubts. No doubts at all.

"I have to ask this question, Greg. Is that the true reason behind your proposal? *Do* you want to marry me just to get your son under the same roof with you?"

Greg dragged a hand through his hair. "I knew this was coming."

"Can you blame me?"

"No, I don't blame you," he said in a defeated tone. "I guess I was an idiot to think you could trust me so soon after all the lies. But I was hoping you'd understand the motivation behind the lies and give me another chance."

"Giving you another chance and marrying you are two very different things."

He saw her eyes instantly glisten with unshed tears. He stood up, strode quickly across the floor to her and cupped her shoulders. He compelled her to look at him. Gazing steadily into her pain-filled eyes, he said, "All I can do is tell you the truth. If you can't believe me, there's nothing I can do about it. You have to take this on faith.... I love you, Mikelle. I'd want to marry you even if Jamie weren't in the picture. You've changed my whole outlook on life. You balance me, anchor me. I want you to be my wife and the mother of my children. Jamie is just an incredible bonus and the beginning of a family I suddenly can't seem to live without."

"And what if I can't believe you, Greg?" She spoke with obvious difficulty, swallowing past emotions he understood only too well. "Will you reverse your decision about giving me Jamie?"

"The decision is irreversible, but even if it weren't, I'd never take him away from you. I'd still want to see him. I'd settle for visiting him...and you...when I could. But what I really want is for the three of us to be a family."

"I can't believe this," said Mikelle with a humorless laugh. "Here you are, handing me my dream on a silver platter, and I can't—" She shrugged free of Greg's grasp and walked to the window, looking out over the browning grass and layers of fallen leaves. "I just can't believe it's true. I'm afraid that if I reach out to take what I want, it'll just disappear like... mist, or something." She turned to look at him with a plea for understanding in her eyes. "You think I'm crazy, don't you?"

"I think you're not ready to trust me." He paused, wondering if he dared tell her everything he was thinking. He took a deep breath, then let it slowly out. "We agreed to be honest, so here goes.... Maybe you're not ready to trust anyone yet. I've done things to make you doubt me, Mikelle, but I'm beginning to suspect that your fear of committing to marriage again has as much to do with Jim as it does with me.''

Mikelle looked surprised, then irritated. "What do you mean?''

"I mean, you expected Jim to be around for a long time. You were both young and loved each other very much. He left you and you're afraid that I'll leave you, too, whether it's because of a fatal accident, or because we simply can't make things work. Marriage is damned risky business, even when you love each other as much as we do.''

"You're saying it's me that has trouble committing now, not you?''

"That's exactly what I'm saying. I took you by surprise, Mikelle. You thought you wanted a marriage proposal, but when you got it, suddenly you were scared stiff.'' He made a grim smile. "In other words, be careful what you wish for, 'cause you just might get it.''

She spread her hands in a helpless gesture. "So what do we do, Greg?''

"That's up to you, Mikelle. I know what *I* want. When you decide what *you* want, let me know. You know where to find me.''

LEAVING MIKELLE ALONE to make up her mind had seemed like a good idea at the time, but now Greg wasn't so sure. It was the Wednesday before Thanksgiving and he'd heard nothing at all from Nantucket since Jamie's birthday. Although it was a secondary consideration, he was feeling a little bummed about the holiday, too. He had nowhere to go.

Greg loosened his tie and moved to stand by the window that looked down thirty floors to the busy streets of downtown Manhattan. People were scurrying like so many ants, trying to get out of town and home to their families.

In past years, Greg had always been involved with some woman or other and had ended up at her house or her folks' house for the usual turkey dinner, napping and football. Or he'd been invited by a friend to spend the long weekend skiing in Utah or cruising the Caribbean.

This year he'd received his fair share of invitations, but he'd turned them all down for lack of interest. And, deep down, he'd been hoping for an invitation from the people who mattered the most...*his* family, Mikelle and Jamie. But here it was, four o'clock in the afternoon the day before Thanksgiving, and still no word from the Little Gray Lady.

His telephone buzzed and he moved lethargically to the desk, pressed the speaker button and said, "Yes, Ms. Barnes?"

"There's a woman here to see you, Mr. Chandler."

Greg's heart did a triple Lutz deserving of an Olympic medal. "Who is it?" he asked hoarsely.

"She said to tell you it was Hayley."

Greg's heart settled back to its usual plodding rhythm. "Send her in."

Twenty seconds later, the door opened and Hayley breezed through it. Today she was wearing a green wool blazer and a plaid skirt with black boots. Her cheeks were pink from the chilly forty-degree weather and her hair was attractively windblown. She brought Obsession and the smell of the outdoors in with her.

She should have been as welcome as the proverbial breath of fresh air, but she just wasn't the visitor Greg had been hoping for.

"Gee, Greg, good to see you, too!" she quipped. "Or do you always look like you've just been to the dentist when a lady drops by? Don't worry, I'm not here to do a root canal, I was just wondering how you were doing."

"Sorry, Hayley," he said, managing a weak smile. "I guess it's obvious how I'm doing."

Hayley sat down in one of the chairs in front of Greg's desk and crossed her legs. "I take it you haven't heard a peep yet from Nantucket?"

Greg sat down in his own plush chair behind the desk. He propped his elbow on the arm of the chair and rested his chin in his hand. "I'm beginning to think I never will."

"Then maybe it's time you made a little noise on your end."

"What kind of noise do you suggest? I've given up Jamie completely—an action I don't regret because he's where he belongs—and there's no legal action that would force Mikelle to give me a second chance."

"Isn't there something like a restraining order, only in reverse?" joked Hayley with an encouraging smile.

Greg grimaced. "I know you're trying to cheer me up, but—"

"But my jokes are falling flatter than the state of Kansas. Well, you can't blame a girl for trying. What about calling her? I know that's a difficult concept for a lot of men, but you could give it a shot."

"I left the decision up to her, Hayley," said Greg. "I don't want to pressure her. She needs time and space."

"I'd say you've given her plenty of time and space...nearly a month and hundreds of miles, in fact. They say absence makes the heart grow fonder, but it's also been known to help people forget other people who may have caused unwelcome ripples in the smooth sea of life."

"My, aren't we poetic today? I thought you came here to cheer me up."

"You said that, not me. Actually I came to ask you if you want to spend Thanksgiving with me."

Greg was speechless.

"Don't look so terrified, Greg," said Hayley, laughing. "I wasn't suggesting you spend the day at the Van der Linden family funny farm. I'm planning on escaping the traditional histrionics by flying down to Florida for the weekend. Believe me, I can do without turkey and all the trimmings—you know, mashed potatoes and accusations. Stuffing and re-criminations. Peas, carrots and a healthy helping of sibling rivalry."

Greg looked across his desk at the stunning blonde sitting in his office. She was vital and witty and warm. And, as it now occurred to him, very vulnerable. She had been checking on him ever since his return from Nantucket. They'd had dinner together once, and had gone out for coffee several times. She'd been truly concerned about his dilemma with Mikelle and Jamie. She'd listened to him go on and on about his problems. Now it suddenly occurred to him that Hayley could probably use a listening ear from time to time, too.

"You're something else, Hayley," he told her.

"Pardon?" she said, cocking her head to the side.

"You're nothing like Connie. Nothing at all."

"Quit flattering me, Greg, and answer my question...do you want to go to Florida, or not?"

"You know how I feel about Mikelle—"

"Don't worry, this is a group thing," she assured him with a twinkle in her eye. "You'll be well chaperoned, and I promise not to get out of line even when you strut your stuff in a bathing suit."

"I appreciate the offer, but—"

"But there's only one place you want to be."

"And if I can't be there, I'd just as soon stay home and eat a TV dinner and swill beer in front of the boob tube."

Hayley's brow furrowed. "Are you sure you'll be all right, Greg?"

"Sure I'm sure." He stood up. "You don't think I've given up, do you?"

She smiled and stood up, too. "I'm glad to hear you haven't. That would be major stupid. Be patient a little longer."

"I'm not a patient man, but I suppose I have enough patience for something as important as this."

He walked her to the door and she stood on tiptoe to kiss him on the cheek, then wiped away the lipstick with her fingers. "I hope Santa's good to you this year, Greg."

"So do I, kid. And I hope he's especially good to you. Thanks for everything, Hayley. You've been a lifesaver. Have fun in Florida."

After Hayley had gone and only her Obsession lingered, Greg sat down at the desk and started loading up his briefcase with work to take home with him. He might as well do something constructive with his free time.

His telephone buzzed again. He glanced at the clock; it was almost five. He picked up the phone. "Ms. Barnes, why are you still here? Don't you have a date in Connecticut with your grandchildren for the weekend?"

"I'll have plenty of time to catch the train, Mr. Chandler" came Ms. Barnes's voice over the phone. "Thank you for being concerned, though. You have more visitors out here."

Greg frowned. "I don't have any appointments, do I?"

"No."

"Do I know these people? It isn't Hayley again, is it?"

"No, it's not Hayley." Her voice was hesitant.

"Who is it, Ms. Barnes? Didn't they give you a name?"

"The young woman wouldn't give me her name, Mr. Chandler. She said to tell you it was 'family.' My guess is, the little guy is your nephew. He looks just like you. He's got the cutest—"

But Greg would never know what Ms. Barnes thought was so cute. Before she'd finished her sentence, he dropped the phone and flew out the door.

Chapter Fourteen

Mikelle had never been so nervous in her life. Ever since the friendly Pakistani cabdriver had picked them up at the airport, he'd kept up a chatty, mostly one-sided conversation. But because he continually turned and expected at least a nod of the head to indicate she was listening—adding to her frayed nerves by barely missing other vehicles on the busy New York City streets—Mikelle couldn't immerse herself in her own anxious thoughts. If she'd had more opportunity to think, she might have turned tail like a coward and gone straight back to the airport.

It was too late to chicken out now, because she was in Greg's office, sitting in a chair near his secretary's desk, while "Ms. Barnes" buzzed "Mr. Chandler's" office. Mikelle had been surprised at the formality between the secretary and Greg, although there was definite warmth mixed with respect in Ms. Barnes's voice. She was silver haired and probably a grandmother, and was dressed very elegantly in a tailored suit and high heels.

Mikelle was secretly relieved to see that Greg hadn't hired a miniskirted girl fresh out of business school, then reminded herself that she was there in New York because she *trusted* Greg. Because he was so attractive, he'd be constantly flirted with by women of all ages. What mattered was how Greg responded to the flirting. The bottom line was, she trusted him, she loved him, she believed him, she wanted to marry him.... Did that cover it all?

Trouble was...had he changed his mind? She hadn't heard a word from him in three weeks and it had taken her that long to straighten out her jumbled thoughts and come to some pretty enlightening conclusions. She hoped she wasn't too late....

While Ms. Barnes talked in a low voice on the phone, Mikelle glanced over at Jamie to make sure he wasn't trying to climb inside the large aquarium in Greg's reception area. The instant they'd walked in the door, Jamie's attention had been caught by the brightly colored tropical fish swimming in circles through miniature sea caves, treasure chests and pirate ships. At the moment, he had both palms and his nose pressed against the glass.

Then, while Ms. Barnes still appeared to be in the middle of a conversation with her boss, Greg's office door opened and Greg himself strode into the room, dressed in a gray pin-striped suit and a white shirt. His tie was loose and slightly crooked, making him look sexier than a man had a right to be. Mikelle's already erratic heart rhythm skipped a few more beats. The expression in his gray-green eyes was intense, expectant, guardedly hopeful....

She didn't remember standing up, but suddenly she and Greg were facing each other, her head tilted back to adjust for all those extra inches of gorgeous male as he towered over her. They were close, but not touching. Joy filled her heart as she looked into his eyes and knew with a certainty that she wasn't too late.

"God, it's good to see you," he said.

"Ditto," she breathed.

"Why didn't you call? I would have come to you."

"Your exact words were, 'When you know what you want, let me know. You know where to find me.'"

He smiled. "I had no idea you paid such close attention to what I say."

"Well, I did that time." She stepped closer and laid her hands against the smooth fabric of his lapels. Against her palms she could feel the fast, strong beating of his heart. His hands slid up her arms and rested lightly on her shoulders. Even that minimal contact made the blood race through her veins like quicksilver.

"For example," she continued, "I was listening when you suggested that I was as afraid of commitment as you were at one time, and that it was because of losing Jim. I spent a lot of hours on the widow's walk working that one out, and I decided you were right. But now I know exactly what I want. It's risky, but it's worth it, and I know Jim would approve."

"What do you want, Mikelle? Because whatever it is, kid, you've got it."

"I want a white picket fence."

"My pleasure."

"I want a bunch of kids."

His hands slid down her arms and around her back. He pulled her closer. His voice got lower and husky. "Definitely my pleasure."

"And I want a marriage certificate with your name on it."

He raised a brow. "My name and . . . yours?"

Her hands crept up the front of his jacket and around his neck. She smiled coyly. "Definitely."

"My pleasure," he said, lowering his head till their lips were nearly touching.

Mikelle closed her eyes and was anticipating *her* pleasure, when Greg suddenly pulled back. They both looked down. Jamie was leaning against Greg and had his arms wrapped around Greg's leg. He was gazing up at them with wide-eyed wonder and curiosity. By making his presence known, Jamie had also reminded them that there was another person in the room—Ms. Barnes.

Mikelle glanced toward Ms. Barnes's desk and that lady hurriedly ducked her head and pretended to be busy rearranging papers. Greg and Mikelle looked at each other and smiled. They had their whole lives ahead of them. There was time later for kisses . . . for a million of 'em.

Greg picked up Jamie, gave the smiling toddler a hug and a kiss on the head, then put his arm around Mikelle's shoulders. They turned and walked to Ms. Barnes's desk.

"Ms. Barnes?" said Greg, grinning like a lottery winner. "I want you to meet . . . *my family.*"

Epilogue

Their first Thanksgiving together was wonderful. Greg accepted the honor of carving the turkey with so much smiling pride you'd have thought he'd been awarded a Nobel prize. There was Rose's famous walnut stuffing, plenty of side dishes for those of the vegetarian persuasion, and enough love for second helpings all around.

Christmas was even better. Just as Hayley had wished for him, Santa was real good to Greg. He gave him and Mikelle a Christmas Eve wedding. Jamie was the best man, Rose was the matron of honor, and "Aunt" Hayley was an honored guest.

A year later, Greg had accomplished the move of Chandler Enterprises to Boston without a hitch, and the branch office in Manhattan was doing well under the auspices of one of Greg's junior partners.

Because they needed the extra rooms for Jamie and his hoped-for siblings, Mikelle had closed the bed-and-breakfast. Now the Little Gray Lady was a single-family home. The wrought-iron fence out front was replaced with white pickets.

Rose continued to cook and clean house for them, but she was more like a family member than an employee. This left Mikelle with more time for her painting, and the "task" of honeymooning and being a mom at the same time. Judging by her constant smiles during the day and the long, loving nights they spent in each other's arms, Greg didn't think Mikelle considered the task too arduous.

It was Thanksgiving again, but instead of carving a turkey, Greg spent the day at the hospital with Mikelle helping her deliver their child. Just hours before, Greg had been a happy man, convinced that life couldn't get any better. But when the nine-pound, squalling infant was put in Greg's arms, he was astounded to discover he'd been wrong. Life just kept getting better and better... and better.

After a quick trip home to pick up Jamie, Greg walked down the sterile halls of the hospital with his son's fingers tightly curled around his. Now a bright, sturdy two-year-old with an ever growing vocabulary and endless curiosity, Jamie took in everything he saw with wide-eyed interest.

Jamie tugged on Greg's hand. "Daddy?"

Greg stopped and looked down with a smile. "What, son?"

"Mommy's here?"

"Yes, Jamie. Just down the hall in that room with the pink balloons tied to the door handle."

Jamie looked confused. "Where's th' baby?"

"The baby's with Mommy. Come on, I'll show you."

Greg thought Jamie looked a little tense about the fact that he was about to meet his baby sister, even though they'd spent lots of time preparing him for the new addition. He picked Jamie up under the arms and swung him back and forth like a pendulum till they reached Mikelle's room. As he'd hoped, the horseplay erased Jamie's worried frown and they both entered the room smiling like kids out of school for the summer.

Mikelle was sitting in the bed, propped against a couple of pillows, and looking to Greg even more beautiful in her white cotton nursing gown than she had in her wedding dress. She was holding their baby daughter. When Mikelle looked up, her face was radiant.

"Amanda," she whispered to the baby. "Wake up, sleepyhead. Your daddy and your big brother, Jamie, are here."

Greg bent and kissed her on the head, while Jamie hung back with a shy smile and a finger in his mouth.

"How are my girls?" asked Greg.

Mikelle smiled up at him. "We're fine. We both just had lunch. How are my boys?"

Greg cocked his head toward Jamie. "Maybe feeling a little anxious," he whispered.

Mikelle leaned forward, patted the bed and said to Jamie with a huge, reassuring smile, "Come sit with me, Jamie. I've missed you. And I want to show Amanda what a big, special brother she has."

Jamie went hesitantly at first, but after Mikelle had showed Jamie the tiny pink face of his sleeping sister, then discussed how Jamie was going to be such a good helper, then laughed with him at the funny way baby Amanda's face wrinkled up when she yawned, Jamie's anxiety was a thing of the past. Now the only problem would be to keep him from taking over Amanda's care completely.

Greg marveled for the umpteenth time at his luck in finding such a wonderful woman, despite the unorthodox way they'd started their romance. Mikelle was not only a fabulous mother, but the sexiest, smartest, most loving, most talented wife a man could ever hope for. And to think he used to sneer at marriage and fatherhood. Who was that fool? he wondered now. Who was that guy that couldn't commit?

Mikelle looked up at Greg, her gray eyes alight with warmth and love. "Look, Daddy wants to sit with us, too," she said to Jamie. "Move over and make room for Daddy."

No fool, Daddy moved right in.

Once in a while, there's a story so special, a story so unusual,
that your pulse races, your blood rushes. We call this

HART'S DREAM is one such story.

At first they were dreams—strangely erotic. Then visions—strikingly real. Ever since his accident, when Dr. Sara Carr's sweet voice was his only lifeline, Daniel Hart couldn't get the woman off his mind. Months later it was more than a figment of his imagination calling to him, luring him, doing things to him that only a flesh-and-blood woman could.... But Sara was nowhere to be found....

#589 HART'S DREAM
by
Mary Anne Wilson

Available in July wherever Harlequin books are sold. Watch for more Heartbeat stories, coming your way—only from American Romance!

MILLION DOLLAR SWEEPSTAKES (III)

No purchase necessary. To enter, follow the directions published. Method of entry may vary. For eligibility, entries must be received no later than March 31, 1996. No liability is assumed for printing errors, lost, late or misdirected entries. Odds of winning are determined by the number of eligible entries distributed and received. Prizewinners will be determined no later than June 30, 1996.

Sweepstakes open to residents of the U.S. (except Puerto Rico), Canada, Europe and Taiwan who are 18 years of age or older. All applicable laws and regulations apply. Sweepstakes offer void wherever prohibited by law. Values of all prizes are in U.S. currency. This sweepstakes is presented by Torstar Corp., its subsidiaries and affiliates, in conjunction with book, merchandise and/or product offerings. For a copy of the Official Rules send a self-addressed, stamped envelope (WA residents need not affix return postage) to: MILLION DOLLAR SWEEPSTAKES (III) Rules, P.O. Box 4573, Blair, NE 68009, USA.

EXTRA BONUS PRIZE DRAWING

No purchase necessary. The Extra Bonus Prize will be awarded in a random drawing to be conducted no later than 5/30/96 from among all entries received. To qualify, entries must be received by 3/31/96 and comply with published directions. Drawing open to residents of the U.S. (except Puerto Rico), Canada, Europe and Taiwan who are 18 years of age or older. All applicable laws and regulations apply; offer void wherever prohibited by law. Odds of winning are dependent upon number of eligibile entries received. Prize is valued in U.S. currency. The offer is presented by Torstar Corp., its subsidiaries and affiliates in conjunction with book, merchandise and/or product offering. For a copy of the Official Rules governing this sweepstakes, send a self-addressed, stamped envelope (WA residents need not affix return postage) to: Extra Bonus Prize Drawing Rules, P.O. Box 4590, Blair, NE 68009, USA.

SWP-H595

In June, get ready for thrilling romances
and FREE BOOKS—Western-style—
with...

WESTERN *Lovers*

You can receive the first 2 Western Lovers titles FREE!

June 1995 brings Harlequin and Silhouette's
WESTERN LOVERS series, which combines larger-than-
life love stories set in the American West! And WESTERN
LOVERS brings you stories with your favorite themes...
"Ranch Rogues," "Hitched In Haste," "Ranchin' Dads,"
"Reunited Hearts" the packaging on each book
highlights the popular theme found in each WESTERN
LOVERS story!

And in June, when you buy either of the Men Made In
America titles, you will receive a WESTERN LOVERS title
absolutely FREE! Look for these fabulous combinations:

♦ Buy ALL IN THE FAMILY
  by Heather Graham Pozzessere (Men Made In
  America) and receive a FREE copy of
  BETRAYED BY LOVE by Diana Palmer
  (Western Lovers)

♦ Buy THE WAITING GAME
  by Jayne Ann Krentz (Men Made In America)
  and receive a FREE copy of
  IN A CLASS BY HIMSELF by JoAnn Ross
  (Western Lovers)

**Look for the special, extra-value shrink-wrapped
packages at your favorite retail outlet!**

HARLEQUIN®

A M E R I C A N ◆ R O M A N C E®

Spend your summer with Strummel Investigations!

STRUMMEL INVESTIGATIONS

American Romance invites you to read Victoria Pade's Strummel Investigations trilogy! Three top-notch P.I.'s in the Strummel family—Quinn, Lindsey and Logan—solve mysteries and find love.

Look for:

#588 THE CASE OF THE BORROWED BRIDE
in June
Quinn Strummel puts his P.I. skills to use when he looks for a missing groom—and accidently falls for the bride!

#590 THE CASE OF THE MAYBE BABIES
in July
Lindsey Strummel helps a bachelor who's found twin infants on his doorstep. Will she solve the mystery— and become a mom?

#594 THE CASE OF THE ACCIDENTAL HEIRESS
in August
Logan Strummel doesn't exactly believe that his new client's had an out-of-body experience—but she's sure got a body *he'd* like to possess!

Strummel Investigations—only from American Romance!

HARLEQUIN®

A M E R I C A N ✦ R O M A N C E®

A NEW STAR COMES OUT TO SHINE....

American Romance continues to search the heavens for the best new talent... the best new stories.

Join us next month when a new star appears in the American Romance constellation:

Charlotte Douglas
#591 IT'S ABOUT TIME
July 1995

When Tory Caswell attended her sister's wedding in a magical old Victorian resort, her mind was filled with images of bouquets and garters. But when she awakened the next morning, she thought she was still dreaming. A gray-eyed hunk was next to her in bed! And he claimed he'd come from the 1800s....

RISING STAR

Be sure to Catch a "Rising Star"!

STAR4

THREE BESTSELLING AUTHORS

HEATHER GRAHAM POZZESSERE
THERESA MICHAELS
MERLINE LOVELACE

bring you

THREE HEROES THAT DREAMS ARE MADE OF!

The Highwayman—He knew the honorable thing was to send his captive home, but how could he let the beautiful Lady Kate return to the arms of another man?

The Warrior—Raised to protect his tribe, the fierce Apache warrior had little room in his heart until the gentle Angie showed him the power and strength of love.

The Knight—His years as a mercenary had taught him many skills, but would winning the hand of a spirited young widow prove to be his greatest challenge?

Don't miss these **UNFORGETTABLE RENEGADES!**

Available in August wherever Harlequin books are sold.

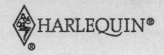

HARLEQUIN®

Announcing
the New Pages & Privileges™ Program
from Harlequin® and Silhouette®

Get All This FREE
With Just One Proof-of-Purchase!

- **FREE Hotel Discounts** of up to 60% off at leading hotels in the U.S., Canada and Europe

- **FREE Travel Service** with the guaranteed lowest available airfares plus 5% cash back on every ticket

- **FREE $25 Travel Voucher** to use on any ticket on any airline booked through our Travel Service

- **FREE Petite Parfumerie** collection (a $50 Retail value)

- **FREE Insider Tips Letter** full of fascinating information and hot sneak previews of upcoming books

- **FREE Mystery Gift** (if you enroll before June 15/95)

And there are more great gifts and benefits to come!
Enroll today and become Privileged!

(see insert for details)

PROOF-OF-PURCHASE

Offer expires October 31, 1996   HAR-PP2